SEX

and the

SINGLE
ZILLIONAIRE

SEX

and the

SINGLE

ZILLIONAIRE

A Novel

TOM PERKINS

REGAN

An Imprint of HarperCollinsPublishers

A hardcover edition of this book was published in 2006 by Regan, an imprint of HarperCollins Publishers.

HarperCollins books may be purchased for educational, business, or sales promotional use. For information please write: Special Markets Department, HarperCollins Publishers, 10 East 53rd Street, New York, NY 10022.

For editorial inquiries, please contact Regan, 10100 Santa Monica Blvd., 10th floor, Los Angeles, CA 90067.

First paperback edition published 2007.

Designed by Kris Tobiassen

The Library of Congress has cataloged the hardcover edition as follows:

Library of Congress Cataloging-in-Publication Data
   Perkins, Thomas J.
     Sex and the single zillionaire : a novel / Tom Perkins.—1st ed.
       p. cm.
     ISBN 0-06-085167-8 (alk. paper)
     1. Billionaires—Fiction. I. Title.

PS3616.E748S49 2006
813'.6—dc22
                                       2005056402

ISBN: 978-0-06-085977-0
ISBN-10: 0-06-085977-6

07 08 09 10 11 RRD 10 9 8 7 6 5 4 3 2 1

TO DANIELLE STEEL

WITH THANKS FOR THE PUSH, RENEWED RESPECT, AND LOVE.

AUTHOR'S NOTE

*T*his story is pure fiction. Both the plot and all the characters are my invention.

Except that, exactly like my fictional character, I received an invitation to try-out for the star part in a TV reality show. While I haven't modified the tone, I have changed the names, disguised the studio, and fictionalized the actual letter sent to me. But, the basic proposition of the letter at the beginning of the novel is entirely factual—the premise of this book is taken from real life.

And, for better or worse, no "ghost" did the writing.

—*T. P.*

SEX

and the

SINGLE
ZILLIONAIRE

*T*he doorman delivered the FedEx envelope to Jeffrey, the live-in chef and household manager who set it down on the breakfast table in front of Steven Hudson's *Wall Street Journal*. Steven was just finishing a couple of delicious eggs Benedict. He put the newspaper down. The morning sun glinted off the gold-rimmed plates and polished silverware as he opened the envelope.

The letter read:

ACME STUDIOS

Dear Mr. Hudson,

I have a fantastic idea! I am the Executive Producer of Acme Studios, and I want to make you the star of our new reality television show. I want you to meet and play with a dozen twenty-year-old stunningly beautiful girls and at the end of our thirteen week series you will marry the one you choose—she will become your bride on national television!

Clearly this is an outrageous idea—matching an older, single, wealthy man with young, sexy women—but it will be wonderful for the right man who adores women and who has a sense of adventure.

We will select the young ladies from an alluring array of models, actresses, athletes, and others based upon their appearance and personality. You will have the opportunity to know them in your home and at various glamorous locations, to see them competing for your love and attention. Of course, if at the last moment, you don't, or your chosen bride doesn't want to proceed, the wedding won't happen. But, you must understand that marriage is the whole point of the show, and you should enter it in that spirit.

This is not a frivolous proposal. We are authentic producers with a long track record, and this show has a very high probability of being aired. If you are the right man, with the right chemistry, please call me. I am offering you a life enriching experience that will be impossible to duplicate.

Very truly yours,
Jessica James
Executive Producer

"My God, Jeffrey! What a letter! Can you believe this?" Steven passed the letter over to Jeffrey, who was starting to clear the table.

The portly, young chef read with an ever widening smile. "Boss, I'm sure it's for real." He passed the letter back to his employer. "You'd be a natural for the show, you know. You're rich, single, handsome, and well-known. Since Mrs. Hudson died, you've been pretty lonely, and you haven't had a lot of fun. It looks like a great idea! You going to follow this up?"

Steven wasn't sure if his long-term cook had gone barking mad.

"Jeffrey, despite what you may think of me, I do have a shred of dignity left. Can you imagine me cavorting around in front of a TV crew while a gaggle of gold-digging bimbos make me look like a fool? You know the saying 'There's no fool like an old fool.' Well, it ain't going to be me."

"Come on boss," Jeffrey said, removing the bone china plate. "You aren't that old. What are you now anyway? Sixty-one, sixty-two? You don't look a day over fifty. Those girls wouldn't be able to keep up with you."

"Thanks for the compliment, but this is a crazy idea and I'm going to deep-six it right now. Just chuck it out with the garbage, please."

Jeffrey took the letter with the remainder of the breakfast dishes and headed back into the pantry muttering to himself. "I wish they were looking for someone like me. Why do rich guys get all the action?"

Steven smiled. He settled back in his chair and returned to the *Journal* with one elbow on the breakfast table, his second cup of coffee within easy reach. It was one of those cold, clear winter mornings when the sun glittered off windows of midtown office towers and white clouds of steam rose from the roofs of nearby buildings into the crisp air. The view from his forty-seventh floor penthouse was as spectacular as ever. Five years ago he'd closed the big house on Long Island and moved into this sleek, ultra modern, minimalist, yet somehow very comfortable, glassed and terraced condominium. It had taken five years to hunt down and buy a fortune's worth of contemporary art, paintings, and sculptures to furnish the penthouse. Yet his lavish attempt to create a new, different home for himself had utterly failed to replace the empty longing that now occupied the center of his soul. The contentment he'd once taken for granted had been replaced by a gathering gloom.

Steven and his wife, Yvonne, had been a dazzling couple, constantly photographed for the society pages at openings, the opera, and charity balls. He was tall, slim and strong, with a movie star's chiseled looks. Yvonne had been marvelous, a lovely woman who created beauty in everything she did. Then came the doctor's diagnosis of cancer. A painful two years' struggle had been followed by death and, for Steven, a grief that seemed endless.

Steven had always assumed he would be the first to go. After all, he had the high-pressure career. Hadn't *Time* once dubbed him "America's Power Investment Wizard"? Type A guys like him were supposed to drop like flies, weren't they? But not women like Yvonne. Yvonne had been so wonderful, never losing her charming French accent. Her grace, her beauty, reminded people of the film star Catherine Deneuve.

Could he have spent more time with her? Could he have traveled more often with her back to her beloved Paris? And could he have spent more time with their two children, Henry and Helen, while they were growing up? Sure, he'd risen from a working class background—God rest his parents' dreary, unimaginative spirits— and become a "Titan," a "Wall Street Lion," but had he been neglectful? The guilt gathered.

"Boss, I'm keeping the letter." Jeffrey broke into Steven's downward spiral of thoughts, and he looked up, mildly startled. "You might not want to be a curmudgeon forever, even though lately you're getting really good at it," Jeffrey added.

"Jeffrey, don't nag," Steven growled but then had to smile. Though only thirty-six, Jeffrey had worked for the Hudson's for almost fifteen years. A naturally gifted and brilliant cook, Jeffrey had sometimes seemed like another teenager in the family. Frequently in hot water with credit cards, lost passports, and a never-ending string of speeding tickets, the minor troubles this rotund culinary genius seemed to encounter usually required Steven to step in and resolve the problems, one way or another.

Jeffrey had worshipped Yvonne. When she died, he suggested to Steven through a voice choked with emotion, "You and I could become like Wooster and Jeeves—I would like to stay on and help." Steven said that Jeffrey had gotten it backward. Wasn't Jeeves the suave and all-knowing problem solver? But ever since, Steven sometimes called him Jeeves. And like Bertie Wooster and his man Jeeves, Steven and Jeffrey depended on one another.

"Jeffrey, you know I think I'll take that crazy letter with me when I go to the office. Some of the guys might get a kick out of it. Imagine those girls!"

Jeffrey laughed at the idea too. Then he asked: "Do you want the Bentley brought around or will you take the subway?"

"I'll take the subway. I probably won't hang around downtown too long—hardly worth starting the car."

The famous boss of Hudson and Partners, a top firm with over four thousand employees, still went down to Wall Street most days. In order to spend more time with Yvonne during her illness, he had delegated almost all day-to-day responsibilities to his partners. They were a hardworking crew, and Steven had not sought to reestablish himself as the chief. Of course, his partners deferred to his opinions on the rare occasions when they asked for them, but increasingly he felt isolated, even useless. "The Lion of Wall Street" had become the lion in winter, he sometimes thought.

Steven, wrapped in a stylish blue, long cashmere topcoat, set out from his building, touching the brim of his blue, felt Borsalino hat in a friendly salute as he responded to Eamon, the doorman's, "Good morning, sir. Cold out there today, sir."

Steven took in a deep breath of the bracing air. God, he loved New York. He loved the drive, the sense of urgency. He liked rubbing shoulders with the people around him, as the subway rocketed and clattered its way down to the heart of the world's financial center. After ascending the Wall Street station's narrow stairway and emerging into the canyon-like street, he glanced up as he always did. He still got a charge from seeing his name emblazoned in bronze letters above the archway to the building, which his firm owned. He arrived at his tenth-floor office with a healthy glow from the nip in the cold air, looking as confident, purposeful, and in control as ever.

Hudson and Partners occupied multiple floors in an old, gray stone-clad building, grimy with the accumulated decades of soot of lower Manhattan. On the trading floors, there was the buzz of excited young people at their computer terminals buying, selling, hedging, and noisily interacting with one another, but on Steven's floor it was serenely quiet, splendid and tasteful in the expensive and conservative style of the city's private financial temples. Deep carpet, mahogany paneled corridors, tasteful antique furniture, and old marine paintings flanked the offices of the senior executives. Some of the doors were open, and as Steven walked past on the way to his corner office, he nodded to several of his partners. Many were working the phones, handling mergers and acquisitions required by his firm's clients.

Everett Ross and Dick Jennings, two of his junior partners, were in a discussion by Mrs. O'Brian's desk. Mrs. O'Brian, Steven's secretary and assistant, was very competent and totally professional. Even after twenty years, they still referred to each other as Mr. Hudson and Mrs. O'Brian.

"Steven, where do you think the prime rate is headed?" Everett asked. "Where do you think it'll be in six months?"

"I don't know, guys," Steven responded, "but let's find out." Turning to his secretary, he asked, "Mrs. O'Brian what will the prime rate be six months from now?"

"Mr. Hudson," the unflappable woman replied, "I don't have the slightest idea."

"Well, there you have it," Steven said with a grin. "If Mrs. O'Brian doesn't know where the prime rate is headed, then no one does—don't even try to guess!"

Steven entered his office, scarcely glancing at the huge polished brass chandelier that dominated the imposing paneled sanctum with its elegant cherry wood desk. It could have been the lair of the iconic J. P. Morgan, except for the wall of electronic screens that continuously displayed an array of financial data, streaming in from around the world.

Steven had just hung his hat and coat in the closet and was about to add the letter to the small pile of papers on his desk when Pierce Crowninshield, one of the senior partners, strode in. Pierce was all business.

"Morning, Steven. We finished the new Delta Fund last night

at exactly three billion dollars. It has a total of ninety-three investors, including a few institutions that are new to us. We buttoned it up just before midnight, right on schedule. I thought you'd be pleased to know." Pierce was about fifty with thinning black hair, tall, and aristocratic in his perfectly tailored navy blue suit, looking exactly like the blue blooded New Yorker that he was.

"Excellent, Pierce. I'm glad you were able to sweat it out on time." Pierce frowned slightly at Steven's purposeful use of the word sweat. Pierce considered himself above those who actually perspired.

"Take a seat Pierce, please, if you have a moment. I'd like to show you a letter I received this morning at breakfast."

Pierce sat down in a leather chair, carefully protecting the crease in the trousers of his elegant suit. His aquiline profile alert, his brow slightly furrowed, betraying his cautious curiosity about the letter Steven was handing him. It could be anything from a problem to an opportunity. Steven, displaying only a little smile, watched as Pierce read the letter with an ever-deepening frown. Steven loved pricking the bubble of Pierce's pomposity. Pierce didn't disappoint.

"Steven, this is disgusting!" Pierce exclaimed. "How did they get your name? Are you going to sue?" His fine-boned patrician cheeks turned bright red. "My God, how could anyone even dream that you would be party to such a stunt?"

"Well, you know, Pierce, it might just be a joke. Maybe one of my friends is setting me up for a big laugh. Maybe this was sent by you."

Pierce let that pass. "No, Steven, this is real. I recognize the name of the production company. Reality TV is hot these days. You know, *Joe Millionaire*, college kids on a desert island, society girls on a farm." He eyed the letter with renewed disdain. "The networks must be frantic for new ideas to have come up with this."

"It's silly, isn't it? Who'd want to watch such a thing?"

Oddly enough, Pierce saw the appeal better than Steven. "Now that you mentioned it, probably everyone! Look at the basic idea: money for sex. Out in the open, upfront. I'm rich, old, and horny, and you want my money and will put up with me to get it! No hidden agenda here. The dumbest Joe Sixpack out there will lock on right away and be drooling through every hour it's on the air. It's beyond crass. It turns my stomach!"

"Don't hide your feelings, Pierce. What do you really think?" kidded Steven.

"Well, I know you well enough to be sure you wouldn't even be tempted to flirt with this farce—am I right?"

"Absolutely. I just thought you would get a kick out of reading the letter." Seeing how offended Pierce was, Steven couldn't help getting in a dig. "I must admit, though, that I'm secretly a little flattered to even be considered for the star part in a sex frolic."

"Don't flatter yourself *too* much," Pierce said with a well practiced sneer. "I'll bet a thousand of these letters were sent out. It probably won't be hard to find some rich publicity-mad geezer who still fancies himself a swordsman."

For some reason, Steven blushed at this comment. He began to wish that he'd not brought up the letter at all. Pierce was not famous for his tact or sensitivity. Nor was his wife, Eunice, who could freeze everyone in a crowded room with one haughty stare.

Then Pierce stood and disdainfully handed the letter back to Steven, holding it by a corner, as if it were a used airplane vomit bag. "Well, Steven, if this amuses you, I suppose you ought to keep it in your desk and read it in secret from time to time. *I've* got to get back to work." With this, he excused himself and escaped, squaring his shoulders at the door, as if recovering from a perilous brush with the great unwashed.

Steven slipped the letter into the pocket of his suit, dismissing Pierce and his airs and began to work through the small pile of papers, notes and phone messages on his desk. He hadn't gotten much beyond reading through the advance information for a dull board of directors meeting he would be attending the following week when Mrs. O'Brian told him that his son was holding on line two.

"*Ciao Bello*," Steven boomed, happy to hear from Henry.

"Dad, what's up? I'm just calling to confirm our lunch. We still on for today?"

"Of course we are, Hank."

"Well, I hadn't heard from you, so I wasn't sure."

"I wouldn't miss it," Steven said, but secretly chided himself for having let the lunch slip his mind. "Where shall we meet? The Links or the Yacht Club?"

"How about The Links Club? They have a better chef and it's not as busy."

"Great. See you there. One thirty okay?"

"Done deal, Dad, see you there."

Steven looked forward to seeing his son, but he hoped that this wasn't going to be another plea for a trust fund handout—those were becoming increasingly common. He supposed this possibility was the reason he had let the lunch date slip his mind.

The rest of the morning sped by with a few phone calls and more business papers to digest. Steven had always worked very effectively with an unerring judgment about people and events. His partners had been attracted to him because of these skills, and he had made nearly two generations of them extremely wealthy. Yet, in a fi-

nancial jungle periodically savaged by scandal, intrigue, and litigation, he and his partners remained the "choir boys," as they were
sometimes called, with unimpeachable ethics; his firm was the blue
ribbon bunch of Wall Street.

Steven cleared his desk by one o'clock and told Mrs. O'Brian
that he probably wouldn't be back after lunch. Before leaving the office, he checked to be sure the letter was in the pocket of his suit
jacket. He would show it to Henry, he thought. It would be good for
a laugh.

The taxi, driven by a real New Yorker—complete with turban
and Punjabi accent—dropped him off uptown at No. 36 East Sixty-
second Street, before a large but unpretentious town house, the
Links Club. Henry rounded the corner at the same time on foot, and
together they descended the few steps to the lower-level entrance.

The club was perhaps the most exclusive in America. Indeed,
all the former presidents were, or had been, members—at least all
the Republican ones. Old leather, old paintings, old wood, old port
wine, and old men could be found within its hallowed portals.

Steven and Henry strode up the spiral stairs to the burnished
dining room side by side. They were obviously father and son, with
the same tall, athletic build. They were so handsome that they could
have made money modeling, if anyone could afford to hire them.
The aura of money seemed to float around them. Perhaps not old
"blue stocking" New York money, but "better new than never," as
Steven sometimes joked.

While the elderly green-jacketed waiter discreetly took their
orders—no "Hi, my name is Jason and I'll be your server today" in
this place—Steven and Henry caught up on things since their last
lunch, about a month ago.

"Hank, how are you getting on with that crazy sports car you bought—a McGuire, isn't it?"

"Dad, you mean the McLaren, the McLaren F-1. It's still the only one in America," the boy proudly answered. "I got it legalized two weeks ago. The importer had to add bumpers and all kinds of stuff to pass the tests, and afterward my mechanics took all that stuff off again, so it looks original. It's gorgeous! People can't get over the gull-wing doors and the steering wheel in the middle. I love it."

Steven shuddered inside. Why had he brought up the damn car for openers? Henry had discovered it in England and had withdrawn over nine hundred thousand dollars from one of his trusts to buy it. Now he supposed there would be another big bill to pay for making it legal. Why would anyone want a car that could go 241 miles an hour? And why couldn't Henry get serious about life?

His son continued to extol the virtues of the car. No doubt it would be a hit with the girls constantly in his orbit. Lately a stunning redhead named Kathy had been sharing his Village loft. She was smart, and Steven really liked her, but he doubted anything would come of the relationship. Somewhat to his surprise Henry had graduated from Yale in good standing, so why couldn't he take life seriously and begin to make a contribution? Steven shifted the conversation toward these concerns, which always arose when they were together.

"Your computers, Hank, are you still putting in time with them?"

"Sure, Dad, I've just released a nifty approach to the problem of identity theft on the Internet."

"Would I understand it?"

"Well, maybe not, but I'm getting lots of kudos from the Linux programmers out there."

"You gave it away! Why didn't you sell it?"

"Oh, that's against the whole idea of open source—I just love to get kudos," his son responded with the most charming of smiles.

"Hank, you can't put kudos in the bank. Aren't you getting a little low on funds this quarter? Am I going to have to top up the trusts again?"

"Oh, Dad, no problem! I just borrowed against next quarter's income—no sweat!"

Henry's cavalier attitude toward money baffled Steven, who had not been born with the proverbial silver spoon in his mouth. He'd had to work for everything, every day, on his way up, and he wanted to make sure his children never had to experience the anxiety of his own upbringing. Henry had everything—lessons of all kinds, sports, resort vacations, private schools, then Groton, and finally Yale. Steven would have loved the boy to join him in the firm, work his way up to become a partner, and perpetuate the Hudson name around Wall Street. After all, doesn't everyone really want a clone of themselves?

He had tried to guide Henry, of course. After his son's graduation from Yale, when the full flow of the trust funds had begun, and with no indication that a career or work of any kind was planned, Steven had intervened, subtly at first. He'd given the boy a subscription to the *Wall Street Journal*, hoping that reading it might trigger some interest in Dad's world of finance.

Nothing happened.

Then, less subtly, over lunch one day, Steven had given Henry a six-figure check with the idea that it should be invested independently of the trusts. Henry would begin to understand, to appreciate how money could be multiplied through a well-reasoned process, Steven had thought. When, a couple of weeks later over another lunch, Steven had asked how Henry was doing in developing an investment strategy, his son's answer had stopped him cold. "Oh, it's already invested," Henry had happily replied. "I called Mrs. O'Brian and she gave me a list of ten companies you're chairman of and I divided it equally among them. You're working for me now, Dad!" Steven hadn't known whether to laugh or cry.

One shouldn't be judgmental, Steven knew. Henry was healthy, happy, well-adjusted sexually (maybe too well adjusted!) . . . why should he have to make a contribution? . . . the trust funds weren't going to expire . . . perhaps Henry really had figured it out perfectly . . . perhaps, perhaps, perhaps. . . . The thoughts spun around in their familiar groove, as his son again expounded upon the fun of contributing free software to the "Linux World."

The food, as always, was superb and the wine a wonderful vintage, Cheval Blanc '97. The polished woodwork reflected the coming and going of the white-haired waiters. The conversation at the other tables was quiet. Steven must have let his mind wander, for when he came out of his reverie, Henry was speaking.

"Dad, Dad, are you with me? Hello! Am I boring you about open source?"

"Oh no son, not at all, really." Steven snapped back to the present and shifted gears. "You know, I got an absolutely crazy letter this morning. Here, I'll show it to you. Just sort of keep it a bit under the table when you read it. You know how fussy the club is about conducting anything that remotely resembles business." He handed the letter to his son.

Henry read with an expanding grin. He seemed delighted. "Dad, this is fantastic! Absolutely fantastic. What a wonderful idea. I can hardly wait to meet them!" Henry's eyes were sparkling with enthusiasm.

"Whoa, slow down. I'm not going to do this. I'm not in the least tempted. Just wanted to give you a laugh."

"But why not, Dad?" His son's excitement was growing. "They'll get a bunch of gorgeous girls. Wow! It'll be great! We can have a terrific time."

Steven started to rein in this runaway idea. "Hank, this isn't about us." He was amazed that a sudden agenda seemed to be in Henry's mind. "I'm not going to dignify this thing with an answer. You keep the letter. Maybe you can talk them into starring you."

"No, it's about you Dad—you getting some action—and I think it's brilliant." Steven felt himself blush again. He was becoming a little flustered.

"Hank, slow down." Steven tried to let the hot air out of this balloon. "I don't need a TV circus in my life. Everything's just fine as is."

"Just fine? Are you sure, Dad? Aren't you lonely living by yourself?" Henry's expression turned serious. "Dad, really, you ought to follow up. Why not give the studio a call?"

They threw the idea back and forth, but Steven didn't budge. He ended the conversation by taking the letter back from Henry and returning it to his pocket. By this time they had finished their lunch. Father and son returned to the street in the late afternoon sun to walk off in their separate directions. They gave each other a brief hug and promised to do lunch again soon.

Steven was almost home when a Shakespeare quote crossed his mind. "It is a wise father who knows his own child." How well did he really know Henry, and since when had his son been concerned about Dad's loneliness rather than his own fun, cars, and girls?

CHAPTER TWO

A few weeks earlier Jessica James was bundled into a long, gray winter coat of crushed lamb's wool with a silver fox fur collar. She was moving too quickly to pay attention to the approving glances from men as she hurried from the taxi through the crowd on the sidewalk to Acme's office. It was miles uptown from Steven's Wall Street headquarters, in the heart of Manhattan's new media district at Forty-third Street and Broadway. Her building was a recently built glass skyscraper festooned with huge neon signs and a pulsating news zipper running around the lowest floor. It was typical of the Times Square location. The polished stainless steel framing the windows glinted in the glaring light of the cold winter morning, and she was happy to get indoors, through the electronic security gate and into the crowded chrome and mirrored elevator, which soon opened to her twenty-third floor office.

Brittany, the attractive Asian-American receptionist, pressed the buzzer to let her boss through. Jessica hurried through the large open office floor with people at dozens of desks. She strode toward her corner office smiling and acknowledging the various friendly greetings along the way. It was only a few minutes past nine, but already the place was buzzing. As she entered her flashy glass fish bowl of an office, she was deeply worried. How was she going to keep it all going? She needed a hit or she'd be out of a job.

Where was the next idea that would revive the fortunes of Acme Studios? TV was such a brutal and unforgiving business. A chef was only as good as his last meal, and a TV producer was only as good as her last ratings book, she often thought. She sat down behind her chrome and glass desk. The drama series and situation comedies that she'd been so successful in grinding out like sausages were dropping in their ratings. The shocker had come with the recent debacle of her two-hour pilot of *Courtroom Conquest*. In spite of a great premise, a good cast, adequate investment in production, advertising, and a favorable time slot, viewers had bailed in droves. One hour into the pilot, their market share had dropped to under 3 percent. By the end, the network was virtually broadcasting into the empty ether.

She'd been brainstorming for weeks with her assistants, searching for something new. Acme's owner, Saul Gross, was getting restless, and when Saul got restless, he got aggressive, in a sexually predatory way, just barely contained. She hated that and she hated to have to report her lack of progress to him in his office that reeked of blue cigar smoke, even though it was illegal to smoke in the office building. Clearly, reality TV was the stuff audiences wanted, and it was not going to go away. But Acme was behind.

The Brits always seemed to be on the crest of new reality ideas, just as they had been in rock and roll with the Beatles and the Stones.

When Jessie heard that the British TV creative fireball, Willard D'Arcy, might be unhappy with his present situation, she tracked him down and offered him a first class ticket to New York just to meet, to test the chemistry. He was very friendly on the phone and the complete opposite of the stereotypical reserved Brit. She had trouble getting a word in edgewise, in fact. He agreed to jump on a British Airways flight the next day and come over. "The Concorde may be too old to fly, but I'm not!" he said.

Twenty-four hours later, an hour or so after lunch, Willard burst into her office. She'd just cleared her desk of messages and paperwork. His energy was incredible and his appearance rather astonishing, even for the relaxed standards of the industry.

Willard D'Arcy, thirty-two years old, was the size of a small teenage boy. His youthful appearance was accentuated by spikey hair dyed royal blue on top with a pink tinge around the sides, gold earrings, and royal blue fingernail polish. He was still short even in his high-heeled cowboy boots but all this was overwhelmed by his perpetual motion. He didn't walk, he darted. He didn't sit in a chair, he fidgeted and wriggled. And he talked constantly. Fortunately he repeated himself frequently, as his East London accent was sometimes hard to understand.

"I rushed over because you have the best telephone voice I've ever heard," he gushed. "At last I meet the famous Jessica James, the mistress—no, the dominatrix of situation comedy. I loved *California King Size*, never miss a rerun. How do you do it year after year? What are you cooking up now? What's in the 'hopper'—as you Yanks say— but shouldn't you be in Hollywood? Does anybody actually have ideas in New York?" While talking he scurried around her high-tech office, peering out the windows, picking up and replacing a photo on her desk, and sizing up all the plaques and trophies on her glass shelves. "Great place, though, and unlike L.A. you can breathe the air. What can I do for you? Never thought I would be in the inner sanctum of Acme Studios."

Jessie had to interrupt him to get a word in. "Willard, I'm stuck. Situation is dead these days, and we want to try our hand at reality even though we're coming late to the game. We wondered if you could help."

"Oh! You really meant what you said on the phone!" His hands fluttered up, as if fresh story ideas could pop out of them. "Reality is a smashing way to tell any story you want, but it's best built around money and sex. Sex and money is always with us, like death and taxes." He was distracted by a new thought. "Say, I'm starving, I'm absolutely starving. Can we get something to eat?"

It was mid-afternoon, but Jessie knew they could find a good sandwich and some quiet in the Blue Bar. They made an odd couple as they walked together down Forty-fourth Street to the Algonquin Hotel. Even in her bulky winter coat, Jessie's tall figure was striking, and her black hair shone around her extraordinarily beautiful features. Willard virtually skipped along at her side. He was childlike in so many ways that she had to resist the temptation to take his hand as they walked. He reminded her of Mark, her now gangly teenage son, when he was a little boy.

The dark, oak-paneled Blue Bar was nearly empty, and Jessie ordered a club sandwich for Willard and a black coffee for herself.

"Reality programming has always been with us—it's not really new," Willard continued in his frenetic manner. "All the way back to the early days of radio with quiz programs, hobby shows, and such— it's always been around. Now we are just better exploiting what the audience has always wanted. Does our *Pop Idol*, which has dominated UK ratings, really differ much from your Ed Sullivan show from decades ago? Or *Major Bowes Amateur Hour* on radio before that? No, but now we're much better at telling a story, the 'arc' that fiction writers always talk about."

Jessie wasn't clear about this. "What do you mean, Willard?"

"Well, we decide up front the story we want to tell. We write a script for a thirteen-week series, episode by episode. There will be a good guy and a bad guy. A good girl and a naughty girl; there will be some tears, some crisis, a resolution, and eventually a happy ending. It's the arc of life, just the way a fiction writer would put it down on paper!"

"But how do you make it happen? The people in these shows aren't actors, they aren't following a script, are they?"

The waiter arrived with Willard's sandwich, and he took a tremendous bite out of one corner, like a shark attacking a smaller fish.

"No, of course not. Sometimes nature takes its course and we depart from the script and we let it happen, if it's interesting. But, basically we screen the contestants—let's call them that. It's easy to find people from real life who will fit exactly into the roles we have set for them. There really are good girls; there really are bad blokes out there. We just give them the opportunity, and let's face it, some pushing in the right direction."

"What do you mean, pushing?"

"Jessie, that's why these reality shows cost so much to make! They're so labor intensive. We have about a dozen associate producers to follow our contestants through almost every hour of their lives—we help them to follow our script! You don't for a minute think that we just turn on the cameras and wait to see what will happen, do you? We give them ideas, we coach them off screen. Someone follows every second of their conversations, and when they say and do something that fits our chosen direction, we mark that snippet of tape and work just that part in. For every hour of finished work there's at a minimum of one hundred, maybe two hundred hours of tape behind it." He went back to his sandwich, and in two more huge bites he'd demolished it.

"I had no idea it takes so much coaching, Willard. Do the contestants just go along willy nilly?"

"Well maybe Willard nilly! Ha ha! Actually a key part of the process happens off-screen. The interaction with the producers and the contestants is all-important. We question them. When, for example, the guy says, 'I was really pissed off when I found out that Sheila had put that dead fish in my underwear,' looking angrily into the camera, it's because moments before, a producer asked him just how he felt and even asked him to repeat the statement. We plant ideas in their heads. We help them to realize that what they want to do, think, and feel is what we want them to do, think, and feel."

Jessica took a sip of her coffee, mulling over what he had said.

"You mentioned cost—what *does* it cost to shoot a reality show?"

His head bobbed back and forth as he calculated, converting pounds to dollars. "Oh, for an episode on the top end, about nine hundred thousand dollars to a million. And, of course, we don't pay the contestants anything. They do it for all kinds of reasons—the glory, the opportunities it might open for them afterward, to show off. It's really expensive if there's much travel involved. You're flying about one hundred people around. With all those extravagant junior producers—it starts to add up!"

By the time the first early drinkers had drifted into the place, Jessie and Willard had hit it off very well. Willard explained that he lived and breathed reality television. He was the first to cry at the sad stuff that he himself had worked into plots. "After all, you can't make the audience believe it if you don't believe it yourself." Last month, he told her, he'd married a contestant from his most recent show. "Sally became real for me when I saw her on screen doing the stuff we had cooked up for her."

Jessie was fascinated. How could he get so involved? After the waiter delivered a Brandy Alexander for Willard and another coffee for Jessie, they decided to go out for the evening. Willard remembered to include Sally—he had brought her to New York.

A cell phone call from Jessie to her fiancé, Gregory, confirmed that he would be able to join them. A second call to Daniel's confirmed a table at eight at the famous chef's midtown restaurant, a favorite of Jessie's.

She had a feeling she was about to strike gold.

*G*regory came by the apartment at seven thirty and mixed himself a drink while he waited for Jessie, who always ran a little late when she was getting ready to go out. The place was small, on the ninth floor of a new condo building on the Upper East Side. Gregory sat in an expensive chair upholstered in soft corduroy and idly watched the evening news on a huge flat panel display sitting on the half-filled bookshelf opposite him. A big black and white photograph of himself was smiling back from its leather frame next to the TV. Jessie was always too busy to be much of a homemaker. A decorator had furnished the place for her in a quiet, tasteful modern style, but the personal touch that only she could have provided was missing. The apartment was suitable to be photographed for *Modern Living* but the photos wouldn't reveal much of the owner's personality or career. The tiny kitchen was also a decorator's showpiece. The highly polished copper pots and their lids hung on a black wrought iron rack above the gas range. None of them had been used, nor had the strings of now dried out garlic, which hung from a rustic hook. Jessie wasn't much of a cook. She and Gregory were both busy professionals, so eating out was easy and natural; they could afford it. And Jessie was away every weekend in her parents' Scarsdale home with her son, Mark.

As she rushed about, she filled Gregory in on Willard and thanked him for agreeing to help entertain the colorful Londoner and his new wife. She'd decided to try to hire Willard by the time they left the Blue Bar together. Gregory would be an asset in helping her make that sale. Gregory had such an attractive personality that for him making friends was effortless. Being voted president of his fraternity and making captain of the college tennis team were typical fruits that had fallen to him naturally.

As Jessie emerged, looking stunning in a gray, wool tailored suit, she thought once again how lucky she was to have him in her life. Gregory was exceptionally good-looking, tall, athletic, and ten years younger than her. Yet at twenty-nine, he had the self-confidence of most men her own age, or even older. He'd pursued Jessie as if she'd been the only woman in existence and she had not been easily won. Jessie had been badly wounded from her first marriage and had resolved never to marry again. But Gregory had charmed her so that she now wore an engagement ring, even though they hadn't yet set a date. Only the difficulties surrounding her son stood in the way of the new marriage. Mark didn't like Gregory at all, and no matter what she said, he wouldn't warm up one bit. To him Gregory was "stupid." Jessie worried about the relationship, when she slowed down enough to think about it. Like most women, she tried to find time to examine the inner clockworks, but like most young men, Gregory didn't relish relationship talks at all.

They found Willard and Sally already at Daniel's, and after introductions, they all started chatting happily at a corner table. Sally would have been spotted by anyone as Willard's other half: tiny, with frizzy hair colored a sort of reddish-orange, and festooned with huge, bright, plastic costume jewelry.

Willard was very interested in Gregory, wanting to know if he was a stage actor or maybe in television, but the answer was even more intriguing. Gregory was, as Jessie put it, an apprentice guru.

Gregory readily explained that he was working for Anthony Tower—the world-famous *Discover Your Inner Self* author. His original book was now in its seventh edition with over eleven million copies in print. It had been followed by *Unleash Your Inner Self* and *Control Your Inner Self*. Gregory's smile conceded that Tower was controversial, but that working for him was interesting. Gregory now pretty much ran Tower's seminars around the country with huge audiences, and the ideas were as appealing as ever.

Jessie didn't like Anthony Tower personally, though, and let the others know it.

"Gregory, remember the dinner when you introduced your boss?" Tower had carried on about a smattering of ideas from across the spectrum, held together only by his magnetic and charismatic personality. The silliest of his theories was that food had electrical frequency, which you could measure in kilohertz. Thankfully, Gregory was not caught up in too much of this. He, however, sincerely believed that he was helping his audiences.

As expected, the conversation returned to the afternoon's topic: reality television.

"Jessie, I've been thinking about a new idea," Willard enthused. "We've had *Joe Millionaire* where the contestants thought they would be marrying for money, but he was a fake millionaire. He was so good-looking though, that it didn't matter—and the audiences loved it. And we had *The Bachelor* more recently—single guy, a bunch of pretty girls—and again, the audience couldn't get enough of it. I think we're ready now for the next step. A guy with real money."

"What's the special angle, Willard?" Jessie wondered.

"Well, the guy is an old man! That's the point. He's loaded, but over the hill. The girls will be chasing him only for his dough! We could call it 'Gold Diggers' or something like that," he said laughing. "It would be fun to watch the competition between the girls. They can't be too obvious, of course, because he'll pick the one he thinks really loves him."

"Pick one for what?" Gregory asked.

"Why, to marry, of course!" Willard was positively gleeful in his excitement.

Jessie and Gregory exchanged glances.

"Oh, I don't know, Willard. Marriage is a serious proposition—not a game." She didn't wish to dump cold water on Willard's brainstorming, but this idea didn't appeal to her. "Plus, how could we ever find a guy to participate? Any serious person would laugh at us."

"Oh, you'd be surprised, you'd be surprised! I'll bet that within thirty days we could line up a half dozen older millionaires—all single, of course, and straight. Widowers would be best."

"You can't be serious," was her reply.

Willard immediately tried to overcome her objections.

"Listen, Jessie, people like to be noticed, flattered. They're bored. They'd like to be the center of attention. They want to be important. We provide a vehicle for all that and make it fun. Besides, sex is always appealing as long as there's life in them bones." His delighted cackle stopped short as he considered a new thought. "The best guy would be the one least likely, the one who isn't desperate. One who doesn't need us. You see what I mean?" He mulled over another angle before he added: "The girls are really going to have to try for it, for the show to be interesting to an audience, but I think if we get it right, it could be a real smash! Think of the demographics! Think of the ad rates the networks would be able to charge!"

Their orders were served and Daniel's cuisine was as delicious as ever. Willard and Gregory ordered the chef's recommended sweetbreads and found them delicious. The women both settled on grilled salmon, and they compromised on the color of the wine by ordering a rare 1997 Haut Brion rosè. The discussion of Willard's idea continued into dessert and then into after-dinner sauterne. By then both Gregory and Sally were sold on the idea. But Jessie still voiced doubts.

"Willard, I can't get over the feeling that there is something icky about this. An older man agreeing to marry one of these bimbos—a guy the age of my father, with lots of money but no dignity—just drooling over the young women that we dish up? Personally, I'd have no respect for such a man."

"But, Jessie, the audience will be fascinated. The ickiness, as you put it, will be part of the appeal. Awful, perhaps, but like a train wreck, you just can't look away."

She saw that he couldn't be denied once he got on a roll.

"Well, let's sleep on it," she said. "Maybe we'll have other ideas when we meet tomorrow."

*T*here were other ideas that Jessie and her staff chewed over with Willard, but he kept pulling them back to his rich old man plot. Over the next two days, the team decided to work up the idea into a story line. Jessie accepted, at last, this majority opinion. She and Willard prepared a presentation for Saul Gross. If Saul green-lighted the proposal, she would hire Willard as a special assistant, and then they would pitch the idea to an investment group, hopefully, to get some extra production funding.

The meeting with Saul was awful. Willard and her boss took an instant, visceral dislike to each other—they were like creatures from different planets, Jessie thought. Willard made no effort to flatter and kowtow the way Saul expected. Shortly after arriving in Saul's office, Willard insisted that Saul extinguish his cigar, which had already deposited a trail of ash across the smoker's vast vest. Yet Saul understood quickly that Willard's ideas had proven to be huge moneymakers for others, even though reality shows were expensive to produce.

"This is your call, Jessica." Saul said. "It's your responsibility entirely." She maintained a brittle smile as he continued. "Win or lose, it's on your shoulders, and that's what I'll have in mind when your contract is up for renewal in May." He grinned, truly savoring this idea. "Line up some investment money to coventure with us; try

Theatrical Capital. Now, unless you have other guests from Hell for me to meet, let's get on with making some money for Acme." Jessie nodded. As so often in the past, her boss was expecting her to carry the Studio forward singly. Well, she'd done it before and she could do it again.

As they left Saul's office, he called after them: "I'll call Atherton at Theatrical—should be a piece of cake for you to pick them up as an investor."

As soon as they were out of earshot, Willard hissed, "What a revolting pig! How can you stand working for him, Jessie?" Deeply affronted, he complained all the way back into Jessie's fancy glass office. "I would've helped you with this one, but cannot work for that human ashtray! Sorry, Jessie, but it's off."

However, Jessica's soothing voice and cheerful attitude about the show's prospects dispelled Willard's aversion over the next few hours. Later that afternoon they jointly worked up a PowerPoint presentation to give to Mrs. Lamont Atherton the next day.

*G*regory and Jessie met as often as possible on weeknights when his travel schedule permitted. That evening, in her apartment, he rustled up a light dinner of shrimp salad that they shared in candlelight with a chilled, soft French Chablis. Jessie brought him up to speed on the day's events and Saul's tough attitude.

"Do you have a plot for this thing yet, a title?" Gregory asked.

"We're going to call it *Trophy Bride* or *Spring for September*. And yeah, we do have a plot, sort of. We will have thirteen episodes including an introductory evening with a bunch of girls. We'll cast a mixture—all eager, but some 'country innocent,' if you know what I

mean, and some very sophisticated. We'll try to alternate the seduc-
tresses with the girl scouts. We'll shoot, for example, for a soft and
naïve type to match against a sophisticated, hard-edged city girl."
She took a sip of her wine. "Oh, we have a whole agenda on who
we'll be looking for in the contestants. And we'll have cooking contests, shopping sprees, and so forth. I am thinking of them all taking
an art lesson, and then having to create something. Our hero will
have many ways to eliminate a girl each week."

"But what about the guy? Who are you going to get for your
mildewing millionaire?"

She laughed at the phrasing. More unkind monikers had been
floating around the office.

"That's tougher. Much tougher. The guy is the key to the show.
The women in the audience are going to have to like him—be attracted to him even. And the men in the audience are going to have
to relate to him—to want to *be* him. We've been on the Internet
searching for hours. I have a bunch of my staff on this and we have
come up with about twenty likely names so far. We need, I suppose,
about fifty. Willard has no idea what our hit rate might be."

"How are you going to approach them?"

She sighed slightly because this was one of the tricky parts.

"I'm thinking to use a very personal letter, delivered by FedEx,
to each one. Then I'll follow up with a phone call and if possible a
personal visit." She shook her head. "I'm worried about this, though
Willard says it will be easy. I can't imagine a decent, reasonable, and
especially wealthy man wanting to have anything to do with us. I
wouldn't respect any man who did, and I'm concerned the audience
will be as put off as I am." She saw that Gregory didn't think this

would be a problem and she shrugged. "Willard says I am being too old-fashioned. I don't think that I am; I hope he's right."

"You have a lot riding on this, don't you?" he asked. "I think that with the right man it could be very interesting. But you're correct—with the wrong guy, it'll be a major turn off." He paused. "I'm glad you and I didn't have to meet in such a complicated way, babe." They rose from the table, and he held her in a long, loving embrace.

She pulled away and smiled at him.

"Right. I took one look at you in your tux and I was sold. You closed the deal with 'Hello,' you smooth talker," she said fondly. "I remember everything about the rest of the evening—the Ballet Black Tie Ball."

"I thought you were the most beautiful, the most interesting woman I'd ever seen in my life. And you know what? I still do."

Sometimes Jessie wondered how the chemistry worked between them. Their two busy lives didn't leave them long periods of time together, and often Jessie dismissed Gregory's "inner self" mantras, but he was incredibly attentive, calm, and loving. Gregory didn't have deeper, or darker, aspects to his 8×10 glossy photo personality. What you see is what you get with him, she thought. On the physical side, well, she didn't think that it could get any better.

They headed to the kitchen to clean up the dishes.

"Anthony Tower would say that Saul has an unharnessed inner dynamic," Gregory noted, "and his people potential is contra focused."

"Yeah, you could say that," she said lightly. "But I prefer to think of Saul as a real prick."

"Energy of Saul's kind is rare, Jessie. You need to understand and channel it for better organizational alignment."

She was glad she had her back to him so he couldn't see the look that crossed her face.

"I will, Gregory, I will. If I don't kill him first. If he pinches my ass one more time, he'll be decked so fast I'll be out of there and in my lawyer's office filing a sexual-harassment suit before he hits the ground." She continued to load dishes into the dishwasher. "Oh, you should have seen Saul and Willard together! The fire-breathing whale and the English ferret. God! It was hate at first sight. Natural-born enemies."

"But Saul went along with the idea."

"Of course, because there's money to be made, but Saul wants us to split the risk by raising some production money from Theatrical Capital. Willard and I will call on them tomorrow." Finished loading the dishwasher, she dried her hands on a towel and drew close to him. "So, I'm going to need my beauty sleep tonight. After, that is, you show me once again why I permit a younger man in my bedroom. Although you look great in a tux," she said, winking slyly, "you look even better in nothing at all."

*I*n the taxi on the way downtown to Theatrical Capital, Jessie and Willard reviewed the pitch they would make to Mrs. Lamont Atherton. Jessie explained to Willard that Acme Studios and Theatrical had a long-term relationship. Mrs. Atherton was a wealthy widow whose hobby was Broadway stage productions and their financing. Most of Theatrical's stage investments were flops, but the activity was good entertainment and a nice tax write-off for the rich old woman. On the other hand, Theatrical's investments with Jessie had been returned many, many times over. Jessie was always welcome to pitch a new idea.

"It's only ours to lose, Willard," she stated confidently. "Remember, you make the basic presentation on the reality concept, and I'll follow up and ask for the money."

"What will you be asking them to invest?"

She'd been down this road before.

"Well, I think I'll offer to go fifty-fifty in a partnership. We'll shoot the pilot and the first two episodes on a total budget of three and a half million dollars and split the cash down the middle. If the show tests well, we'll continue with ten more episodes at one million dollars each, with them putting up the money. If we run over our budget, it's on our nickel. We should clear a million profit up front before we split the network broadcast proceeds fifty-fifty."

Willard's eyes lit up. "Wow! If I follow you, Acme risks a total of one and three quarters and makes back one million dollars before the first broadcast. Not bad. Not bad."

She'd always liked that feature as well.

"Right—assuming we continue after the first three. Remember, Willard, we've a great track record. Many people would like to invest with us. We are good, and as Gregory would say, 'Our inner selves are laser focused.'"

"Yes, that's what he would say." Willard frowned at the memory of so much self-help gobbledygook at the restaurant that night. "Does he always talk like that? Is he always so calm and kind?" he asked, amazed. "Doesn't he ever lose his temper? If you suddenly woke him up in the middle of the night, would he *still* be that way?" The cab swerved to the curb and came to a gut wrenching halt. "Why have we pulled over? Are we there?" Jessie merely grabbed Willard by the elbow and guided him out of the cab, glad to escape jihad by taxi on this bitter cold Manhattan morning.

Theatrical's offices near Union Square were on the sixth floor at the top of an old imposing stone structure that carried the name Iroquois Building over its bronze doors along with some carved, feathered Indian heads with very sooty faces. The clanking elevator carried them up to the offices, rich in old-world charm. Paneled oak wainscoting ran below walls covered in burgundy tooled leather. The office was far larger than was needed for Mrs. Atherton and her small staff. Jessie knew that they made only a handful of investment decisions each year. Still, the profits she'd generated from their past series of partnerships had paid for the splendor of the offices and the beautiful conference room into which they were now led. It was decorated with paintings of old New York in carved, gilded frames.

Mrs. Lamont Atherton, the chairwoman and CEO of the company, one of many she had inherited from her late husband's huge estate, was seated at the head of the polished rosewood table. Jessie had always liked her, and she watched with interest as Willard skipped around the table to take her hand briefly to his lips in a gesture outdated by at least a hundred years, but somehow exactly appropriate at this instant.

"Please, Mr. D'Arcy, call me Agnes, and may I address you as Willard? Jessica tells me that you have become England's reality television superstar."

The meeting was quickly launched by Willard in his usual antic fashion. He covered all the high points of their thinking on *Trophy Bride* or *Spring for September*, the tentative working titles Jessie had hastily coined. It sure beat Willard's *The Old Man Gets Laid*

Show. He discussed the budget. The hero wouldn't get paid much—
"Even Donald Trump got peanuts the first year of *The Apprentice*"—
and the contestants wouldn't receive more than their expenses. He
explained that sex and money always proved a better draw than the
early action reality shows of cops and dangerous animals. "I hate animals anyway. They're too predictable compared to humans." Also,
secrecy was vital; there could be no leaks, and thus audience testing
had to be circumspect and clever.

As Willard talked, he darted about from the printed Power-
Point cards he had set up on an easel, to the windows, where he
made his points with large arm gestures. Jessie could tell from
watching Mrs. Atherton that they, or rather, Willard was making the
sale. Their target investor was an attractive, silver-haired woman in
her mid-sixties; she was smart, but gentle and generous by nature.
She'd learned early in her career that good business could be done
in good fellowship.

As Willard rattled on and on, Mrs. Atherton began to nod in
agreement and smile as she increasingly warmed to this very odd but
very charming, elfin dynamo. Her two assistants, a terribly pale and
fragile looking young man and a somewhat older woman, looking se-
vere in horn-rimmed glasses, took their signals from their elderly
boss, and they too began to relax and even permitted themselves to
laugh a little at Willard's jokes. Jessie could see that it was time to nail
down the financial arrangements, but how was she supposed to stop
Willard, who seemed to be gaining altitude by the minute?

". . . and of course, we'll have everyone tested medically," he
was saying. "We don't want to have any responsibility for untoward
results from shagging."

"Shagging, Willard? What do you mean?" Her assistant's stifled laughs, but Agnes was puzzled. Jessie guessed she must be unfamiliar with the Austin Powers movies.

"Well, we won't show the actual shagging on camera, of course."

"But what are you talking about?"

"Oh, it's the term we Limeys use. You know, bulls serve, stallions cover, dogs line, chickens tread, sheep tup, foxes clicket, and people shag, Agnes. They fucking shag!"

Jessie needed to jump in quickly but couldn't before a deep blush rose to Mrs. Atherton's face. But then—thank God!—she started to laugh.

"Oh Willard, this old lady still has a lot to learn." Her smile was genuine. "But I think this reality idea could be fun! How do we start?"

Jessie smoothly explained the basics for the partnership she had in mind. This part was much more familiar to the investors, and after an inquiring glance to her two assistants, Mrs. Atherton confirmed agreement with a smiling nod.

"Jessie, you have a deal. Only, I think everything depends on finding the right man. How are you doing with that?"

Before Willard could respond, Jessie gave him a wink and said, "Well, we have a list being compiled now. We want to avoid the obvious playboy types, no Warren Beattys or George Hamiltons. We need a genuine guy that the audience will believe in and will like."

"Is Steven Hudson on your list?"

The name rocked Jessica back in her chair.

"The Lion of Wall Street?"

"Yes, I know him socially," Agnes said. "His wife died a few years ago, you know. He's a wonderful man and very attractive."

"Agnes, I'll add him to the list. Thanks for the idea." With a few further interchanges, Jessie and Willard said their good-byes and headed back out to the street.

Jessie stuck out her hand.

"Thanks, Willard, we did the deal."

"I like her Jessie," he said, shaking. "By the way, is her Steven Hudson a good prospect, do you think?"

Jessie gave him a doubtful look. "Well, I'll write to him because she asked us to but, no, a man of his stature would never play our little game."

CHAPTER THREE

*S*teven woke up feeling clearheaded and refreshed. Well, why not? He hadn't done much of anything the night before, besides nodding off while watching a TV show. He couldn't even remember what it had been now, but this was Saturday morning and Steven looked forward to getting out and cruising the uptown and Madison Avenue art galleries. Collecting contemporary art had gradually become an obsession, and there still was a blank wall in the foyer that yearned for something special.

It had started with the need to furnish his apartment. The Old Masters still hanging in his shuttered Long Island mansion would have looked out of place in this new high-tech glass, steel, teak, and concrete penthouse.

He hadn't known much about pictures. Art was his daughter Helen's field. In the past, he'd pretty much bought famous names—

Van de Velde, Caillebotte, and so forth. He even had a rare Bruegel shut away in the dark old suburban house.

Even when he was a young man, Steven had a philistine's notion of contemporary art. Until recently, the splotches, dribbles, torn paper and such had seemed silly to him. When he decided to collect it and learned the prices, he was appalled. Were people who bought this stuff just showing off how rich they were? Maybe it was like that Indian tribe in the Pacific Northwest who gathered things all year long—the better off accumulating the most—and then burned it all in a great communal fire, just to show how rich they were and how little it all mattered. The Potlatches, he remembered they were called.

Yet on his first visit to the Allan Stone Gallery way uptown, his eyes had been opened. Stone's knowledge, humor, and passion for cutting-edge creations changed Steven's mind, and as his taste improved, he began to buy. Now his weekly Saturday wanderings had become a habit.

Steven took a second cup of coffee his Jeeves had brewed and carried it with him as he wandered through the penthouse admiring his collection. A sculpture by Matthew Barney molded in wax was on a massive slab near the steps in the sunken living room. Another, a sculpture of a vacuum cleaner in a big Lucite case by Jeff Koons stood by the triple wide doorway leading into the dining room. One of Bill Viola's video pictures of a huge cascading waterfall was running on a matrix of multiple plasma screens in the living room opposite the enormous fireplace. And he enjoyed looking at his numerous paintings hanging on the waxed and polished walls, like those walls found in the finest old Italian villas. A pair of moody and haunting oils—self-portraits by Trampedach—were among his favorites. A giant painting by Squeak Carnwath displayed dozens of blotches of paint in varying shades of the color red. It hung on the living room's inner wall, perfectly augmenting the modern leather and steel furniture.

He no longer bought by name but by eye, and his eye was becoming good. He wished Yvonne could share his new passion with him. What would she have thought, he often wondered, of these extreme, challenging pieces? For that matter, would she have been surprised at this previously unexplored side of his personality?

He was happy to note that by shifting a few things around, perhaps the Roy Lichtenstein oil parody of a comic book hero, he could liberate some more wall space. Like many collectors Steven knew, it would be hard to stop. He hoped he would never be finished.

His gallery forays allowed him to share a common interest in art with Helen, now almost finished with her master's in art history at Columbia. Sometimes she joined him on these Saturday mornings, and he was delighted, in response to his spur-of-the-moment phone call, when she said that she would love to join him.

"Jeffrey, I'm going out. I won't be in for lunch, but I'll be back for dinner."

"Okay, boss. You have a date tonight? Want anything special?"

"No date unless you round one up for me," Steven joked as he summoned the elevator, which opened directly into the expansive marble-floored penthouse foyer.

Yesterday's bright clear cold had given way to high overcast skies, and Steven thought snow might arrive with it. Fortunately, he was wearing a full-length Gianni Versace suede coat with a lamb's-wool lining. It had a deep pocket into which he had slid the Acme Studio's letter before departing. He wanted Helen's opinion of the letter. He didn't seem that desperate without Yvonne, did he? He wondered if Helen would be as enthusiastic as her brother.

They met at eleven at the corner of Madison and Sixtieth Street. His daughter had taken the subway, and Steven gave her a big hug and a peck on her cheek. As always, she looked great. She had her mother's beauty and sophisticated taste in clothing. An art student and aspiring artist she might be, but she didn't display artistic rebellion in her appearance, Steven was happy to note. Where her talent had originated was a bit of a mystery to him. While he had an appreciation for art, he couldn't draw a circle. And Yvonne, while having a marvelous feeling for space, shape, and color in her interior decoration and garden design, wasn't much better at drawing. But with just a charcoal pencil and sketchpad, Helen could capture a person's likeness perfectly, including some insight into the sitter's personality.

She had, on two occasions, surprised Steven with oil portraits of himself on his birthday. Too modest to commission a professional painting of himself, he hung Helen's wonderful pictures with pride, one in his downtown office and the other in his office in the penthouse. He took the greatest pleasure, though, in the loving painting she'd done of Yvonne—it hung in his bedroom. Yvonne had seen it a few weeks before she passed away, just after it was finished. It captured his wife's beauty and personality perfectly. All three of them had cried when Helen unwrapped it at her bedside. The memory of that afternoon was still poignant as he looked at his vivacious daughter now.

Wandering together into a new gallery a few blocks up Madison, they encountered an arresting work. He wondered, what would you call it, painting or sculpture? It was a huge canvas covered with several dozen big house painters' brushes stuck to the surface and sticking out nearly horizontally—each flowing in a solid color downward to another brush to create a multihued whole.

"Wow," said Steven, "what do you think of that? Even I could make one of those. Is it really art?"

Helen was fascinated by the piece. "It's the essence of art. You might call it conceptual art, but look how the artist carried it off— huge! No tentative, partway ideas here. I think it's really great. I don't know who did it, but it really has balls!"

Steven could see why it appealed to her. "You always go for the big idea in art, don't you, Helen—all the way with no holds barred?"

She gave him a friendly thump on the arm. "Yeah, Pop, you're right. But you've taught me that, haven't you? Look at the life you've led—no half measures, right?" A brochure on a table nearby had a photo of the artist in front of his creation, a bearded, fierce-looking man. Helen turned from it to her dapper but straightlaced father. "Well, maybe not as wild as that guy."

"Let's see what the asking price is," Steven said, with his acquisitive instincts in full flow.

Unfortunately, according to the ethereal young man in charge of the gallery, the work called *Paint* by a rising Dutch artist had been sold just yesterday. Art movers had been called and the piece would be gone on Monday.

"Do you think I could commission him to do a copy?" asked Steven.

Before the boy could reply Helen cut in, "Pop! I'm shocked! Conceptual art is just that, totally unique. It's got to be one of a kind. Just like a life, it can never be duplicated. The artist is already moving on. It's great that you liked it, though."

Disappointed, Steven allowed his daughter to shepherd him back out onto the busy avenue. He suggested a sandwich at the Carnegie Deli over on Seventh Avenue. When they arrived, they found it as insanely busy as ever. After a five minute wait, they were seated at a tiny table in a long row of tables. A surly, old waiter took their orders.

"So, Pop, how's it going? What are you doing to keep busy?" The buzz all around them was so pervasive that there was privacy in the noisy anonymity. New Yorkers had learned to live this way.

"Oh, my partners run the place better than I ever did," Steven said, unwrapping his Reuben sandwich. "I go to the office most days, but it's not very exciting anymore."

"That sounds sad, Pop," she said, picking up on the trace of discouragement in his voice. "What I really meant to ask, though, is how's your social life? I know you go out sometimes, but is there anyone you're serious about these days?"

"Well sure, you know who they are. Madeline, Louise, Bonny, and Rosemary. I go out from time to time with all of them." Steven was referring to a list of widows and divorcees, friends of Yvonne who had emerged—bright and sparkling upon her death.

Helen's question triggered dark thoughts of Yvonne's memorial service. They filled him with a sadness so deep that the buzz of the busy deli was forgotten for the moment. Hundreds and hundreds of friends and associates had attended the memorial service, seemingly filling the immense Cathedral of St. John the Divine, bathed in the deep-hued light of the stained-glass windows. After a family lunch with Helen and Henry, all of them nearly numb with pain, Steven had returned alone to his estate, Ivy Columns, near Oyster Bay on the Island.

Steven would never forget that afternoon. He had sat in the inviting drawing room, surrounded by photographs of Yvonne and the children in leather and silver frames perched on the tables and the Steinway concert grand piano. The late afternoon sun had cast rays into the room, lighting up linen-fold, carved oak paneling and the rich furnishings, the tapestry, and the huge, soft pastel Persian rug Yvonne had found and persuaded him to buy. It was a beautiful room in a beautiful mansion overlooking a beautiful rose garden, all of which emphasized Yvonne and her inviting, warm, superb taste. But she herself was gone.

As he sat in the fading light, he'd heard a car approaching the circular drive at the front. One of the staff showed Stella, a realtor and Yvonne's closest friend, into the room. She gave Steven a comforting hug, then sat and talked reassuringly about the loveliness of the memorial service. Steven listened, but his thoughts were far away.

Only when Stella began to talk about "making a new life" did he begin to listen. Stella let him know that she was exceptionally fond of him. Her marriage to her ne'er-do-well husband, Sebastian, with whom she had four nearly all grown-up children, had never been satisfying. Steven couldn't believe his ears as what she was saying began to register. She at first hinted and then said explicitly that she would like a divorce from Sebastian in order to marry Steven. "We could make a powerful team, you know. Yvonne was never interested in business, but I am."

Steven didn't remember actually saying a thing to Stella. The horrified look on his face said it all. Stella left and he never saw her again. The anger still smoldered. He had never mentioned it to his children.

His thoughts snapped back to the clamor of lunchtime at the Carnegie. Helen was watching him with mischief in her eye. "Earth to Pop, Earth to Pop."

He remembered what they had been talking about. "I like them all really, those ladies I mentioned. We go to the opera and so forth. They keep me in the social scene, I guess."

"I don't mean one of your escorts. I mean a woman you want to live with. Oh. Pop, have you slept with a single woman since Mom died?"

For the second time in twenty-four hours, Steven blushed deeply. Lunch with his kids was turning into a contact sport.

"Honey, I . . . I do okay." He fidgeted with his half-eaten sandwich. "Isn't that question getting a little personal?"

"Not at all, Pop. Hey, I worry about you. I don't think you're having any fun. As your daughter, I inherited worrying rights."

She was trying to help. "Yeah, I guess your guesses are hitting the mark pretty accurately. Except for scouting around for art with you, having lunch with Hank sometimes, board meetings, and dropping in at the office, I don't have much else going on."

"Pop, think about it. There must be some way to meet women who aren't just after your money. What about taking up dancing lessons? Arthur Murray is still in business. Or you could start going back to church. You could meet a saint there. Or golf, didn't you play golf once? Plenty of women around a golf club. There must be other ways as well."

"Helen, you'll be happy to learn that I have a possible solution right here in my pocket." Steven extracted the letter and handed it to her across the table. "I showed this to your brother yesterday. Tell me what you think." He assumed it would just provide a laugh to wind up their lunch.

Helen read the letter with an ever-increasing expression of delight. "Pop, this is fantastic! Absolutely perfect! I couldn't dream of a better idea!" Helen was always quick to react, and then sometimes just as quick to change her mind.

"What? Have you gone nuts? I thought we were trying to find a way for me to meet women not after my money, and now you want to throw me straight into the shark pool!"

"But that's exactly why this is so great! It's so totally pure and open. No pretense at all. It's only about picking a woman who will be the best buy! You get to choose. Just like shopping," Helen said, laughing.

"Helen, this is a television show," Steven said, becoming flustered. "Everything would be shown to everybody. My privacy! My dignity! My reputation! All the stupid little things I say or do would be flaunted on TV. You can't be serious."

"Pop, you'd be totally in control. Like a work of art," she said, animated. "This is a big blank canvas. They're offering you the materials. It's up to you. What do you want to make out of it? The artist doesn't care who's watching, why should you?"

Helen wasn't going to let go, Steven could see that. He reached across the table, grabbed the letter, and hastily put it back in his pocket.

"Helen, I love you very much, you are a great kid, but I think you've gone totally bonkers. You want your dad to make an ass of himself? Let's get back to talking about art, and I mean the kind you need brushes for."

Steven pushed away the remains of his sandwich and reached for his wallet. He wanted to get out of there.

"Okay, Popkins. I'll let you off the hook. Don't be surprised, though, if I send you ten coupons for dancing lessons. I want to get you back in some action. And by the way, I love you too, Daddy."

They elbowed their way back onto the street and continued their browsing through a few additional galleries. Soon Helen informed him that she needed to get back uptown. She had a date that evening. He was tempted to ask questions about the mystery man but didn't. He didn't want to reopen the door to any further intimate questions.

The sun was setting and a few scattered snowflakes were beginning to fall as Eamon the doorman punched in the security code and gave Steven his usual welcome.

"Any mail, any news?" Steven asked.

"No, sir, it is very quiet today. Will you be going out again, sir? Be needing the Bentley?"

"Thanks, Eamon. No, I'll be staying in tonight."

Upstairs, Jeffrey was bustling about in the pantry. He began shaking a martini for the boss as soon as he heard the door open. The wonderful scents of a roasting duck were coming from the kitchen.

Well, Steven thought, with a couple of martinis and an excellent dinner under his belt, a Saturday night alone wouldn't be too bad. Would it?

The letter and his kids' reaction to it remained with him as he sat at the candlelit table, all the way through his after dinner coffee. His only companion was his own reflection in the dark window of the dining room. Both Henry and Helen had given him an endorsement to bring some madness—no, excitement into his life. Probably Henry's motives were not pure, but there was no denying it, he was lonely. A smile crossed his expression as the passages of the letter again crossed his mind. Should he give Acme a call?

No, no, what was he thinking? Steven Hudson would never do such a thing.

CHAPTER FOUR

"*B*limey, isn't this fun?!" said an enthusiastic Willard to Jessie, the day before Steven received his letter. "I told you we wouldn't have any problem lining up our girls."

Acme's offices were teeming with stunningly attractive young women. As soon as the news hit the grapevine that contestants were needed for a new TV reality show, photos and resumes began to flood in.

"No doubt about it," responded Jessie. "We have plenty of talent to choose from. You were right—it isn't that hard to find personalities to fit our script." They sat together in Jessie's fancy corner office equipped with the electronic glass walls set so they could look out unseen into the open area where assistants, now calling themselves associate producers, were interviewing several lovely aspirants. Girls that made this first cut then had a screen test and interactions with more senior staff. Jessie and Willard made the final selections among the candidates. So far they had decided on only three finalists—a ditzy, blonde "country girl"—who was actually from Cincinnati; a potential gold digger from Chicago; and a ravishing professional model from New York. Willard remarked, "Even a man as old as Ramses the Second—you know the Egyptian mummy— would fall in love with her. And he's been dead for thousands of years!"

After lunch, they hoped to have their first group meeting with the three girls already selected, plus one or two more from the morning's work. However, the key problem remained: finding the man to be their star.

Jessie skimmed through the possibilities with distaste. Picking up one reply, she said, "Robert Sullivan just leaves me cold, Willard. The fact that he accepted before the ink was barely dry puts me off. It is a good letter, sure, but come on, you don't jump into something like this so quickly."

"Well, I sort of agree with you. But worse," he said, cringing, "he's really long in the tooth. Look at that ghastly smile! Those have to be dentures. And his enormous ears! He's ugly enough to give old age a bad name." With a blue fingernail, he flicked the photo off the desk, falling just short of the wastebasket. He picked up another glossy. "I thought Austin Campbell might be a possibility."

"You can't be serious, Willard! We met him only yesterday, and I've already forgotten what he looks like. He is so *boring*! That hypnotic monotone would put our young ladies to sleep. No, Willard, I would go with Silvio Lucca before him."

Willard nearly bolted out of his chair. "No way, Jessie! That old dog is just an oily Latin letch. He's been married seven times, for heaven's sake! Plus, he isn't really rich enough for us. Rumor has it that he lives on an allowance from Silvio Junior." He sat back down again, tucking one leg underneath him. He mulled over the possible list again, not encouraged by what he saw. "It's only been a few days," he said dispiritedly.

"I suppose," she murmured. "Willard, maybe we need a better recruiting technique. More of a personal approach."

"Yes, possibly . . . what about Agnes and Mr. Hudson? Why not have her call him?"

Jessie shot that down fast. "I think she would be too embarrassed. And, anyway, his letter is in the works." She glanced over at the door, where she left her packages. "It's part of the second batch FedEx picked up an hour ago. He'll have it today or tomorrow morning. I think we'll have to keep our fingers crossed." She reviewed the prospective list, but they'd already gone over it a dozen times. "If an appealing rich guy doesn't cross our radar soon, well, Willard, I think it's back to the drawing board . . . God! I hate to have to tell Saul that we may be changing directions."

"Speaking of the Devil!" She followed Willard's gaze and saw Saul in the outer office. He was hovering over a very pretty contestant being interviewed at one of the desks. His few strands of long, black hair were carefully combed across his perspiring bald head, and as she watched, his smile morphed into a revolting leer. Saul permitted his fat fingers to slide down from her shoulder toward her breasts, but the girl sprang to her feet almost instantly, glowing in anger and humiliation. She slapped his face, very hard. Only slightly stunned, Saul turned and headed to the door.

Willard was nearly a blur as he shot out of Jessie's office. By the time Jessie caught up with him, Willard was nipping at Saul's heels as her notorious boss beat a retreat through reception to the waiting elevator. "Don't you dare interfere with our show again," Willard snarled.

Saul found his usual bluster as he turned to confront them, his face beet red, a vein throbbing at his temple. "I own this place, and I'll do as I damn well please! I'll be back after lunch!" he shouted as the doors slid closed.

"How can you bear that man?" Willard was radiating anger. "Jessie, I'm not going to permit that slob to ruin this show. I am not. Let me settle the girl down . . . and then you can take me to lunch and settle me down too. . . . It will be a three Brandy Alexander session, I suspect."

But the lunch was not to be. Moments later Jessie's assistant rushed in to exclaim, "Saul just collapsed! His secretary called and the paramedics are on the way."

"I'll go up. Willard, you stay here!" Jessie hurried to the boss's office on the floor above, where she found a scene of controlled pandemonium. Saul was conscious, lying on the floor, breathing rapidly, pale, in pain, and very, very frightened. Jessie knelt by his side, and her velvety voice purred encouragement. She held his hand, and her calming magic seemed to work. Saul's trembling lessened, and when the paramedic team struggled to lift him away on a stretcher and place him on a gurney a few minutes later, he was reluctant to release her hand from his grasp.

After briefing Willard and her key assistants that Saul had probably suffered a heart attack, Jessie grabbed a cab and hurried to Mount Sinai Hospital. The emergency ward nurse told her there was no news yet. She sat waiting, wishing that she had brought her computer as she distractedly leafed through a six-month-old issue of *Popular Mechanics*. Then she spotted Hadassah Gross rushing in through the doors. Jessie knew her only slightly, since socializing with Saul was an agony performed only when absolutely required, but Jessie gathered the small, anxious woman in her arms and comforted her as best she could.

"Hadassah, he's still with the doctors. I was with him in his office, though. He was conscious and if it was a heart attack, it was mild."

Mrs. Gross, now in her fifties, had once been pretty. She clung to Jessie. "He's all that I have," she sobbed. "We have no children— what would I do without him? I've tried to help him lose weight, but he cheats when I'm not around . . . and he never exercises."

A tired-looking ER doctor emerged to tell them that Saul was sleeping in the recovery room, and their relief was profound. The doctor, a light-skinned, nice-looking Jamaican man in his thirties, said that it would be several hours before Saul would be taken to a private room and they couldn't see him until then. "He's going to be okay. The TPA we gave him dissolved the clot. With any luck, he will treat this as a warning and get his diet and exercise on track." He paused and gave Hadassah a sympathetic smile, "If I could've given him a prescription for a heart attack to scare him back into health, this would've been it."

Jessie managed to get back to the office briefly, and then returned to the hospital to spend a half an hour with Saul and Hadassah after he was established in his room. He beamed when she arrived. "Jessie, it looks like I'm going to make it—praise God."

"Wonderful, Saul." He looked dreadfully pale, but his breathing was normal and he was not in pain.

"But I won't be back at Acme for two or three months. The cardiologist here says I need complete rest and a new lifestyle."

Two to three months? She'd be free of him for two to three months?

"It will do you a world of good," she said, comforting him.

"But, Jessie, I won't be able to help you run Acme. What will you do without me?"

Inside Jessie was jumping for joy at the prospect, but she managed to act concerned. "Saul, it will be very tough. Very hard. But with what you have taught me, well, I think I'll manage. I'll give it my all. You'll see." After more small talk, a squeeze of Saul's hand, and a comforting hug to Hadassah, she was out of the hospital, nearly ecstatic with her newfound freedom.

Still, she was running late. She hailed a cab to Grand Central to meet Mark. He was coming in from Scarsdale on the 5:42 train. The really hard part of the day was about to begin.

*J*essie waited on the lower-level and watched the people filing through the exit gate, scanning the crowd for Mark. There! When she spotted him, her heart gave a little leap—she hadn't seen him since Sunday night. He was her joy, the most important person in her life. She waved, trying to catch his attention. He was deep in his own thoughts as usual, looking quite adult in his navy pea coat and wool watch cap pulled down over his ears. He was tall enough to be a young enlisted man, but that would never happen.

She gave him a big hug that he ignored.

"Hi, sweetie, how was the ride in?"

"Boring. There are 137 signal lights between Scarsdale and here."

She could imagine him counting every one.

"Well, didn't you have your pocket chess computer with you?"

"That was boring, too. I always win. It has a program error. It always accepts a knight sacrifice."

They headed together from the platform until they reached the vast main room. "Anyway, I thought we could stop at the McDonald's on Forty-second Street for a burger and shake before the lecture. The auditorium is pretty close." Locking her arm through his and giving him a little loving squeeze that, as always, he did not reciprocate, they headed up the wide Vanderbilt Avenue staircase at a brisk pace.

McDonald's was hot, steamy, and very busy, but Mark secured a tiny table while Jessie ordered and brought the food.

"I feel guilty not providing better food, sweetie."

"The sign says that they've sold ninety-nine billion burgers."

She started unloading the hamburgers from the plastic tray. "Well, nobody ever said they taste bad."

"Is it ninety-nine billion burgers for this store?"

"I think it's probably the number sold worldwide since they began about fifty years ago." Jessie knew her answer had to be precise.

"When was the hamburger invented?"

"Long ago." She inserted a straw into the lid of his chocolate shake. "Sweetie, why do you want to know?"

"I would like to calculate the percentage of the total that McDonald's made."

That made her smile. Who but her precious Mark would ever think of such a thing. "Well, let's say the hamburger was invented in 1900—the turn of the last century." Mark's expression turned into a look of intense concentration. Jessie knew that inside his handsome, black-haired head, behind his intense blue eyes, he was computing rates of population growth, beef vs. chicken consumption and God knows what else. He wouldn't hear a word she said until he'd reached an answer. She waited patiently.

"Two point two percent, I think."

"That's good to know," She nudged his hamburger toward him. "But now let's finish up. We need to hurry to get to the lecture."

As he started eating, he announced, "I don't like Gregory. I'll play my chess game instead. I need to know if it'll always fall for a bishop sacrifice, and then I'll test for a rook sacrifice."

Jessie's heart sank at Mark's response. Tonight was an important part of her effort to try to bridge the void between her son and fiancé. Mark had dismissed Gregory offhand within minutes of their first meeting. He thought everything Gregory said was stupid. Jessie believed that if Mark could see Gregory in action, running one of his inner awareness programs, that he would realize that Gregory was a person of real substance.

As they walked together to the hotel ballroom where the program "Strengthen Your Inner Self with the Anthony Tower Method" would be held, she tried hard and eventually got Mark to agree that he would listen. They arrived only five minutes before the lights in the room dimmed. They found places among the chairs grouped in front of a huge TV projection screen and a small podium upon which a lectern was mounted. About three hundred people were there.

Shortly, the giant image of Anthony Tower shimmered before them, and his magnetic, mellifluous voice boomed out in the recorded introduction to the evening. Gregory would carry the program after his boss's canned inspirational opening, and inspirational it was! Tower had perfected the art of stirring up emotions, bringing to light the fears, doubts, failings, and insecurities one normally kept bottled up. He was brilliant at hitting every key, pulling every stop, and pushing every pedal on the emotional organ. Soon, everyone in the audience seemed to feel that, within, each of them contained at least a Wurlitzer-sized worth of emotional troubles. According to him, a person's problems originated from an inner childlike self, a self full of fears and contradictions. By strengthening this self— helping it to "grow up"—one could become mature and happy. Most important, this could be accomplished only if one closely followed the program that would be taught over the following seven sessions. "A happy, happy future awaits you all! You have taken the first step! You are here!"

As the recorded image faded and the lights came up, Jessie found herself brushing away a tear. Mark had a look on his face of inexpressible boredom. Then Gregory bounded onto the little stage.

A much younger, taller, and strikingly handsome version of his boss's ephemeral image, he picked up the message without missing a beat. Gregory was wearing a lapel radio microphone on his crisply tailored, blue blazer, so he was able to stride into the front rows, never faltering in the presentation. As he talked, he clicked on slides projected onto the screen. They presented simple ideas; it seemed that tonight's lesson—the first step—was to discover and make friends with the inner self, the child within.

As Gregory's words flowed over the audience, gaining their total confidence, Mark took out his computer chess game.

Mark seemed completely detached—not just bored but totally absorbed into his world of numbers, of counting, and ordering things—a world Jessie could not understand or penetrate. He was soon fully engaged with the chess game. After a few minutes he informed her quite loudly, "I knew I could sucker it with a bishop sacrifice. I'm sure it'll fall for the rook too!"

Gregory paused briefly and looked at Mark, but the boy didn't notice.

After an hour—the time seemed much less, Gregory was so skilled at holding the audience's attention—he held a brief question and answer period. Another assistant, who Jessie hadn't noticed previously, moved smoothly through the group with a portable microphone. Most of the questions dealt with "how" to nurture the inner self, and Gregory confidently assured them that the "how" part was the essence of the following six sessions.

The final question was asked by a woman in her forties. She stood and hesitated before speaking, long enough to capture everyone's attention—even Mark looked up from his game.

"I lost my husband a few months ago to throat cancer." The room grew hushed; she reminded Jessie of Hadassah and the life and death drama of the real world. "He and I had been married for twenty-two years. We have . . . I should say, I have, two children from our marriage." Her eyes were glistening as she made the effort to continue. "I am overcome with grief. I don't see how I can continue. I came here looking for help. Will you be able to help me?" She buried her face in her hands as she sat back down. The assistant, very gently, removed the microphone from her lap.

Gregory silently moved to her side and rested his hand upon her shoulder as she looked up to him with tearful eyes. His presence was reassuring but his answer—about learning to acquaint her inner child over the lessons of loss and grief and helping that child grow into a happier child, one accepting of grief—struck Jessie as far short of what was needed. The package was so much more impressive than the contents.

As the meeting was breaking up, Jessie complimented him on his performance, but as she and Mark walked through the cold night back to Grand Central, she was troubled by his rote response to the woman's grief. And the effort to build a bridge between Mark and Gregory had flopped completely.

To her astonishment, Mark seemed somehow aware of her feelings. It wasn't possible she knew, because the psychologists had told her so a number of times. So why did he turn to her as he walked to the platform and say, "Mom, I love you"?

CHAPTER FIVE

*O*n Monday morning Steven had nearly finished shaving when he was alerted by the commentator's mention of the name McLaren. He quickly focused on the little TV set on the wall in his bathroom. The picture was being taken from a news traffic helicopter, and it showed a burning car which was blocking miles of traffic on the Triborough Bridge. He could just make out the distinctive gull-wing doors through the black smoke. Jesus! It had to be Henry's. It was the only one in America.

He rushed to the telephone in his bedroom, fumbled to put on his reading glasses, and grabbed the plastic card containing key phone numbers. He dialed Henry's mobile. It rang and rang, and Steven was nearly frantic with worry when, finally, Henry responded with a quavering "Hello?"

"Hank, my God! Are you okay?"

"Yeah, Dad, I'm fine! But the car isn't—it's still burning. How did you know?"

Steven relaxed, a little. His son seemed more worried about the damned car than himself. He must be okay.

"What happened? You aren't hurt? I saw it on TV."

"No, I'm fine, really. We were just driving back to town when the car started to sputter. The engine was misfiring badly, and in the mirror I saw flames shooting out of the tailpipes." The story was horrifying, but Steven relaxed a little more and wiped the shaving cream off his face onto the sleeve of his terry-cloth robe. Excitedly, Henry continued his explanation: how he'd jumped out, popped the lid over the huge rear engine, saw that the exhaust pipes and the muffler were white hot, how the heat had radiated from them and set the exotic carbon fiber body aflame. He abruptly stopped and said, "Dad, Dad, a fire engine is here! Gotta go!"

At three o'clock that afternoon, Mrs. O'Brian ushered a sheepish Henry into Steven's office. His son was very embarrassed. It's not every day that one manages to burn a million-dollar automobile.

"Hi, Dad." Henry smiled weakly. Steven erased his own frown and quickly moved around his desk to give the tall, errant youth a strong hug. Fatherly love always prevailed.

After they settled back on either side of the desk, Henry began describing the morning's catastrophe. "I'm really lucky. The fireman put it out right away and only part of the back end is destroyed. The engine and the chassis should be okay. I talked with the factory, and they think that they can make it as good as new. I'm going to airship it this week."

"You're going to fly it back to England?" Steven's lifestyle was hardly cheap, but Henry always seemed a step ahead.

"Yeah, the insurance won't pay for that part, but it'll save weeks. And, Dad, I'm going to need you to top up the trust again, after all. Sorry, but I didn't expect this expense and also everything burned up in our suitcases."

Steven sighed. Mrs. O'Brian would give Henry a mid-quarter check, as she'd done so often in the past. It was hard for him to lecture his son on economy when, so obviously, he would never notice the withdrawal. But it was too bad Kathy also lost her clothes.

"Sorry about Kathy's suitcase. Was she badly shaken?"

Henry squirmed a little in his chair. "It was Jill, actually. She's pissed about losing her stuff but otherwise she's okay. We had a great weekend together in East Hampton. Bunny Phipps throws a super house party."

"What happened to Kathy?" Steven really liked the vivacious redhead.

"Well, she's spending a couple of weeks with her parents in Chevy Chase. Uh . . . it's best if you don't mention Jill. Kathy doesn't need to know about her."

Another sigh, before Steven responded, "Hank, when are you going to get serious about life? Settle down into a career, marry a wonderful girl, and start a family?"

"Hey, not as long as I've got a rich father!" Henry's grin was irrepressible. "We're not poor yet, are we? But, if you want to have a serious father-son talk, let me bounce one off you, Dad. When are you going to get your own act together? How long are you going to live like a monk?" Henry turned very serious before he continued, "Dad, when Mom died we were all crushed. I know how much you loved her. But, it's been five years. It's time for you to have a life again."

This time it was Steven who squirmed uncomfortably in his

chair. Henry pressed on, "What about that letter you showed me at the Links Club? Call that studio! Hey, you need to have some excitement. Maybe we could do it together!"

Steven was not happy to have the tables turned so quickly in this conversation. The letter was in his desk drawer at this moment, but he had been trying to put it from his mind. And he didn't trust Henry's enthusiasm on his behalf, not when gorgeous young women were to be involved. So he said, "Hank, I'll certainly think about it. Thanks for your concern. Now, about that check?"

After some further conversation about the amount required, he stood and guided Henry out to Mrs. O'Brian's desk. The "top up" check did divert his son's attention, and shortly Henry left happily with it in his pocket, without further talk about Dad's personal life.

In the past few days both his kids had pushed him. Without talking to each other, they were reading from the same page. Were they right? Was he letting grief become a habit?

*A*t nine o'clock on Wednesday morning, Tony, his regular driver picked him up in the black Bentley Turbo-T, and Eamon closed the door on the gleaming supercar with his usual courtesy. Steven settled back into the comfortable contoured rear seat, paying little attention to the aromas from the supple, rich leather and the beeswaxed-marquetry inlaid woods, masterpieces of craftsmanship. The thick lamb's wool carpets and the solid body muffled the sounds from the streets and the powerful engine was but a whisper, as Steven wound up his reading of the *Journal*, scowling at the day's political outrages from the editorial page.

The relatively traffic-free drive out to Space Technologies, near Oyster Bay on Long Island, didn't take long at all. Steven had been the chairman of the company's board of directors for years. In fact, all the way back to when he first financed the now giant company. The firm had prospered greatly under his guidance and on his sixtieth birthday the board had waived the requirement for mandatory retirement.

Steven actually didn't like board meetings. A good board meeting should be very, very boring, Steven always thought. The lawyers, accountants, and management should have thoroughly discussed every possible issue beforehand so that business ought to be routine. An exciting board meeting meant that something was out of control. The meeting Steven was attending that day was being held to review and approve next year's operating budget.

Thomas Clark, the dynamic, youthful CEO, had reached the details of the budget when lunch was laid out in front of them. They typically worked through lunch. He had raised the need to float another bond issue to finance capital equipment, when Aaron Adler, a combative and outspoken director, started to challenge Clark. "Do we need to spend so much? Wouldn't a stock issue be less dilutive to earnings than interest on bonds?" And so on and on it went, with ever growing impatience and irritation.

Finally Clark blurted out: "Look, Aaron, if you're so damn sure of how to run this show, maybe you should just take over." He said it with a smile, but the tension was only thinly disguised.

"Oh, come on, I'm just making you earn your outrageous pay," Aaron barked.

Then he did the unthinkable. He tossed a bread crust at Clark, hitting him squarely in the chest.

The CEO was taken aback, but only for a moment. With a sweeping motion, Clark snatched a bread roll from the table and hurled it back at Aaron, who caught it in midair and flung it directly at the astonished Steven! Within a second or two, the entire board broke into a high school cafeteria bun fight. After every roll and napkin was thrown and lay on the floor, the directors collapsed in fits of laughter, including Steven, who couldn't believe that he'd been one of the more active participants. Thank God none of the waiters or outsiders had been present. The investing public's confidence in big corporate America would remain unshaken. Interestingly, the board moved the CEO's agenda and ended its affairs on a congenial note.

As Tony drove Steven back to Manhattan in mid-afternoon, the friendly driver said, "Mr. Hudson, we're not far from Ivy Columns. Would you like to swing by and have a look? It's only about fifteen minutes from here."

Steven caught his breath. Was there no escaping the past? But maybe it would be best to deal with it, so he'd answered calmly, "Sure, Tony. That's a good idea. I've got plenty of time."

The scene of that awful afternoon after the memorial service rose in his mind again. It had been such a happy house when Henry and Helen were growing up. Every weekend had been busy with tennis parties and the kids' friends around. Steven always remembered it in the bloom of summertime, with the scent of roses in the air and Yvonne working in the garden, which was her delight. Once Steven had had to go looking for her with a flashlight long after the sun set, she was so loath to leave her beautiful roses. In one of Steven's favorite photos, Yvonne was standing under an umbrella in the rain and at the same time watering some fresh planting with a garden hose, silly to anyone who is not a gardener. He remembered her sitting at her desk late into the winter evenings, poring over her books on roses and flowering shrubs.

A friend once said, "You don't 'get over' the loss of a loved one, but you learn to live with the loss." As they neared the house, Steven thought that he must be a very slow learner.

The Bentley passed through the wrought iron gate with it's gold-tipped finials and motored up the long, private road flanked by tall, stately oak trees to the circular drive around the fountain, where it stopped in front of the ivy-covered columns supporting the entrance portico. The place was flawlessly maintained. The lawns had been swept of the fallen leaves, and the spotless windows of the closed house glinted darkly in the fading winter afternoon light. No one was about. The gardeners probably had left, and the housekeeper must have been in her quarters.

Tony hopped out to open the door, but Steven didn't move. After a few moments, he was able to swallow the lump in his throat and say, "Thanks, Tony. But I'm not going in. Let's drive back to town."

*N*ow, back sitting at his empty desk, Steven realized that he had finished up his week's work. Mrs. O'Brian, bless her, was so efficient in organizing everything, eliminating the inessential, that Steven sometimes thought he had become a mere rubber stamp in her capable hands. She seemed to know what he should do next before he did. He reflected that the day's drive and the board meeting was probably the high point of his week.

A bun fight, the most fun he'd have. Pathetic.

He slid out the thin drawer in the center of the desk and the letter was lying there. He read it again.

He summoned Mrs. O'Brian. Handing the letter to her, he asked if she could track down Jessica James.

Why didn't he just dial the number himself? Steven wasn't sure. Did a part of him want Mrs. O'Brian to read the letter? He knew she would never offer any opinion unless asked. If he was the Lion of Wall Street, she was the Sphinx of Wall Street.

After a few minutes, Mrs. O'Brian appeared at the office door to say that Ms. James was holding on line one.

Before Steven had a chance to say more than "Steven Hudson here," a rich, smooth woman's voice purred over the line.

"Mr. Hudson, I am *so* delighted, so wonderfully delighted that you called. I was about to call you, in fact. Obviously you received my letter."

The alluring voice intrigued him. "Well, I guess you're real then," he said. "I halfway thought the whole thing might just be a joke."

"Oh, I'm real, all right," she said with a laugh. Steven never knew that honey could actually flow through the telephone wires. "Of all the men I hoped might respond to my invitation, you are without a doubt my first choice." Her voice became sweeter still. "We need to meet. I personally want to introduce you to the wonderful world we are preparing for our show."

There was some sort of sexual magic in that voice. In spite of himself, Steven couldn't resist wanting to see the person with this caressing, intoxicating voice.

"Well, oh, I suppose we—uh, could find a time, maybe." Steven was having trouble saying yes without seeming too anxious. Ms. James heard the yes clearly, however.

"Mr. Hudson, it's four o'clock now," she whispered. "I will be in your office in twenty minutes—we simply have to talk."

This was going too fast, thought Steven with alarm. If her body looked anything equal to her voice, he didn't think she would pass unnoticed within Hudson and Partners, not to mention Mrs. O'Brian.

"No. Uh, you're uptown, aren't you? It would be better if I stop by on my way home. I'll drop by before five. Is that okay with you, Ms. James?"

"Call me Jessica, please. That will be perfect, Mr. Hudson. Just perfect. I'll be waiting."

Steven put down the phone feeling strangely exhilarated. Why should he wait until five? He could go right now. He grabbed his briefcase and stopped by Mrs. O'Brian's desk to retrieve the letter—it had the address.

"Mrs. O'Brian, please call down to Tony. He needs to drive me uptown for a meeting and then home."

"A screen test, Mr. Hudson? Is that your next appointment today?"

Steven looked closely at Mrs. O'Brian. If you divided the Mona Lisa's smile by one hundred, it would have exaggerated the expression on Mrs. O'Brian's face. But it had to be. Yes, a smile, or at least the Darwinian ancestral predecessor of what is now known as a smile.

"I guess you glanced at the letter, Mrs. O'Brian."

"Mr. Hudson, you know me better than that . . ." and she winked.

Mrs. O'Brian winked! Bun fighting boards and a winking sphinx. Steven's world was transforming before his eyes, as he fled down to the waiting car.

CHAPTER SIX

*S*teven arrived at Acme's building a little after four thirty and calmed his jittery nerves with a few deep breaths while riding up in a chrome and mirrored elevator to the twenty-third floor. An attractive Asian receptionist summoned Ms. James, and Steven waited while sitting on the edge of an expensive leather chair in a tasteful but not over-the-top reception area. He was having second thoughts—and third thoughts—about the meeting. He felt foolish, increasingly sure that this was not the way to deal with the bitter residue of long-standing grief.

She walked in briskly. Ms. James was stunning and her smile friendly and genuine. She was startlingly beautiful: tall, black hair, brilliant blue eyes, and a look in her sculpted face of refinement and intrigue. Her complexion was extraordinary, her figure marvelous. Steven was nearly overwhelmed by the initial impact.

"Mr. Hudson, I am Jessie James."

From out of nowhere came the wisecrack: "Gosh, are you? I came unarmed."

Instantly, Steven felt like an idiot. Of course, Jessica James would be called Jessie. She must be sick to death of dumb comments like that about the train robber and gunslinger from the Old West. She didn't seem to mind, however. "Oh, you'll be safe with me, Mr. Hudson!" Her velvet voice sounded even better in person. "I am so happy to make your acquaintance. Will you please join me in my office? Perhaps for a glass of sherry as well? It's almost five."

As they walked, Steven didn't notice the wink she gave to a tiny man with rainbow colored hair, who winked back. And he couldn't have guessed how the two of them had tailored a sales pitch just for him, right down to the sherry.

Steven followed her as she passed through the open office behind the reception area. He managed to mumble a response. "Sherry would be a great idea. I always like to mix business and pleasure." God, that was another dumb clunker comment, he thought. He felt as awkward as a teenager on his first date.

She was a lovely woman—thirty-five? Forty?—and as he followed, he admired the long, confident strides of her walk. She'd achieved the look of a powerful woman executive without diminishing her extraordinary beauty in any way. The smart blue suit, no doubt by some top designer, was set off by fashionable, delicate high heels, her dark hair was swept back—but not pulled back too tightly—and an attractive pair of glasses hung on a thin silver chain around her lovely neck.

Her corner office was nearly all glass with floor-to-ceiling windows and glass inner walls dividing her domain from the acre of surrounding desks. The others working there were young and dressed very informally. Her secretary had blue and pink slashes in her hair. This sure was different from Wall Street, he thought. As they entered, Jessie flicked a switch near the door and instantly the interior glass walls became opaque. Steven had read about liquid crystal glass walls in the Science Section of the *Times*, but he had never seen them before. In the midst of the office activity outside, they were suddenly alone.

Jessie sat on a small couch behind a low, circular glass table and crossed her shapely legs, clad in gray-black stockings. Steven sat in a comfortable deep chair nearby. He tried to focus his eyes on her face and only her face.

"Ms. James, let me apologize for that dumb remark about your name. You've probably been hearing that joke since you were a little girl."

"Oh, don't worry, James was the name of my ex-husband. I actually like the desperado idea, so I kept the name after I got rid of the man. And I haven't had two seconds to change it back even if I wanted to. The TV business really keeps one on the go, and that's probably why I'm still single." She slid easily over this bit of personal history, but Steven spotted what looked like an engagement ring on her left hand.

"Mr. Hudson, before we start, would you mind if I called you Steven?"

"Of course . . . Jessie," he said, trying to sound informal.

"Let me begin by telling you what we're all about." Following her script, she briefly outlined the history of Acme Studios, stressing the fact that they were one of the strongest independent TV producers in America. She dropped the names of some of their most important shows. Steven had actually heard of a few of these, even if he'd never watched one.

While she was talking, Jessie poured two small glasses of sherry from a cut-glass decanter and placed them on the table. Steven liked this—it was not what he'd expected at all. Boy was she beautiful, he thought.

"The problem all producers face these days is that the public is sick of the stuff we've been grinding out. New sitcoms seem to flop. So do new hospital dramas and police shows. Meanwhile, the old war horses like *Friends*, *Buffy*, and even *Law & Order* have been beaten into the ground after running for years. The only thing the viewers never seem to tire of is *The Simpsons*." She glanced up expectantly, but he didn't respond. He wasn't a fan.

"Enter reality shows. *Joe Millionaire* was a mega hit and so was *American Idol*. *Survivor* broke all records. *The Apprentice* was huge. *Amazing Race* continues to win Emmys. If we can come up with a reality hit, we can sell it at a premium to the networks because a hot program at prime time will keep the audience tuned to that channel for the whole evening. That's the way it works. In theory." Gesturing with her sherry glass, she filled him in on some other industry knowledge. "Reality may be the only way to stem the decline of the network audience. There's just too much competition out there—cable, the Internet, video games. People are working long hours to make ends meet. Leisure time is at a premium. We are always seeking a fresh idea, and when we get it, we can sell it quickly."

"That's interesting," said Steven, who downed a little of his sherry. "How do you go about selling such a show?"

"Oh, that's the easy part," she said with a dazzling simile. "You just talk to the moguls, plus, of course, General Electric. Between Michael, Rupert, and Sumner, you have Disney/ABC, Fox, and CBS, and GE gives you NBC."

Steven knew Sumner Redstone and had met Rupert Murdoch.

"Do these men actually get involved in stuff like this?" he wondered out loud.

"You bet they do," Jessie enthused. "Rupert was in England and happened to see their show *Pop Idol*. I know for a fact that he bought the U.S. rights to it on the spot and it became the Fox hit *American Idol* in no time."

Steven was impressed with Jessie's grasp of her field. She was certainly dynamic, he thought as she expanded upon the importance of reality TV. Who did she remind him of? It came to him—a very beautiful English actress who had caught his eye recently on a flight to London. They hadn't talked, but had "slept together" across the aisle in the British Air first-class section. The steward told him later that she had played the Devil in a popular Hollywood movie comedy. Her name was Liz something. Yet Jessie put her in the shadows. Everything about Jessie James was lovely. Her smile was warm and her teeth perfect when she laughed. Her features looked chiseled, and her business suit couldn't hide a figure of wonderful promise.

She was still a businesswoman, though, and one of some importance, judging by the swanky corner office. Although it wasn't as big or as formal as his own, with the outrageous price of Manhattan office space, she was clearly a top earner for her firm to justify this much square-footage extravagance. Plus those on-off glass walls! That technology didn't come cheap, he was sure.

There was no wall space for art, but some sort of polished stainless-steel Mobius strip stood on a marble stand in the corner. Steven's office contained a wall of trophies, mementoes of his trade—New York Stock Exchange bronzes of the proverbial bear and bull mauling each other, one bronze for each company he'd built and then listed on the exchange. The business awards on Jessie's glass bookcase were of a different kind—plaques and cubes—but she had lots of them. He thought that a couple of them might be Emmys.

He refocused on what she was saying. He wondered if she'd decided that the best way to capture his attention was by coming at him from the business angle. He did feel himself being drawn and wanting to help this attractive woman with her problem. Then he remembered the letter, but before he could ask about it, make polite excuses and then extract himself, Jessie James moved on ahead of him.

"Steven. Now, I need to get very personal with you. The fact that you called me and that you are here gives me some hope that you will at least listen to our idea. You should know that I have talked with several wealthy and prominent men so far, and I have a couple of them ready to participate." Steven fleetingly wondered if she was trying to stir his competitive instincts.

"But, Steven, they aren't right. *You* are right for this show, from our selfish viewpoint. Frankly, you have the looks. You are an extraordinarily handsome man, Mr. Hudson! The cameras will love you, you will fill the frame, you will look great on television." Steven hadn't experienced such open flattery in quite some time. He couldn't help blushing again.

"And," she said, ticking off points on her fingers, "you have the stature, the class, the presence, the sophistication, the accomplishments, the charm, and the knowledge of one man in a million. No, I lie—make that one man in one hundred million."

Steven couldn't see any red warning flags through this wonderful haze of compliments. He could listen to Jessie sweet talk him with that caressing, lovely voice forever, even if her charm was rehearsed.

"So, Steven, you are the answer for us. But why would you consider participating? Clearly not for the money. It will mean nothing to you, although you could donate our couple of hundred thousand dollars to the Hudson Family Charitable Trust, if you wished." She had obviously fired up Google and had done her homework on him, he realized.

"No, the only reason you might want to explore this with us, Steven, is for the best reason possible. To have some fun and excitement and to enhance your life with a fabulous new partner."

Steven stirred in his chair and was about to protest when Jessie cut him off by holding up her hand.

"Wait, Steven! Let me show you."

Moving quickly to her desk, she retrieved a large manila folder. Laying it on the table in front of him, she flicked it open and fanned out over a dozen black-and-white photographs. All professionally shot, they displayed the most incredibly beautiful young women imaginable. How could there be so many gorgeous girls, all different but equally attractive?

"Athletes, models, actresses, all in their twenties, none famous yet, none committed in a relationship. All of them wanting to meet you, Steven," Jessie said enticingly. "I have interviewed them all, plus many more. They are wonderful girls, all quite different but with the same innocence of youth. Steven, youth!"

He sat unmoving in his chair, transfixed by the photographs. A sudden dryness in his throat made speaking difficult.

"Imagine the fun of getting to know them. To dine and dance and party. To know them in your own home. To try them on for size, as it were," she said. "To get to know a few of them better than the others. To know them well, to *know* them really well. To perhaps narrow the field, over time, to one or two to whom you are strongly attracted and have known fully. And then, at last, letting nature take its course to find 'the one.' *The one*, Steven, who has changed your life. The one, Steven, who you can't dream of parting with. The one you can't bear never seeing again, of knowing no longer. The one, Steven, who will become your knowing bride!"

The dryness in his throat made it impossible for him to respond, although he felt like giving her a standing ovation for her performance. And he was blushing. He could feel it rising as Jessie's speech had gathered momentum. He hadn't blushed like this since he'd been a boy. God, all this talk about knowing and youth and youthful knowing, in the biblical way of knowing, he knew. Nervously, he grabbed his tiny glass of sherry and knocked it back, all while thinking about *knowing*. Knowing one or more in his bedroom, naked and knowing the whole night through. Lots of knowing.

"Wh . . . what about the cameras?" he stammered.

"Oh," she laughed, "they just become part of the background."

"You mean, they're around all the time?" Steven could feel the blush move from pink to somewhere south of crimson.

"No, of course not," she assured him. "Just enough with you and each girl so that the camera gets to see your personalities a little. Observe how you interact with each other. It's sort of like peeking through a window, from time to time, to see how things are progressing. Don't worry, you and the girls will spend lots of time by yourselves, in your homes, in your clubs, on your jet, whatever. Off camera."

Steven felt himself sinking in deeper and deeper, but he couldn't seem to find a way to stop it.

"But that's getting ahead of the story," she continued. "We will start the show with a big fancy dinner party—you in black tie, they in

SEX AND THE SINGLE ZILLIONAIRE 81

formal evening gowns. That's the only sequence we'll shoot in the studio because it will be a big important scene, when you first get to meet all the girls. And before then, you and I will have narrowed the field to only eight girls. We think that's about the optimum number for a thirteen week series."

"How will we do that?" Steven wondered.

"Easy," she smiled. "You take these photos with you and pick out the eight you like best. Your eye won't fail you. Tomorrow I'll call you and answer any questions you have about personality or background."

Jessie, with a master saleswoman's sense of when to lighten up, began to assemble the fabulous photographs and put them back into the folder.

"My, it's just past six," she purred. "Can I refresh your sherry, Steven?" She really did look a lot like that beautiful actress who played the part of the Devil.

He had to put a stop to this madness. "Oh, no," he said hastily. "I'd no idea it had gotten so late. I really shouldn't keep my driver waiting." He took the proffered envelope, gathered his topcoat and hat from the adjoining chair, and prepared to leave. He was in a daze as Jessie flipped the switch, making the walls to the office transparent again, now only half full of the hip young people. She walked him back to the reception area with her hand lightly touching his elbow.

"Steven, I can't tell you how much this has meant to me, meeting you this afternoon. It is so rare I get to meet a man of your caliber. I am overwhelmed that you like our project. It will be such fun! You will enjoy yourself so much! Take care, I'll call you tomorrow."

Her perfume lingered on his clothing. He could smell it mixing together with an odd whiff of sulfur in the empty elevator. A match lighted by a smoker too eager to wait until he was outside, no doubt.

Tony was waiting in the Bentley. He put on his chauffeur's cap and sprang out of the car to open the door for Steven, leaving the radio on. WQXR was playing some opera. *Faust*, Steven thought.

In reality, it was *Figaro*.

*J*essie, how did it go? I can't wait to hear—he looks perfect for us!" Willard could hardly contain his excitement and his curiosity.

"I agree, Steven Hudson would be ideal," she replied. "The poor guy blushed like a teenager when I showed him the girls! I followed our plan pretty well—I really gave it my best shot, Willard." She blushed herself, thinking of how she'd reduced him to such a state. He was a very distinguished, prominent man and still damned attractive, she thought. "But, let's face it," she went on, "he's going to wake up tomorrow morning and realize how absurd our plot is. This guy is not some nouveau riche dope who wants to be on TV."

Jessie and Willard continued to talk about Steven while she collected her things, preparing to go home. She agreed, as planned, to follow up the meeting with a phone call in the morning. "Wouldn't it be amazing if he said yes?"

"You have to work him, Jessie. You can do it, girl," he said, giving her an appraising look head to toe. "I know you can."

*H*is elevator opened into the dark foyer. None of the lights were on anywhere. The myriad sparkles of the Manhattan skyline shone through the vast windows of the dark penthouse. Where was Jeffrey? Where was his five o'clock martini? Muttering to himself, Steven stumbled into the darkened sunken living room and nearly took a flyer as he knocked into a modern, free-standing floor lamp. The folder flew from his grip and the photos scattered all over the travertine marble floor.

Steven had just found the light switches and was turning lights on when a bleary-eyed Jeffrey walked into the room, barefoot, in boxer shorts, and with a white T-shirt not quite covering his ample waistline.

"God, boss, it's you! I thought somebody had broken in. Gee, it's dark outside. I must've fallen asleep." His attention turned from the window to the mess on the living room floor.

"Holy shit, boss! Look at these pictures! Where did you get them?" Jeffrey busily gathered them up one after the other, smiling and muttering, "Fantastic! Wow! Look at this one, will you?"

"Jeffrey, stop babbling," Steven grumbled, embarrassed all over again. "Let's just get these photos put away. And put some clothes on." By now Jeffrey was staring at him with open curiosity, and Steven tried to deflect his question. "What do you plan to do about dinner? It's close to seven."

Jeffrey snapped his fingers. "I know! The letter. You're actually doing it—that's fantastic, boss! I can't believe it. I'm proud of you."

"Listen, Jeeves . . ."

"Ouch," he said, pretending to be wounded. "I know when you call me Jeeves it's either going to be very funny or very serious. This is serious, huh?"

"Yes, it's serious. It's nearly two hours after martini o'clock! I'm starving." Steven sighed. "Hell, to tell you the truth, I don't know what I am doing."

Jeffrey held up the pictures in his hand. "Well, boss, you got the photos. Did they send them to you?"

"Worse. I called the studio and went to their headquarters just now." Jeffrey didn't seem bothered, though, and Steven continued. "The producer is the most beautiful woman I've seen in a long time. She seems like a wonderful person too, bright, successful — the kind of woman I should maybe have in my life again." An image of her, with those great legs, came to him and he shuddered. "But, as to these girls . . . I think that I let her carry me away. I can't understand what's come over me. I can't even believe I've gone this far."

"Boss, you're bored. You're lonely. And you're a man. You deserve some excitement. It's only natural." He began gathering up the rest of the photographs. "I'll get hustling. Martini coming up. How do Blue Point Oysters sound? Followed by a nice little steak?"

Steven nodded, grateful Jeffrey was letting him off the hook.

It was a good dinner. Afterward, Steven sat on the comfortable couch in the darkened living room with a neat glass of single malt scotch in hand. Looking out at the tens of thousands of lights around him in the city beyond, Steven mused about the lives going on all around him. All that living. Plenty of *knowing* as well. He smiled at the thought. He got up, turned on a lamp, and picked up the folder with the photos from the massive stone coffee table, then sat back down again. He opened the folder and began to study the smiling, alluring photos. The girls truly were knockouts. No wonder he'd been struck dumb. Yet even as he reviewed the stack, he was thinking about Jessie James. She'd been so attractive and yet so accomplished. She was no dummy. A woman like that, he thought, was someone he'd like to know better.

*T*he next morning, Steven delayed going to his Wall Street office, and by ten thirty he'd decided to work from home instead. The office in the penthouse was extremely comfortable.

He was going through routine reports, some backlogged phone calls and legal papers when his daughter called, to his pleasant surprise.

"Pop, Mrs. O'B. said you were at home. That's great. I'm coming by with something you'll like. I'll be there before noon. Ciao."

*L*ess than an hour later, Eamon rang up from the lobby saying he'd cleared the elevator through to the penthouse and that Helen and two delivery men were on their way up with something big. He had also rung through to Jeffrey to meet them.

Soon Helen and the delivery men were setting a tall, thick package down in front of a blank wall in the foyer. As Jeffrey showed the guys out, Helen started to tear off the brown paper covering carefully. Shortly, she had exposed the painting/sculpture called *Paint*, which they had seen on their art jaunt of last Saturday.

"Pop, I went past the gallery yesterday, and this was going in through the front door. Turns out the wife of the guy who bought it hated it and sent it back, so I had it brought here for you. It's on a trial loan, you aren't committed, but I love it."

"Helen, so do I," said her pleased father. "Jeffrey, please see if Tony is down in the garage. He can help us hang it. This is a perfect spot."

With Tony's help, Steven and Jeffrey mounted the piece. Both father and daughter were delighted with its extravagant flamboyance. Behind their backs, Tony and Jeffrey exchanged a raised eyebrow and a shrug of shoulders.

Steven and Helen were finishing cappuccinos and chatting about *Paint* hanging before them, when Jeffrey reentered the foyer and announced with a question in his voice, "There's a woman calling herself Jessie James on the telephone for you, boss."

Helen turned to her father. "That's a new name. Who's she, Pop? Have you taken to robbing banks instead of founding them?"

"Oh, just a business acquaintance that I met yesterday." Steven felt his face beginning to get warm and fled toward his office, leaving Helen wondering about his peculiar behavior. Jeffrey motioned her into the grand living room, where the folder was still lying closed on the big stone table. He handed it to Helen, whose expression changed from puzzlement to mischievous delight as she leafed through the photographs.

"Did he tell you about the letter?" Jeffrey asked.

"He showed it to me. Did he actually contact the studio? He must have. Jessie James must be the Jessica James from the letter. This must mean he's going through with it. My God, I never thought he would!"

At that moment Steven entered the room. "Jeffrey! What are you doing?" he said, flustered and angry. "Those are private, you shouldn't be showing them to Helen."

Helen started to laugh. "Gee, Pop, how private can it be when a million people are going to be watching you on TV with these girls?"

"Well, it's not going to happen," he said with firm dignity. "I just told Ms. James I hadn't made up my mind, but now that I see you two smirking and cackling, it's perfectly clear. I'm not going any further with this!" He was mortified, as though Helen had caught him red-handed, about to engage in *knowing*.

Jeffrey decided this would be a very good time to be silent for once, and he edged his way back toward the pantry.

Helen studied her father intently for a moment and then with her typical impetuosity she said, "Sit down, Pop, we need to talk."

CHAPTER SEVEN

"*R*emember how happy you were, Pop, not how sad you've been lately. What makes you think that you can't do it again?" Helen was sitting next to Steven on the couch, and she was enthusiastic in her pitch. "Sure, Mom was a unique and wonderful woman, but you brought a lot of skill and understanding to the marriage too. You can do it again." They both knew that although Yvonne had been an extraordinary, loving woman, she wasn't always easy to get along with. Because he had adored her, he'd been tolerant of her little quirks.

As Steven listened, he recalled the happy times. Soon he participated with Helen in reconstructing the picture of his decades of happiness with Yvonne. He and his daughter reminisced and laughed again, thinking of the fun times at Ivy Columns as the happy family they had been. Maybe his psyche abhorred the emotional vacuum in which he lived. And maybe Jessie had provided the answer, and the means, of how to fill it.

Helen made the sale. But really, Steven was ready to be sold.

He agreed to meet Jessie for lunch at the yacht club, only a block and a half from her Times Square office. He'd called her after his "sit down" with his daughter. Helen wanted to tag along to make sure that he didn't change his mind again, but Steven had wanted Jessie to himself. Helen finally agreed, without his explaining why.

He took the folder of photos with him, and when Jessie arrived, she carried an envelope containing a contract. She looked stunning in a smart cranberry business outfit that complemented her dark hair. As he took her in, he noticed just a couple of silver-white strands of hair. He felt a tremendous attraction to her; it swept over him powerfully. He felt at the same time challenged and at ease with her. He hadn't talked to a woman like her in a long time.

"I've never been inside the New York Yacht Club," Jessie said, "though I pass by it all the time."

With its stone bay windows on Forty-fourth Street, carved to look like the transom of a galleon, architect Whitney Warren's pile was a national treasure, though very few of the nation's people would ever be permitted through its portals. The land had been given to the club a century ago by its then commodore, J. P. Morgan, and the interior contained the grandeur to suit the upper crust of the gilded age. She said that she wasn't much interested in clubs or the New York social scene. "I'm away every weekend, always."

Jessie seemed impressed, Steven noted, as they climbed the marble staircase and passed the dockyard model on the landing of an

English first rater, which Morgan had also presented to the members back then. The famous Model Room, a few steps farther up, was the club's crowning glory. The huge room with its stained-glass skylight was anchored by an enormous fireplace, richly carved with dolphins rampant and a masterpiece marine painting of racing schooners above. But the room's predominant feature was the models of yachts. Hundreds and hundreds of them. Half models going back to the nineteenth century were mounted nearly floor to ceiling, and glass cases contained models of all the boats that had ever raced for the America's Cup. As Jessie and Steven strolled around the room, he explained the history of the Cup, the world's oldest continuous sporting event.

Back downstairs, they had lunch in the dining room, designed to resemble the interior of an old sailing ship, with curved oak walls between ribs and overhead beams cut to the camber of a ship's deck. Some twenty tables were set with rich linen and blue and white chinaware carrying the club's emblem. At the big table near the door seven or eight members were in jovial conversation. Steven and Jessie were seated at a small, quiet table away from this group.

"Steven, I was thrilled when you decided to come aboard and join our crew." Her lovely smile was so genuine. "As I said, we'll get started right away. The background stuff will be easy to do."

He had to shake himself out of his happy daze. "Right. Um, what do you mean, exactly?"

"Oh, we have to set the stage, so to speak, with the viewers. I want them to get a feeling for the kind of man you are. I would like the camera to visit your office, look around your apartment, and your Ivy Columns out on the Island. I've studied your penthouse in *Archi-*

tectural Digest. It must be fabulous! We will also want to shoot a couple of your favorite restaurants. What are they, by the way?"

Steven experienced a growing sense of what was to come. "Ah, well, Aquavit, for fish. The 21 Club, I suppose. I go there a lot; maybe we could go there together sometime? Babbo's in the Village; The Palm for steaks. And of course, my clubs—Harvard, the Links, and here."

Then Jessie proceeded to explain the contract. Pretty simple, he didn't have to sign in blood. It contained a release for the studio to use all the tape of Steven they would be shooting. It stated that the money would be going to his charitable foundation. He could quit at any time, though Jessie surely hoped he wouldn't be doing that. Plus, he was under no legal obligation to see it through all the way to the altar, though the projected wedding would, of course, be the high point and the last episode.

"You just wait, I think you will be swept away."

He would normally have scoffed at the idea of love at first sight, but that had been exactly the case with Yvonne, those many years ago. They had met over a ski weekend in Stowe, Vermont, shortly after she arrived from France. Yvonne had planned to stay in the United States for only a couple of months—meeting Steven changed that plan!

So why not play along now? It might be fun. He could get to know Jessie better. Steven found himself nodding along, and he was rewarded by her most radiant smile. He was indeed swept away—but by her, not by what she was selling.

It only remained to narrow the field down to the beauties the show would actually star in the series. Steven, however, found that impossible to do. "Jessie, I've been through those photos dozens of times," he said. "I can't make up my mind without meeting them."

"I understand." She paused. "Okay, here is my solution. We'll shoot the first episode in a few days, and I'll have twelve of the girls there. It will be clear where the chemistry works and where it doesn't. Narrowing it down to the final eight should then be easy." Jessie was so sure of herself, he thought dreamily. "Don't worry, Steven! The fun is about to start!"

As coffee was served, he signed, letting out a long sigh as he did. He had never been more unsure of a deal before. He couldn't believe it; he'd just signed up to star in a television show.

O ver the next few days, things began whirling at a speed that Jessie was used to, but which never let Steven stand back and think clearly. Maybe that was Jessie's intention. She had accompanied the production crew out to Ivy Columns, but Steven didn't go along: too many memories. His clubs, except for the Harvard Club, wouldn't let her in, even when she told them it was for charity. The club secretary at the Links, with uncharacteristic, sharp manners, hung up after saying "No, madam, that will never be possible." Even the more plebian Harvard wouldn't let her film more than the club's lobby. But all the restaurants were more than delighted to let Jessie's crew shoot as much as they wished.

Mrs. O'Brian wasn't a very good sport, Steven thought, when the TV camera crew arrived to shoot "background." She didn't want to let them into his office and when they started to photograph her, her snarl wasn't deemed suitable to tape. Steven had to explain and then explain again that it was all being done for charity. That the money Acme Studios would be paying him would be going to charitable causes. This was the basis Jessie had finally found most effec-

tive; the one he preferred to justify the madness of it all to himself.
Charity. Philanthropy. The family foundation. For the greater good
of all. Apparently, Mrs. O'Brian wasn't buying it. Eventually, they got
a few seconds of her stony faced but not openly hostile. He was grateful that she hadn't seen the photographs of the girls!

But the taping at Hudson and Partners had nearly unhinged
Pierce Crowninshield. No one had really explained what was going
on, and he was riled at the sight of the ill-kempt back-clad video crew
clipping microphones to the pinstriped suits of some amused associates. Pierce tried to slide manfully toward Steven's office through the
confused mess of blinding lights, criss-crossing cables, big cases of
video equipment, and large booms held by burly soundmen. Silver
duct tape held everything together. The more his progress was im-
peded, the angrier he became. If he'd taken a moment to observe, he
would have seen that the chaos was controlled, and that the TV crew
was actually highly professional. Just before he reached Steven, a
cameraman focused in on him, and it was comical to watch Pierce
trying to decide whether to huff or preen. Being the peacock that he
was, preening won.

"Pierce," Steven said, trying to hide his unease behind a confident voice, "I'm happy that you could join us for this TV taping—it's
for the benefit of my foundation, you know." He was misleading
Pierce by miles, but what the hell, nothing might ever come of it and
it was his own affair, after all. He continued, "Perhaps you could help
us out by showing these folks around, introducing them to who we
are and what we do." He wasn't surprised to see that Pierce's attitude
changed immediately, and that his arrogant associate was more than
pleased to undertake a celebrity turn like this. Pierce said, "Sorry, I

misunderstood, Steven. Of course, I'll be happy to do anything for charity." Pierce happily wandered off with lights and cameras in tow.

Back home, Jeffrey hammered it up for the camera. He dressed in his chef's checkered trousers, and with a toque on his head, he looked the part of the perfect celebrity chef. He happily rattled on about the boss's favorite wines—Lynch-Bages, Haut Brion, Cheval Blanc, which he proudly displayed in the steel and glass, humidity-controlled wine cellar off the pantry.

The kitchen was a wonder of high-tech design and culinary gadgetry. Stainless steel cabinets, black granite work surfaces, and an enormous modern steam oven flanked by an induction heated stove with six burners, plus a restaurant salamander to keep food warm—it lacked nothing. He proudly showed the crew around his domain, rattling on about the food he prepared, including the crack, "The boss loves oysters. Guess that's a good thing, huh?"

Steven was filmed showing Jessie, who introduced herself on the tape, around the penthouse. She raved about his modern art collection, genuinely impressed, and she was fascinated by *Paint*, the piece that he and Helen had found. She was nearly overwhelmed with the high ceilings, the sweep, and scope of the place and, of course, its astonishing views.

Steven's yearnings were stronger than ever over the next couple of days, but he didn't see very much of Jessie. She was forever fielding a continual stream of phone calls and dashing to and from her office. As the producer, she was responsible for the girls. The girls were eager to do the show, she told Steven. Extremely eager. It was the chance of a lifetime to appear on TV. The audience might number in the millions, and even if they missed the big prize of catching

Steven, they could still make a name for themselves. The show could be the career break they all needed.

The following Wednesday afternoon, Henry and Helen arrived to participate in Jessie's background filming, adding to the hectic activity in the penthouse. They were both excited about the sudden twist in their dad's life and they took to Jessie right away.

Henry looked particularly sharp, camera ready, the cream-colored cashmere sports coat and black silk shirt complementing his blond hair. He was grinning from ear to ear. As soon as Jessie spotted him she said, "Steven, this must be Henry. He has your good looks." Her honey-toned voice purred on as she turned to Henry. "Have you ever done any acting? Really handsome young men like you are always in demand." He glowed in anticipation. Jessie was delighted to have these two attractive kids as additional eye candy for the show — things were beginning to shape up very well.

"Okay, everyone," she announced. "I have to fly, but all of you be at the theater by nine tonight. We shoot episode one with the girls, and Steven, remember it's black tie."

*W*illard was a tornado of activity, as he tried to be everywhere at once getting the cameras, the lights, and the set ready for shooting on the stage of the little theater Acme had rented. But he dropped everything to chatter excitedly with Jessie when she arrived. "How's our lover boy doing? Will he be here on time? I can't wait to get started! This is going to be great reality television, better than the real thing!"

"Yes, yes, Willard, he'll be here." Jessie paused, thinking of the fabulous penthouse and wonderful art collection. "I still can't believe it. How can a man like Steven Hudson be so attracted to girls his daughter's age?"

Willard elbowed her with a grin. "Well, he's a healthy male animal, I guess!"

She smiled in return then raised a curious notion. "I get the feeling he's attracted to me too—yet he has seen my ring, I noticed him looking at it. Can you *believe* this guy?"

"Same question—same answer."

She nodded. In a way she was pleased by the idea. "But you're right, he sure looks the part. Maybe we can write in a bigger role for me on the show," she said, and they both laughed.

*S*teven arrived looking elegant in a stylish Hermes tuxedo he had picked up in Paris. Jeffrey came with him, very excited to be a witness to *Trophy*, as everyone but Steven now called the unfolding event. The new and very jittery TV-star-to-be was ushered into a small, shabby dressing room where a woman from the studio, who was responsible for his makeup, took charge. His objections were overruled and Pan-cake and hair spray were applied with a sure dexterity. Before she was finished, Henry burst into the little room, very excited; Steven was startled to see him so early. He could smell some alcohol on his son's breath.

"Dad, where are the girls? I've looked everywhere."

"Hank, I don't know—but calm down, you're making me nervous!" Maybe kidding around with his son would help to relieve the tension. "Hey I have an idea. Why don't you take my place for the whole thing?" he said as straight-faced as he could. Henry's face lit up with the idea. Steven frowned. "But, of course, the women would have to be old ladies to keep to Jessie's basic plan." As Henry grasped for a suitable reply, Jessie entered the dressing room, which was now getting pretty crowded. She was wearing a stunning, low-cut, red satin evening gown. Wow! Steven's heart soared at the sight of her.

"Come on, Steven." Jessie was beaming. She seemed excited herself. "Let's give the cameras the pleasure of your company." The make-up lady was still brushing powder off his shoulder as Steven followed Jessie out the door and toward the action. He wondered if actors ever experienced stage fright like this.

Henry tagged along. They walked out behind the stage area where Jeffrey and Helen, who just arrived, were standing. Steven had only a second to give his daughter a quick hug and to whisper in her ear, "Keep an eye on your brother, he's had a few." Helen absorbed this piece of information with a wry nod.

The stage was surrounded by batteries of lights shining down from above. Camera crews and attendants were in place, busy making adjustments and performing sound checks. Steven spotted an elfin man in cowboy boots with blue-and-pink dyed hair, darting about. The seats in the theater were mostly empty, but some of the studio staff were sitting in the front row, and that's where Jessie indicated Helen, Henry, and "Jeeves," as she had also begun to call the bubbling chef, should sit for the taping. Henry was still muttering that he wanted to meet the girls, but Helen managed to get him off the set and down into the seats without too much difficulty.

Carpenters had constructed two sets on stage for the taping. One featured several Ionic columns made of wood but painted to look like white marble, with a scrim in the background looking like fleecy clouds. Steven assumed it would not look as utterly phony and ridiculous on camera as it did to his eye.

"Steven," Jessie explained in her soothing voice, "this is our Greek temple, where you will meet your lovelies and your future wife to be. As soon as their bus arrives, you will have champagne with these goddesses and we will start taping—discreetly, of course."

Steven, now seriously nervous, was still digesting the idea of Greek goddesses arriving by bus—maybe Jessie was putting them on the cross-town M-27? "You have to imagine, as the girls arrive, the music building in the background, which we will dub in later together with the title, voiceovers, and so forth."

"What *is* the title anyway?" Steven asked.

"Actually, we haven't made a final decision." Jessie instinctively didn't mention *Trophy Bride*, the name they would probably use. It was too early to hit Steven with its blatancy. "I have been thinking along the line of *Spring for September*. What do you think, Steven?"

He thought he was going to be sick. Caterpillars were crawling through his stomach, going through metamorphosis, and turning into butterflies. And he felt the butterflies might be feeling queasy, too. He could feel a cold, clammy fear beginning to take hold.

"Ugh" was all he could say, wishing he had some antacids.

She agreed. "You're right, it's pretty awful." She had just spotted two cameramen wearing T-shirts with the sexy *Trophy Bride* logo on them that Willard had designed, and steered Steven away from them. "Okay, we'll change it. Now, over here is where you will be having dinner."

She directed Steven's attention to the second set on stage left, where a large, circular table was set with enough flowers and candelabras to make Liberace feel at home. As he looked more closely, he could see that the round table was actually shaped like a donut, with a space in the hole filled by a small, single table and chair set with knives, forks, and crystalware, just like the settings around the periphery.

"I don't understand, Jessie. How's this supposed to work?" he asked dismayed. "I thought, well, that I would be at the head of a long table. I'm having trouble keeping up with all this."

"Oh, Steven, my staff has been very clever. If we did a normal setup, you would get to talk with only the girls close to you, on your right and left. We had to come up with a better plan. We thought of musical chairs, where everybody changed position every so often, so they all got a chance to enjoy your close company, but I thought that would look awkward. Then one of our tech staff came up with this idea. The inner part, with your table and chair, is on a turntable! It rotates, slowly, of course. That way you will have a chance to be with each girl two or three times, directly across from you during the course of dinner. We just need two cameras, one shooting you and the other shooting the lovely creature opposite."

That was a terrific idea. "You people astonish me, Jessie. But how do I get into the middle?"

For the first time her face turned sour. "Well, it's not too elegant. Assuming you can't hurdle the candelabras, you'll have to crawl under the outer table. Of course, we won't photograph that part."

She quickly led him across the stage, wanting to get past the crawling idea. "If you look closely, you'll notice that your table is a semi-circle, and it's cut to fit closely to the big table, so you won't be more than a normal table width from any of the girls, as you rotate.

Incidentally, the lights overhead are bright enough so that the camera won't pick up any part of the set not under the light, or anything in the audience."

The confident founder of Hudson and Partners looked totally lost in this world of make-believe. To set him at ease, Jessie added, "Steven, I'll be mingling with you during the temple part. That's why I am dressed this way. If we decide that it's appropriate for the girls to have me sort of like a chaperone, we'll leave me in. If it works better with me not in the series, we'll just edit me out. But I'll be helping you tonight no matter what. Don't be nervous. It will be fun!"

Before Steven could tell her about his butterflies and their illnesses, a buzz was noticeable from the back of the stage. One of the production assistants shouted, "The girls are here!"

The overhead lights blazed even brighter as one of the techs responded to this input, and just as the front row of the theater vanished in the increased glare, Steven thought he saw the image of a tall male sitting next to Helen, holding her hand. A man he didn't recognize.

Then the girls rushed in and the butterflies flew away. Jessie was right. Goddesses they were, dazzling as the bright lights played off their glossy hair, their tanned bare arms and shoulders, their gorgeous faces radiantly made up to cosmetic perfection, their silk and satin long evening gowns—each a different pastel color from creamy ivory to shimmering apricot—all from Valentino, and of course, coordinated by Jessie, as was their minimal but tasteful jewelry. In they came, surrounding Steven with their alluring perfumes and radiant smiles, displaying perfect teeth. Young waiters in formal white tie and tailcoats began to move among them, carrying silver trays with tall champagne glasses. The camera crews circled the temple like dark sharks beyond the pool of light, while the overhead microphones on long booms recorded all the mindless chatter for posterity.

Steven's face was plastered with a silly grin. This was great! Jessie and a dozen incredible beauties! Forgotten were his earlier fears, his self-deprecating doubts, his protective cloak of privacy. It was hot under the lights, and the cold champagne became a necessity.

Jessie had put name cards on the dinner table large enough for both Steven and the cameras to see easily, but here in the temple Steven couldn't retain the names in the blur of self-introductions. Tracy, Tiffany, Cheryl, Crystal, Heather—all seemed to be interchangeable new-age names. He couldn't seem to attach a name to any of them. It didn't matter, though. They all knew Steven's name and everything about him. He had considered himself immune to flattery but all this attention from these beautiful young women could have turned a dead man's head, he thought.

Jessie was in and out of the set. She kept instructing the cameras to roll on and on, to capture enough tape so they would be able to choose from plenty of footage. When Jessie announced it was dinner time and herded them all out of the tacky, fake temple, Steven was floating on the bubbles of a number of champagne glasses.

Before the dining room scene began, the crew put down a clean blanket on the stage, as Steven had to crawl on all fours under the table to get to his place in the center. It was not dignified and he distinctly heard guffaws from the audience, accurately identifying both Henry and Jeffrey. Well, let them laugh, he thought. For him, the fun was just starting.

When Jessie had her bevy of beauties seated at last, Steven found himself opposite a raven-haired Eurasian knockout. As Steven focused on her, really for the first time, noting her name—Stephanie Wong—he said:

"Stephanie, there can't be a more beautiful woman than you in the world, really and truly."

"Actually, Mr. Hudson—I mean Steven—I've an identical twin sister, Melissa, back in San Francisco."

"Well, my dear, I've always said that two Wongs can always make it right."

As this clunker registered, drawing a frown and pursed lips from Stephanie, Steven's table lurched sideways, almost spilling the glass of red wine by his plate. The turntable had weighed anchor, so to speak, and Steven found it a little disconcerting. As he slowly rotated, he couldn't decide whether to start talking with the woman approaching on his port quarter or to linger on in conversation with the lovely turning away on his starboard side.

But it didn't matter. After a while the food arrived—later he couldn't remember what it had been—and the red wine flowed and the revolutions slowly accumulated. On the second pass, Stephanie laughed when Steven said, "Haven't we met somewhere before?" and on the third time around, "We have to stop meeting this way. People might talk."

They all talked with Steven about hometowns, accomplishments and aspirations, schools and courses. They asked questions about him, his children, his career. Their names, their thoughts, and histories began to meld into a continuous impression of youth, innocence, beauty, and desirability. Steven could have gone on forever. In this happy pool of light, the cameras were forgotten. If this was reality, it was very good indeed.

After dessert and yet more champagne to go with it, Jessie called out, "Okay, folks, that's a wrap for tonight! I think we have some great footage, more than enough for episode one."

For Steven, succulent reality turned back into the plain vanilla kind. He had trouble getting out from under the table. The techs hadn't stopped his turntable, and when he tried to crawl back out, the big table's legs kept moving in the way. Muddled by all the liquor, he tried to climb over the top of it, thereby capsizing a section of the outer ring, bringing some plates and crystal crashing to the floor, and decorating one leg of the tuxedo pants with whipped cream. But it didn't matter to anyone. When he finally got to his feet and brushed himself off, Jessie gave him a big hug.

"Steven, you were great! What a wonderful start! You were terrific on camera. You're a natural—so relaxed, so handsome, so sexy." She was very happy. Steven gave her a big hug, happy that she was happy. It was good to be with her. His head was still spinning, but the turntable had stopped, hadn't it?

Willard was passing champagne around. He carried a tray brimming with plastic cups, and the technicians didn't have to be encouraged to participate in the impromptu series kick-off party.

Now the people from the audience walked on stage as well. Jeffrey and Henry eagerly introduced themselves to the girls, and several readily gathered around Steven's tall, handsome son.

Helen was oddly subdued. And she was on the arm of the stranger Steven had spotted earlier. "Pop, I want to introduce you to Professor Aristotle Cohen from Columbia. He teaches my Quantum Principles in Contemporary Art seminar."

"Professor, huh?" Steven was a bit taken aback by the tall man with the black, wavy, shoulder-length hair and darkly romantic look. "What does quantum physics have to do with art?"

"Quantum mechanics actually." Cohen immediately adopted a professorial air. "You know, Heisenberg's uncertainty, Schödinger's duality, Einsteinean relativity, Gell-Mann strangeness, Gödel's incompleteness—everything really that modern art is all about."

But further conversation with this annoying pedant who seemed strongly attracted to his daughter was impossible, as the girls regained control of the space around Steven gushing, "What fun I had," "Can't wait to see you again," "You're everything a girl could dream of."

Jessie managed to elbow her way in and round them up to get back on the bus. It was past midnight and the crew, already in over-time, was packing the cameras and the technical equipment. It was time to go, but Steven was still soaring. He had loved every minute since the girls had arrived. He hadn't had this much fun in years.

Happily he agreed to meet with Jessie in the morning to plan the second episode's shoot. It was happening. He was beginning to have the time of his life.

How wonderful—is there a support group for optimists?

CHAPTER EIGHT

*S*teven awoke later than usual, and then he rolled over and tried to go back to sleep. He could feel a hangover hovering over him, waiting to attack. He buried his head in his satin covered pillow, knowing he was doomed.

He couldn't shake off the dream that had revisited him several times during the night. Yvonne laughing and laughing—fits of helpless laughter, the kind where you can't talk, but only point and collapse in renewed, involuntary waves. Kindly, loving laughter, surely, like a mother's for a child who has just done something incredibly stupid yet somehow loveable and hysterically funny.

The sounds of activity beyond his bedroom suite pressed in on him. Vacuums were roaring and voices were talking above the whir. He remembered that he'd told Jeffrey to call in his cleaning staff. At last Steven got out of bed and looked over the cold, gray Manhattan skyline.

The hangover attacked.

Steven downed a large glass of water after swallowing some aspirin from the cabinet in his marble-tiled bathroom. This morning he took no pleasure from the floor of elegant Italian Portoro marble or the customized sauna and steam bath next to his luxurious shower stall crafted from black-carbon fiber. On the counter was a smiling black-and-white photo of Yvonne. "Well, you really had a good laugh on me last night, didn't you, *mon amie*?" he murmured. Her smile seemed to enlarge somehow before his tired eyes. They had shared everything, even anticipating each other's thoughts at times.

After a long steam bath and hot shower, Steven thought that he had purged some of last night's alcoholic poison. How much champagne had he downed? What inane things had he said? Digital tape recorded everything very clearly, he thought, grimacing.

"Jeffrey, coffee: strong, black, quick," he said as he at last entered the breakfast room in his long, blue silk robe with red piping. He squinted against the morning light streaming in through the skylight.

"Wow, boss, what a night." His exuberant Jeeves hustled quickly to comply, providing a badly needed espresso *subito*. "Henry and I stopped by this great bar in Tribeca after the shoot. I only drank beer, but he put away plenty of scotches. I'll bet he feels worse than you do today, huh?"

"How much of an ass did I make of myself last night? Be honest, Jeffrey."

"Honest, boss? Not bad. You liked the girls a lot, but that was the whole point, wasn't it? Don't worry, they'll edit it way down. It was fun, I thought. You looked just great. For once you were having a good time."

"Yeah, I was, at least last night," he said, testing his forehead with his fingertips. The headache had subsided somewhat.

"Have you picked the one, boss? I mean, is it all over but the shouting?" Jeffrey kidded him. "Do you know already who will be the next Mrs. Hudson?"

"Are you serious? I can't even remember any of their names—they all sounded the same to me. They all were so beautiful, but as they spun me around and around last night, one seemed to blend into the other."

"So that's a no, I guess?" Jeffrey produced a second espresso. "Well, it's all just starting. There's plenty of time."

Steven carried the tiny gold-rimmed cup with him back to his bedroom, passing Juan and Brenda, who were still busy with vacuuming and dusting. As he shaved, he eyed himself in the mirror. He didn't look too worse for wear, all things considered. Feeling a little better, he dressed in slacks and a light wool turtleneck. When, long overdue, he reached his penthouse office desk, it was mid-morning. He had phone messages to call Jessie and Mrs. O'Brian.

He tried Jessie first. She was ecstatic. "Steven, how is my superstar this morning? You were just wonderful last night. I watched the tapes. We're off to a great start!"

"I drank too much and made an ass of myself," he said glumly.

"Oh, don't be silly, you were just friendly. All the girls loved you. The audience will love you too."

He took comfort in her praise. "Maybe it was a good thing I was drunk. Once the girls arrived, I almost forgot everything was being recorded. It helped having you there in the beginning too." After a moment's reflecting, he shook his head. "I still can't believe I'm doing this. I can't pick a mate from that bunch on national television."

"But, Steven, it will go very well. You will start to have intimate occasions with them now," she said, with suggestive promise in her voice. "Have you narrowed it down to the eight we need?"

"Jessie, I can't possibly do that. I don't want to do that," he complained. "I don't even remember their names. They're all just reality girls to me. But they are not real in any way, to me."

"I sort of understand, Steven. I've been thinking about that problem." A beat of silence passed before she said, "Steven, this is an out-of-bounds suggestion for me to make because it's not spelled out in the contract . . . but what if I do the choosing for you?" She hurried on, "I know the girls a little, and I know you a little. I think I can pick eight that will be suitable."

That was a great relief to him. "Jessie, I'm putty in your hands—go ahead!"

"Now don't act too quickly!"

"It's fate, Jessie," Steven said almost mournfully. "Since that letter arrived, I feel like I'm no longer in charge of anything." It sounded like he was feeling sorry for himself, and that was the last thing he wanted to portray to her. Brightening, he went on, "Jessie, you're an intelligent and classy woman. I trust you. I believe you'll do a better job than I would."

"Steven, your confidence means a lot to me." Yet, immediately after she purred that, her pace changed. "All right. I've got to run, got a lot to do today. I have to contact the girls who are in and break it gently to those who are out. Tonight you will meet number one— Crystal, I think." He could almost see her scanning her to-do list. "Have the flowers arrived yet? The camera crew will be along pretty soon to plan their setups. Have you talked with Jeffrey about the dinner? Does he understand that he will be on camera a little? I'll have release forms for him to sign." And on she went with Steven answering, making a note or just grunting in acquiescence as necessary. She signed off with "I'll be by later this afternoon to help you get ready for your first big date!"

After hanging up, Steven circled back to the pantry to collect another coffee. While he'd been on the phone with Jessie, a truck load of flowers had arrived. Jeffrey was telling the dreadlocked delivery guy where to put them all.

"Tonight's your night, Jeeves," Steven announced, shooting a salute to Jeffrey. "You're going to become a TV star, a celebrity chef for a TV girl. Have you decided what you're going to serve?"

Jeffrey had a meal all mapped out. "I thought I would start with a sauteed *foie gras* salad, followed by a tuna tartare entrée, and wind up with *Crepes Suzette*. A nice light red Rhone, maybe Chateauneuf du Pape, then a white Meursault, and for the dessert a Sauterne, probably 1987 d'Yquem. I want it to be pretty simple so that you don't have to be cutting open a duck, or boning a fish, while you talk. I don't want the food to interfere with dinner, if you follow me."

"Sounds great to me. You'll sign their release?"

"Already have, when they were here shooting the background stuff. They want me to wear the toque again. Boss, I love this! Will we be doing it every night? You think they can get me on *Iron Chef!*"

"*Iron Chef*? Going Hollywood on me already? No, we won't be doing this every night—several other nights perhaps. After this, I think, I'm going to a beach setting with Jessie—some place where the girls can show off in swim suits, I would bet."

Jeffrey loved that idea. "This is such fun, boss. Hope you're enjoying it too."

"Yeah, we'll see," said Steven, and he returned to his office to call Mrs. O'Brian.

While she would never betray her thoughts, Steven heard unease in her voice. "Mr. Hudson, Mr. Crowninshield is most anxious to speak with you. He has been by once, and he's called twice since."

"What's troubling him?"

"When the TV crew was here photographing your office, they triggered a lot of rumors that it wasn't just about charity. I didn't say anything to anyone, of course."

"Of course you didn't, Mrs. O'Brian."

"But this morning there was a page one article in *Variety*. It reports that a new reality series is being created, and it alleges that you, Mr. Hudson, are starring in it with a bunch of chorus girls. You can imagine the furor it's causing here."

"They are not chorus girls, Mrs. O'Brian."

For the first time ever she sounded shocked. "Then it's true. Mr. Hudson, I never dreamed you would follow up on that amazing letter you received. So shall I transfer Mr. Crowninshield over to you?"

Steven didn't answer immediately. "No, Mrs. O'Brian," he said at last. "Please tell Pierce that this is a personal matter between me and a national TV audience. If he wants to know more, he should stay tuned."

"Mr. Hudson, he will not be happy. He told me that he would prefer to see you dragged out of here by the FBI in handcuffs before seeing you on TV in some sort of sex scandal. He used the phrase 'cavorting on TV,' as I recall."

"Well, it won't come to handcuffs quite yet, Mrs. O'Brian. He may have to acquire a taste for cavorting instead. Tell him so for me, and please call back if things get out of control."

He put the phone down with a groan. He had sounded so calm and politely firm to Mrs. O'Brian, but he knew his partners would not be so easily dismissed. He could feel his headache coming back as he rose from his desk. He wasn't going to get any work done today.

Sure enough, the phone rang again, and Pierce was shortly sputtering protests to Steven, as Mrs. O'Brian had predicted he would.

"Hudson and Partners has a reputation for sobriety and prudence, Steven." He was pretty steamed. "What has come over you? We're in *Variety*, for heaven's sake! I thought those camera people were doing something for your foundation, not for network TV." Steven listened, his head starting to throb again as his partner ran on.

"Pierce," he replied as last. "I've been very lonely, maybe a little depressed. This is a chance to have some fun. Nothing may come of it, and it won't go ahead unless I am happy. Very happy. And any money really is going to charity. Trust me, Pierce, I won't embarrass you or the firm. Trust me."

This open, honest approach worked with his partner who, after repeating some of his concerns a little more, hung up somewhat mollified. "Maybe," Steven laughed to himself as he stood by the phone, "we'll pick up a whole bunch of new clients from the *Variety* readers—but Pierce won't approve, I'll bet."

Still, no escape from his desk. Moments later Helen rang the private number.

"*Ciao Bella*," he said.

"Pop! My *God!*" She seemed even more agitated than Pierce Crowninshield. "Last night was unreal. I almost didn't recognize you, never thought that I would see you wearing makeup."

"Yeah, it was a little surreal, I admit."

"Those girls," she continued, "they looked like bimbo gold-diggers. I shouldn't have talked you into this."

For some reason Helen now seemed shocked at the prospect of the show itself. It dawned on him that perhaps Helen was jealous. Maybe she just feared losing her dad to a strange woman, her own age.

He shifted the conversation: "Well, it was fun for a while, and I promised Jessie to have a date here tonight—then I think I'll wind it up. Who was that professor you were with? You must have invited him."

She paused briefly, "Oh, Ari. I told you he teaches my contemp art seminar. He's brilliant, Pop. I really love him!"

"You mean, love him as a teacher, right?"

"Yeah, right. Pop, listen, I called you on the run. Class is starting, gotta go. I'll call you, *Ciao*." She hung up without clearing the air at all.

As he walked into the living room, he found the TV crew storming into his penthouse like the Marines invading Normandy. Lights, cables, power boxes, and camera trucks were massed in the foyer with more, they told him, on the way up. The crew was following orders from the weird-looking, manic elf Steven remembered from the previous night.

"Good morning, Mr. Hudson, how's your head feeling?" said the elf with a friendly smile and a down market English accent.

"I suppose everyone noticed that I lost count. I guess I can't, like Bill Clinton, say that I tasted it but didn't swallow."

The elf thought that was funny. "I'm Willard, Mr. Hudson, Jessie's reality consultant."

"When you find reality, Willard, let me know. It must be around here somewhere. I can't believe that this is actually happening."

"Oh, you'll see, reality follows our shooting schedule. Pretty soon the only thing that will seem real will be this show," he said with a grin. "And you're going to have a world of fun."

"Will Jessie be by soon?" Steven said a little too eagerly.

Willard didn't seem to notice. Instead, he consulted his clipboard. "Yes, but she's on a tight schedule, very busy."

"Do you know her pretty well?"

"Only for the last few weeks and by reputation, which is terrific." He finally looked up. "Since we started this project, though, I've practically been living with her."

"I saw a rock on her finger," Steven said, trying to joke. "You two engaged?"

"Oh, she's engaged all right, but not to me. To a male mannequin with a magnetic personality. He's gorgeous."

This sarcastic assessment gave him hope. "Is she happy with him?"

"Don't really know, mate, you'll have to ask her." He placed a light hand on Steven's arm. "Now, if you can spare a moment, I could use your help."

Willard and the crew needed Steven's assistance to plan their setups for that night. They wanted to photograph the *Trophy* girl arriving, looking around the foyer, then get shots of her entering the sunken living room, taking in the art and marvelous views, then into the dining room with its elegant table settings—just for two—with Jeffrey coming and going in the background, and then into the bedroom where they would depart, leaving the couple alone together. Steven didn't think things could go this fast, winding up in bed on his first date, with the first girl. He wasn't sure that he really wanted to, but . . . perhaps . . . maybe? This was all crazy!

Amid the whirlwind, Jeffrey brought him a sandwich and a cup of tea. Steven nibbled and sipped as he worked with Willard and the crew to plan their angles so that they would be taping him and Miss Trophy and not themselves as the evening unfolded. This took much longer than Steven would have expected. As they were winding it up, reasonably satisfied, Jessie blew in, smartly dressed and looking terrific. Steven's face broke into an involuntary smile at the sight of her. She was carrying a cardboard box with a cellophane window in it.

"Steven, glad to see you up and about this afternoon. We're going to try our best not to destroy your beautiful home with all our equipment. We'll be shooting with hand-helds for most of the action, but I always like to have the big stuff to interpose." Whatever that meant.

Jeffrey appeared and Jessie waved him over.

"Here, Jeffrey, please put this corsage in the fridge to keep it fresh until tonight."

"A corsage?" asked Steven. "I haven't seen one of those in years. Are we going to the big dance in the high school gym or something?"

"No silly, it's for Crystal! You'll be picking her up to bring her here for your date tonight. I've already cleared it with your driver, Tony. He's washing and polishing the Bentley right now." Jessie said, always in control.

"Oh . . . okay," Steven said, going with the flow. "Does she live in Manhattan, or is she staying in a hotel? Crystal, huh. What's her last name?"

"It's Style. Her name is Crystal Style," Jessie said without a trace of irony. "Remember her from last night? She is a dazzling blonde. And yes, she lives here."

"They were all dazzling, Jessie. I was overwhelmed. How on earth did you find them?"

She laughed at his naiveté. "I didn't have to. They found me, Steven. Believe me, once the word went out about the show, I've been flooded with headshots and resumes from all sources: agents, scouts and, of course, the girls themselves." All this was business as usual for her, and as she was talking, she was eyeing the clothes he had on. "I came by to help get you ready for tonight," she continued. "Have you decided what to wear? You have to pick up Crystal at six o'clock."

"No, I haven't got that far," he said, looking down at himself uncomfortably. "You don't want me in a tux again, do you?"

"Not for this episode. Let's look in your closet and see what works."

At least he didn't have to worry about clothes. His dressing room had three enormous closets behind beautifully made sliding, teak doors in an open Spanish grating, like something you might find on a yacht. Inside, light flowed from slots in the bottom of the polished steel bars, holding dozens of suits, sports coats, and formal outfits on their wooden hangers.

They spread, on Steven's bed, a number of jackets, shirts, ties, and trousers from the racks of clothing while Jessie pondered the choices. She settled finally on a black silk shirt by Armani with a pink Armani tie, black trousers, and a tightly woven wool Brioni sports coat in a rich dark red. "It's a bold, youthful combination, which fits you to a T." He smiled at her. While it was not a combination he'd ever have chosen for himself, he loved it. He hadn't had a woman pick out his clothes for him since Yvonne died.

"Okay, Steven, I have a million things to do before six, but I'll be back," Jessie said briskly. "Please don't be late picking up Crystal. Tony has the address." And she dashed off.

The balance of the afternoon evaporated in a welter of details, as Steven dealt with Willard, the TV production staff, questions from Jeffrey about the wine, the correct table setting, keeping Juan and Brenda busy cleaning up spilled water from the flowers, and the constant mess from the technicians.

It was close to six o'clock when Steven and the cameraman, who would be accompanying him, descended to the garage. They found Tony flicking specks of imaginary dust off the powerful, gleaming black Bentley.

Jack, the bearded, gum-chewing, overweight photographer, took some tape of Tony in his chauffeur's uniform and cap, then the car from all angles, and of Tony opening the door for Steven to get into the back seat. As they pulled out of the garage, Jack, who was established in the front seat, kept filming Steven until he stuck his tongue out and waggled his fingers—thumbs in his ears—to get the camera jockey to lay off.

Crystal lived farther uptown in a walk-up apartment near the edge of Spanish Harlem. It was starting to get dark and it was really cold. The people around and about were bundled up and walking quickly.

Steven stood by the open car door at curbside with Jack taping, while Tony rang the bell, ready to escort Crystal down. It all seemed so artificial until she emerged from the front door.

She looked great, Steven had to admit. A little shorter than he recalled but so what? She was wrapped against the cold in an enormous platinum fur of some kind. Mink? Sable? She gave him a huge smile and a little hug before he ushered her into the car and climbed into the back seat with her. As he shut the door, a strong perfume engulfed them all. He cracked open his window a little, despite the cold.

Steven thought of pinning the corsage on her coat, again feeling like he was heading to the high school prom. He noticed that it was not fur but some sort of wiry synthetic—the pelt of the rare endangered American Rayon, probably—and before he could decide where to pin the flowers, they were forgotten. Crystal had more or less thrown the coat off her shoulders to expose her extravagantly well-endowed chest to Jack the cameraman, leering in the front seat.

Crystal smiled back alluringly. The camera posed no anxiety for her as it zoomed in strategically on her breasts—no doubt surgically enhanced—and then backed away to survey Crystal—from her bright red cowboy boots, up past her skin-tight jeans, and on to the skimpy, white cotton cowgirl blouse. Steven had never before witnessed such a perfect union between camera and subject. It was almost sacred in its intensity. But then again, he was still new at this.

At last satiated, the camera turned to Steven. When Crystal noticed the camera was no longer on her, she spoke her first words, which, of course, brought the camera's glinting eye immediately back to her.

"Stevie, I thought you were rich. Can't you afford a Cadillac or a Mercedes? What's this thing anyway? Looks like it's made of wood." She pointed to the polished burlwood vanity tables built into the back of the leather front seats.

"It's a custom-designed Bentley, Crystal."

"Oh . . ."

Feeling the camera on them, Steven decided to move along, after exhausting his repertoire of car talk. "So Crystal, where are you from? I don't recall that you mentioned it last night at the party."

"I'm from Cincinnati, Stevie. Where are you from?"

"Well, I was born in Boston, back while the earth was still cooling"—this didn't get a laugh—"but I've spent most of my life here in Manhattan. I love New York."

"Yeah, so do I," she said, becoming enthused. "So many people. Such big buildings. Lots of modeling jobs." She displayed a smoldering smile for the camera upon her mention of the word model. It seemed to trigger some sort of reflex.

"Your name, Crystal Style, is pretty unusual. I hope you don't mind me asking, but is that your real name?"

"I don't mind," she said, her smile dimming somewhat. "I decided to change my name when I left Ohio. I used to be called Emma Zarkowski."

Steven had to control his impulse to laugh. "I see. Why did you pick Crystal, Emma?"

"Don't call me that! I'm *Crystal.*"

"Oh, sorry! Just a slip," he said with a broad smile. "But why Crystal of all the names, and where did Style come from?"

"Well, I believe in crystal power. I always wear one—see?" She plucked a large lump of cut-quartz on a gold chain, which had been indulging itself, nestled deep within her cleavage. "Crystals were found in the pyramids, you know, so they have pyramid power too."

Steven kept a straight face and played along. "That makes sense, I guess."

"And Style, well Steve, that's what I'm all about. So it seemed perfect for my new last name."

"Can't fault your sound logic, Crystal. And it's nice to be called Steve and even Stevie."

Her eyes narrowed, not sure if he was putting her on. "Well, that's your name isn't it?"

They rattled on in this vein until the Bentley pulled into the garage under Steven's building. They were filmed getting out of the car and walking to the elevator, Crystal again wrapped in her fur. She seized Steven's arm as the elevator ascended.

The elevator doors opened into the penthouse foyer, and they were nearly blinded by all the lights—it was hard to see the people behind the glare—but Steven might have caught a glimpse of Henry grinning over a cameraman's shoulder. He couldn't see Jessie anywhere.

The lights were like a stage entrance—a cue for Crystal. Sweeping out of the elevator, she slithered out of her coat—God knows how many Rayons had given their all to make it—and twirled it about like Marilyn Monroe. She was instinctively aware of the cameras focused upon her. Jeffrey jumped out to take the coat from her before she would have cast it adrift into the nether world beyond the lights and cameras.

Then some instinct seemed to take hold, Steven thought, and she became suddenly aware of her surroundings. She focused on the painting-sculpture, *Paint*, which Jessie had so admired, with its dozens of brushes in a state of . . . well . . . erection. It stopped her cold. Steven was sure she'd prepared something clever, witty, and arresting, but the artwork just upstaged her completely.

"What's this?" she said, barely masking her horror. "Did you, uh, *make* it?"

"No, Crystal, it's a unique piece by a modern Dutch artist. Do you like it?"

Crystal looked at Steven like he'd just asked her about the artistic merit of a pile of garbage spilled on the sidewalk.

"It's nice," she managed.

Moving into the huge living room with its high ceilings, the waterfall video art, and the astonishing view over a sparkling Manhattan, Crystal remained mute. She crossed over to the fireplace, alight with Vermont pine logs crackling and sputtering. They were warm and inviting, probably like the fireplaces she knew in Ohio, Steven thought. Then she focused on the enormous Squeak Carnwath painting across the room.

It consisted of a hundred blotches of paint in hues ranging from light pink to the deepest red, each one numbered. Above the blotches, in a brick red background, were several dozen words scrawled in white—such as *cross*, *letter*, *ink*, *hand*, all words associated with the color red.

Steven said, "It's called *What Is Red*. It's a masterpiece, I think."

Crystal stood with her mouth hanging open, then caught herself and turned away. "Do you have anything to drink?" she murmured.

"Of course we do," said Jeffrey as he sprang into the camera's viewfinder bearing champagne. Jessie had instructed Jeffrey only to serve champagne, never hard liquor or, God forbid, beer before dinner. The audience needed to understand, she said, that the rich always drank champagne, no matter what. Being rich, though, didn't stop Steven from craving a martini.

Crystal drank deeply and recovered very well, Steven thought, adapting to these alien surroundings.

"Stevie," she said, regaining her stage presence, "don't you like pictures of *things*? You know, like boats or animals? I think animals are just wonderful." She waved her arms all around. "Don't you have a picture of your spirit animal anywhere?"

"I don't think I follow you, Crystal. What's my spirit animal?"

"Well, for you, it's probably a wolf or a lion. Just like we have all been reincarnated, lots of times, we have all been an animal in the past. The Native Americans call it the spirit animal. Mine is a little baby deer. That's why I love Bambi so."

Steven chuckled lightly. "I've got a lot to learn from you, Crystal."

"Yes, Stevie, and I've got a lot to give, too." She walked across the room with her champagne in hand, a sly wink at the cameras and joined Steven standing by one of the huge windows overlooking the streams of light from traffic on the street far below.

"Can we see Times Square from here, Steve?"

"Oh no, Crystal, that's twenty-five blocks south and a couple of Avenues over. Why do you ask?"

She turned to inform the camera. "Well, my next protest is going to be there."

"Your next . . . protest? And what will you be protesting, Crystal?"

"Anti-globalization."

"You're anti-anti-globalization, is that it?"

"No, Stevie! I'm against killing baby seals and McDonald's and the CIA and everything that's wrong with our planet."

Steven could not help smiling. "That's quite an agenda."

"Yes, I know. But I can't just stand by and let them ruin every-thing, like filling ozone holes and the ocean rising."

Steven was trying to be a good sport but still wanted to egg her on a bit. "You mentioned 'them.' Who are 'they' exactly, Crystal?"

"It's all oil companies and the government," she said passion-ately. "They run everything in secret. It's all a conspiracy, like the Florida vote scandal, the Iraq War, and the rain forests, you know, things like that."

Steven was ready to rise to this bait. As chairman of some of the world's largest businesses, he had always found it hard enough to get people to do what he wanted by openly telling them, writing them, printing it publicly, and endlessly pounding it into their heads. The idea of a vast conspiracy accomplishing everything in secret was ab-surd to him.

But he didn't say anything as Jeffrey entered to announce to them, and to the cameras, that "dinner is served."

Offering his arm, Steven escorted Crystal into the dining room. It looked elegant with the black, leather-topped table mounted on a polished, stainless-steel arch, set with large, burgundy colored, gold-rimmed bone china plates that served as chargers. The candles had been lit and the stemware scattered a soft glow. He seated her next to himself, so that they could easily be shot together on camera. As pre-viously, he found that the TV lights screened them from the others and created a false sense of intimacy.

Jeffrey entered, in his toque—a white tower on his head. He was beaming, on top of the world. "*Foie gras pour Mademoiselle et Monsieur,*" he said with a flourish, setting smaller plates on the chargers before them. The lightly sautéed delicacy, arranged on let-tuce leaves, offered a mouth-watering fragrance. Steven, taking a sip of a light red Rhone Chateuneuf-du-Pape, toasted Crystal, saying, "Here's to you, Crystal. I hope you enjoy your next protest very much."

"What's this?" she asked, pointing to her plate in an accusatory voice.

"It's *foie gras*, miss," answered Jeffrey, who was still standing nearby.

"What's that?"

"It's the engorged liver from a French goose, miss."

"The *what*?"

"The best *foie gras*—it means fat liver—comes from France. They force the goose to overeat by sticking a thing like a funnel down its neck with a hand crank built in, so that they can cram far more down its throat than it could ever eat naturally. It makes the goose's liver swell and really tastes delicious," Jeffrey proudly explained.

Crystal gave a little gasp and started to rise from her seat.

"I can't believe it! The poor goose! First you torture it, and then you kill it. Well, I'm not going to eat it!"

Tears glistened in her eyes, and Steven thought she might bolt, but the cameras probably reminded her of the high-stakes game she was playing and she abruptly sat back down. With a trembling hand, Crystal calmed herself with a sip of her wine.

"I'm sorry, Crystal. I didn't mean to offend you. You don't have to eat it," Steven said reassuringly. He took another bite from his plate before pushing it—regretfully—away, to be polite.

"We don't live like this in Ohio, Stevie. Sometimes I wonder if I'll ever feel at home in New York."

Steven was touched suddenly by her vulnerability. Of course

everything in his world would seem strange to her. Steven gently put his hand on hers, and then her tears really did start to flow.

"Oh, I'm just being silly," she exclaimed after a moment. "I've already been through so much. After all, New York is nothing compared to being abducted."

Steven didn't listen to his little inner voice saying "*Abducted?! Don't go there—you won't like it!*"

But before she could elaborate, a subdued Jeffrey returned with their main course, the tuna tartare, wonderfully prepared with chopped onion and a hint of wasabi. Jeffrey poured the white Mersault into the smaller glasses and then stepped back, awaiting recovery from his earlier disaster.

Crystal stared at her plate. "Is this raw?"

"Ah yes, Crystal," Steven responded. "Tuna tartare. Served with condiments after being lightly marinated, I believe."

"It's raw fish. Do you know what can happen when you eat food that's uncooked?"

Steven said, "Jeeves, I think the lady won't be eating this. Sorry, but I too seem to have lost my appetite," he lied. "Just take this back and we will enjoy our wine. I think you've some nice dessert in the works?" Jeffrey removed the offending tuna.

"Why do you call him Jeeves? I thought his name was Jeffrey."

"Oh, Crystal, it's just a little joke between us. You know Bertie Wooster and his main man Jeeves—from the P. G. Wodehouse novels?"

"No . . ."

"It doesn't matter, never mind." Why had he even bothered? Quickly he changed the subject. "You were going to tell me about being abducted, I think."

"Yes, Steve. Have you ever been abducted?"

"No, Crystal. Can't say that I have."

"Are you sure? I met people at the UFO convention in Detroit who didn't think that they had been either. It was only after talking with those of us who'd been taken that it all came back."

"I'm pretty sure. So what was it like?"

Crystal launched enthusiastically into a long story about how it all happened a couple of years ago back in Ohio. It was a warm summer night and she was having trouble getting to sleep. She saw a blue light, then heard a humming sound, "like a vibrator." She floated up through the ceiling, "as if it wasn't there," into a huge space ship with silver, slender aliens with eyes, "like those nuts, you know almonds." They did medical stuff, "probing, Stevie. And they said I should birth with dolphins."

As he listened, Steven wondered to himself, "How can this be happening? It must be a bad dream." The thought of Yvonne laughing returned.

Crystal was winding up with outrage: ". . . that the government keeps all this secret. You know they have frozen alien bodies in Arizona?"

"Nevada. I think they're in Nevada," Steven corrected.

"Then you know about them too!"

Jeffrey reentered with a flourish and lighted two plates of *Crepes Suzette*. This captured their attention, as the flickering blue brandy flames danced, fluttered, and then died.

"Wow, pancakes. Like at IHOP." Crystal, at last excited about something served at Steven's table. "I love these, they're wonderful!"

She dug in. Jeffrey redeemed himself, partly, by rustling up another serving for Crystal, which was quickly put away as well.

Afterward, they carried their second glasses of the *après* dessert wine, the heavenly Chateau d'Yquem, with them back into the living room. After some further labored chatting, proving they had virtually nothing in common, Steven heard Jessie call out, "Okay, folks, that's a wrap." He had barely seen Jessie all evening.

Now she came forward to congratulate Steven and Crystal with "Well done, kids" and similar flattery. Crystal sank onto a sofa near the fire, pulled off her red cowboy boots, and curled her feet under her. Jessie and Steven exchanged glances. Obviously, Crystal was planning to stay. In the afternoon, Steven had hoped, maybe, to entice the *Trophy* girl into his bedroom. Now he realized that he had no desire for even the most ravishing beauty, if she possessed the mind of a gnat.

"Crystal," Jessie said, detecting his unease, "I think we have to gather up your things and get you back home. The driver is standing by."

Crystal looked up in astonishment. "What do you mean? Stevie and I are just getting along fine, aren't we, Stevie?" Turning to him, with her bosom heaving she asked, "Stevie, you don't want me to go, do you? I know that you want me."

"Well, Crystal, it's sort of getting late. We all have a long day tomorrow."

"What?!" She was flummoxed by his reply. "I thought so. You must be queer! You're gay, aren't you?"

Steven cringed at the ugliness that entered her face. "Hardly, Crystal, it's just that you and I, well, you know, we don't seem to be on the same wavelength."

"It's you and Jeeves, isn't it?" she accused him. "Jeeves, that's some sort of love name you keep using, right?"

Jessie started laughing. "No, Crystal, it's just bad chemistry, okay, no chemistry—between you two."

Crystal looked at Steven with a final plea, but he'd had enough. He headed to the kitchen for another glass of wine.

Helping Crystal to her feet and handing her the red boots, Jessie soothed her hurt feelings. "It's clear that Steven will be looking at the other girls, Crystal, but you were great! What a TV presence you have, and you will be in the first episode! I'll bet modeling, acting, and TV offers will roll in." Jessie guided the softly sobbing girl to the foyer, where Jeffrey was waiting with the platinum faux-fur coat.

"Jeeves, huh? What crap!" was her exit line.

As she stormed into the elevator, Henry—who'd seen it all— slipped in before the doors closed and rode downstairs with her.

*I*t took another hour and a half for the tech staff to clear out most of the cables, lights, microphone booms, and camera boxes from the penthouse. Jessie supervised it all with help from Willard. The crew was still snickering about Crystal when they and the English micro dynamo finally left.

Still amused, Jessie returned and took Crystal's place by the fire. Steven handed her a glass of the wonderful Yquem.

"I had to watch on the monitor in the back," she told him. "I just couldn't stop laughing during that dinner. I was afraid the microphones would hear me."

Steven didn't see it so humorously. "Jessie, how could you have picked her?"

She waved a hand at him not to worry. "I wanted to start off with a very colorful girl who would be fun. I didn't expect you two to click. But it makes for good TV." Seeing how glum he was, she patted the space next to her on the couch.

"Steven, don't be discouraged. You can't expect to hit the jackpot on your first time out. Believe me, I have wonderful, wonderful treats in store for you. We'll talk tomorrow, but I think Bermuda will be next."

Steven sat down on the couch, not close to Jessie. After the failure of the evening, he felt lonelier than ever. Had Crystal really called him gay? He spoke very solemnly. "What would be your reaction, Jessie, what if I were to tell you, now, that Crystal was the girl for me? The girl of my life?"

Her eyebrows shot up. "I would say you were out of your mind!"

They both laughed.

It was nice sitting with her, looking into the dancing glow of the fire. He thought about telling her about his dream of Yvonne, but she might not understand.

He edged closer to Jessie as they stared into the dying flames. He felt as if they were really connecting this time. He mentally rehearsed the next line he was going to say: "Jessie, I'm only doing this for you, you know." Or maybe something more romantic, perhaps . . .

Suddenly Jessie jumped up.

"Steven, I've got to go. I have a million things to do tomorrow." And the executive producer was gone.

*J*essie found Willard in his thin leather jacket on the sidewalk outside helping the crew load the mountain of equipment back into the waiting truck.

"Willard, you don't have to help out. It's so cold and all, and you're not even in the union."

Seeing her, he sparkled to life. "Oh, please. Helping out is the only thing keeping me warm. Jessie, I really wanted to tell you that this is going to be fantastic! He's perfect!" He let out a chortle that rang in the night air. "Did you see the look on his face when she started to talk about the aliens?"

"Yes! I was laughing so hard, I had to bite my hand to keep quiet." They laughed a bit more. As it died away, her expression turned sober. "But, Willard, I don't think his heart is in this. I'm worried that he'll drop out."

"Maybe," he said, nodding rapidly. "That would be a real problem. If we don't get him all the way to the altar, we don't have a show."

She became very serious as she continued. "And we are not following our script. I planned to have him reject her and wind up the episode. I didn't do it because I was afraid he would reject the whole show instead! I think we have to present him with some serious girls to keep him interested."

Willard gave her a nudge. "Well, you know, Jessie, it's you that keeps him interested. Did I tell you he asked me about you and Gregory?"

She stiffened at the suggestion. "Willard, what are you saying? That he's only interested in me?" She thought this over, lips pressed tight. "Believe me, I'm not leading him on, but I have been wondering why any man in his position would do this. He must be crazy."

"No, you're wrong about that, Jessie. He just needs some fun and excitement in his life. If we find him the right lady, we will be doing him a big favor."

She still felt uneasy about what Willard had just said. "Perhaps."

"Sure, I'm right. We just have to work harder on it. Hey, there's a cab! I'm getting cold. Gotta go! I need to cuddle with my Sally."

"Good night, Willard," Jessie called as he hurried to the curb and hailed the taxi. She signaled to the Lincoln Town Car, which had been waiting patiently to take her home. Gregory would still be up, she thought. Maybe she could tell him about how funny Crystal had been, without him explaining some insight from Anthony Tower's seven steps.

Willard's suggestion that Steven might be seriously interested in her weighed on Jessie's mind as the car carried her across town. Had she missed some signals? He did seem to be edging toward intimacy when they sat on the couch. *Had* she been leading him on? She reviewed their brief history. No, she concluded. She'd been totally professional always—though she acknowledged he was an attractive, older guy.

*T*ony expected to be chauffeuring Steven and Crystal back to her place, and he was surprised when young Mr. Hudson entered the garage with his arm encircling the teary-eyed stunner. As he drove the Bentley uptown, he could see in the rearview mirror that Henry's attentions were effective in converting the girl's soft, sniffling sobs into giggles. Henry asked him to wait by the curb as he escorted Crystal up the steps into her building.

He waited.

His surprise was even greater when they both emerged— Crystal carrying a tiny suitcase. Not his business, of course, but Tony couldn't ignore the mirror's view of the boss's son nearly enveloped in the platinum fur, in an embrace and kiss that seemed to last all the way downtown to young Hudson's Village loft. Tony drove away as they entered the old converted warehouse together.

Henry's comfort to Crystal was quite thorough. It lasted until dawn.

Though she may have wondered if Steven was gay, as soon as she entered Henry's loft, she had no doubt as to his son's persuasion. The two large erotic nudes, nearly electric in their impact, painted in luscious colors on black velvet, left no doubt. The figures arched their backs and thrust voluptuous breasts forward—they were nearly as big as hers.

In no time, Henry stripped off his shirt, revealing his buffed up-per body—a most sexy substitute for an aging millionaire, she de-cided. Soon, he had persuaded Crystal to display her own sensuous figure in her skimpy, black lace underwear. A new bottle of cham-pagne popped its cork, arching up nearly to the high ceiling of the loft. It was a huge place, worth a fortune, but the dominant feature was an enormous waterbed against a brick wall toward the back.

Henry was a practiced master in the art of seduction, and he encountered encouragement rather than resistance. Soon they were making passionate waves together upon the aqueous mattress.

"God, I love reality television," he murmured to Crystal, as they lay together upon the undulating surface—before they churned the waters once again. And then still again.

CHAPTER NINE

*J*effrey served apologies along with Steven's espresso, hard-boiled eggs with dabs of mayonnaise, and cod roe. The penthouse was humming with activity again the next morning. Juan and Brenda were busy with their vacuums, after straightening up the mess left by the camera crew.

Jeffrey kept revisiting the failure of his menu. "How could I have screwed up so badly, boss? All she ate was the *Suzette* and she called the crepes pancakes."

"I know, Jeffrey," Steven said, commiserating. "Let's face it. Crystal comes from outer space. But don't feel too badly. Only she, you, and I know about your cuisine crisis—unless you count the national TV audience."

Steven had recovered his sense of humor, but he too was feeling uncomfortable this morning. Crystal was not really on his mind, but Jessie definitely was. Had he let the attractive TV producer talk him into participating in a farce? She was such a persuasive sales-woman that Steven thought she could be a huge success as a partner in his firm. But was he just a spineless softie being manipulated for her purposes? And what about his purposes? This reality show thing was certainly a cure for boredom, but did he want to wind up at the altar with a girl Helen's age? And if so, was this really the way to go about it? Crystal was so mindless, he virtually had thrown her out. Jessie was taking advantage of him. He had to toughen up.

He would have continued to indulge in his guilty, self-deprecating spiral except that Eamon rang the penthouse announc-ing that Mrs. O'Brian was on her way up.

Her arrival was expected. She had papers to be signed and some "housekeeping matters" he needed to review. Steven escorted her past his cleaning staff and into his office.

"Well, Mr. Hudson," she said glancing back at the door, "what's it like to be on TV? Were they here most of the night?"

"No, Mrs. O'Brian. We merely had a quiet dinner. It was all rather unexciting, believe me. You might think of it as a different way to meet new people. The latest since computer dating, I suppose." Steven tried to sound nonchalant, but he doubted that she believed him, since he didn't believe himself.

"I'll watch with interest, I'm sure." Then, all business, she opened her briefcase and spread papers on the desk, which Steven skimmed and signed.

A spreadsheet was then unfolded. "Here is the salary summary for your annual review, Mr. Hudson."

The list comprised about twenty names. His penthouse staff in-cluding Jeffrey, Brenda, and Juan; the staff for Ivy Columns; the Vail chalet; the four pilots required to keep his G-5 available to go anywhere in the world at a moment's notice; the crew aboard his motor yacht berthed at the Caribbean island of St. Martin; and of course, Mrs. O'Brian herself. This had been a profitable year without any unusual inflation, so Steven proposed a ten percent salary increase across the board, which Mrs. O'Brian agreed was generous. She granted her exquisitely controlled smile to Steven's annual joke, "Gosh, it's getting expensive to be rich." Having no further business, he could have excused her, but instead he poured her a second cup of coffee from the silver coffee set on his desk.

Feeling clumsy, he asked, "Mrs. O'Brian, do you think I'm making a fool of myself?"

Her answer was so delayed that Steven at first thought she was going to duck his question. It was perhaps the first personal question ever asked in their long association. But then her usual reserve melted and, with a sad smile, she answered.

"When Mr. O'Brian passed away—it's been twelve years now, if you remember—I thought I wouldn't survive. I was so lonely. And I've seen that in you, Mr. Hudson. Life is empty without a companion. Whether this is the right way to go about finding someone new, I can't say, but you deserve to be happy. Everyone does. It seems to me that you've always been driven to success. But when it comes to achieving happiness, has that been accomplished?"

He had to look away from the intensity of her gaze. "I've achieved a lot, I think."

"Certainly a lot, Mr. Hudson. You are a 'living legend,' as they say. But why have you been so driven?"

"I'm not sure, Mrs. O'Brian. I've always been highly motivated. I think it goes back to childhood. I've been that way as long as I can remember."

"Your childhood, was it a happy time?" He was taken aback by the personal nature of the question, and she added, "I'm only curious. You don't have to tell me."

"Well, I guess I don't mind." He thought about it for a second. "Looking back on it, my childhood was pretty bleak."

He invited her to have a seat before he went on. He hadn't thought about his past in years. He told her that his mother and father weren't really in love with each other. "They made each other mutually unhappy, I suppose." His father was a maintenance man for the Boston MTA, the public transport system—working-class, from his blue collar shirt to his safety boots—and he had no aspirations to anything better than being a union man. Steven's mother always made it clear to her husband that she thought him to be a failure. "Everything in my childhood revolved around money and my mother's yearning for it, and my father's passive resistance to doing anything extra to get more."

Steven realized, early on, that striving and achieving, and particularly making money, would gain his mother's approval. He worked paper routes, grocery bagging, all kinds of jobs. He couldn't ever remember not working, or feeling guilty if he wasn't. As he earned more, it irritated his father more. By the time he worked his way through Harvard, they were hardly speaking.

His mother, on the other hand, loved his success and wanted more. After his father died and Steven made his first million, she wanted it. "She never spent much, she just wanted to think of herself as a millionaire." But he never gave her the million. He figured, why pay a tax on the money when he gave it and another when he inherited it back? He did pay her a "salary" for years, and she too received annual raises. She squirreled it all away. "Years after her death, you probably remember, Mrs. O'Brian, savings accounts turned up in little banks all around Boston. It added up to over a million—she outfoxed me in the end." His secretary smiled slightly as he finished the tale.

"So, that's how I became an A type, striving, achieving, acquiring—the personality that you now know and love." Steven wound up with a tight-lipped smile. But Mrs. O'Brian remained serious.

"Mr. Hudson, I understand . . . perhaps for the first time, I understand. But isn't a TV girl just another acquisition, another trophy?"

Before Steven had sorted out his feelings enough to speak, his secretary stood up primly. Gathering the papers in her briefcase, she became all business once again. "Mr. Hudson, I should warn you, this TV show has raised quite the storm at the office. Mr. Crowninshield is still grumbling."

"Well," he said with a smile, also standing up, "call me if Pierce turns from surly to mutinous." He knew that Mrs. O'Brian would cope with Pierce's moods—she could quell earthquakes with a glance.

She closed her satchel with a snap and headed for the door. Before she left, Mrs. O'Brian turned to him, saying with a smile, "Mr. Hudson, I hope you find her."

*J*essie had shared the Crystal episode with Gregory over morning coffee and croissants at Starbuck's, however, he ran everything through his Anthony Tower filter.

"You have to understand, sweetheart," she patiently explained again, "Steven is *such* a distinguished gentlemen, and she is such a bimbo—we got terrific stuff on tape—but Steven never lost his poise or gracious manners. He was just wonderful." Jessie smiled as she remembered the evening.

Her smile faded when he said, "I still think Steven Hudson has an inner child craving attention." Gregory just didn't get it, she thought, suppressing a sigh. "Look, he needs to be recognized on national TV, and I'll bet that still won't be enough for that craving," he added.

"No, Gregory, if you met Steven, you would understand." Jessie had recently begun to cringe every time the inner child reared its ugly head. "This is not about his inner child. It's about a very classy guy who has gotten swept up in our circus."

"That's right!" he doggedly responded. "You yourself said a reasonable man wouldn't participate. You're proving my point. The inner child rules."

"Gregory, you're wrong." She was grimacing, her patience at its limit. "Damn it, must you bring your boss's ridiculous theory into everything?"

Gregory fell uncharacteristically silent, intimidated by her anger. There was a long pause in their conversation.

Jessie finished her coffee, letting the silence between them lengthen. Finally, she rested her hand on his and gave him a little loving squeeze. His smile automatically switched back on as she said, "Sweetheart, I'm sorry. I guess I'm so close to this that I can't see it the way you do."

They finished their breakfast by talking about other things and parted with a hug. But why, Jessie wondered, had she been so protective of Steven? By the time she reached her office to start a busy day, she still had no answer.

*H*enry knew his father was unaware of his selfless chivalry with Crystal, and Steven was happy to hear from him when he called.

"Dad, how's your TV show coming along?" he asked innocently.

"Oh, Hank, I don't know," Steven said gloomily. "I went on the first date last night with a total airhead. Nothing is going to develop from that."

As Henry had no opinion on Crystal's mental capabilities, he pushed on. "Will you be going on another date tonight?" Henry might have to volunteer quietly to help old dad out again, he thought.

"No, Jessie is planning a beach scene in a couple of days."

Henry heard the lack of enthusiasm in his father's voice. "Dad, why don't I tag along to keep you company? We could have fun sizing up the babes together." Henry casually let Steven know that Kathy wouldn't be returning from Chevy Chase to his Village loft. "She only wants to hear the C-word, Dad. You know, commitment. So we're splitting." Henry left out all of Kathy's anguish over his infidelities. Steven thought his boy might be feeling a little down, so he agreed that it could be a good idea and said he would clear it with Jessie. Henry's positive outlook was always infectious. By the end of the conversation, they both were upbeat about sharing a trip.

*E*arly the following week, Steven and Henry rode together in the Bentley on their way to Teterboro airport. Jessie had easily persuaded Steven to make the Gulfstream Five available for their

trip to Bermuda. She would be meeting them at the executive jet terminal with Heather and Kim, the two contestants also making the
trip. Jessie had decided that it would create better TV to have two
girls competing for Steven during the Bermuda weekend. She hoped
that their rivalry would be interesting, perhaps amusing, for viewers
of the unfolding series. Jessie had been delighted to include Henry.
He would be attractive to young women in the viewing audience, so
he was a great addition.

As they emerged from the Lincoln Tunnel, Steven's portable
telephone rang. It was Helen.

"Pop, I've been trying to reach you all morning. Mrs. O'B. said
that you're on your way to Bermuda with the TV bunch."

Steven acknowledged that this was so. He was surprised by the
urgency in Helen's voice as she continued:

"But you can't be doing this, Pop! You can't marry one of those
pin-ups—an empty-headed, wet T-shirt model barely out of high
school. What about Hank and me?"

"Well, Hank is with me, actually."

"*What?*"

"He thought it would be fun for him to appear in the shoot of
this episode, and Jessie agreed."

"But the whole idea is crazy! I know I suggested you try it on
for size, but I realized my mistake when I saw you all made up on
that TV stage. And those girls . . . Pop, some of them are younger
than me!"

"Helen, I know," he said impatiently. "Remember, you were the
one who told me that life is just concept art and that these girls are
my raw material?"

"But, Pop, if you marry one of those bimbos, she'll be my stepmother!" She sounded horrified.

"Yes, I guess that would be true."

"She might want to have kids—a whole new family. She'll try to disinherit us! How can you be so selfish?"

"Helen, calm down, please. You know that I would never abandon you and Henry."

"Dad, is that Helen?" Henry asked. When his father nodded, he said, "Let me talk to her." Steven, not knowing what else to do, handed the phone over to Hank, who picked up the argument with his sister. "Hey, how is Miss Impulsive this morning? . . . That's funny, I thought you were all for it . . ."

They drove into the area for executive jets and pulled up to the security gate. The guard waved them through. As they came to a stop directly alongside the highly polished Gulfstream Five, Henry stepped out of the car still talking to his sister. "I'm sure he'll have dinner with you when we return. . . . Right, you'll do the cooking, and Ari will be there too." Henry clicked off the phone and turned to his father with a wink. "I calmed her down. The coast is clear." Steven thanked him, though not without a guilty pang about what they were doing.

A light rain had begun to fall, and father and son clambered up the jet's fold-down stairway into its luxurious cabin. Jessie, Kim, and Heather were already aboard.

"Steven, what a magnificent plane," Jessie said, truly excited. "I've never been in an executive jet so big, so luxurious." She gestured around the cabin. "The wood, the leather, the art, it's just magnificent!"

Kim and Heather were seated, side by side, both beautiful brunettes wearing tasteful Loro Piana sports outfits and holding hands—probably nervous about the flight and the upcoming events in Bermuda, thought Steven. Jack, the chubby cameraman who had done the filming of Crystal in the Bentley, was busy capturing everything aboard the plane.

Jessie described her plans. "My tech crew called in yesterday from scouting out backgrounds and locations for our shoot. Acme Studios has pretty much taken over the Royal Victoria Pink Sand Hotel for the next couple of days. They said that the sun was warm and the beaches nice—too cold for swimming but fine for swimsuits on the pink sand."

The pilots today were Tom and Joe, both ex-Air Force Fighter jocks who had each worked for Steven for several years, graduating their way up through his jets, which had increased in size from the original Lear to this G-5, the top of the private jet food chain. They fired up the twin engines as Angie, a part-time flight attendant who had accompanied Steven on other flights, went through the mandatory safety instructions, life vests, oxygen, and so forth, just as required on commercial flights. But, unlike anything in the commercial world, after takeoff they could all sit as they wished in the lavish interior, around the bridge table, or on the couches; they could rotate their seats around to any direction and use the full lavatory, complete with a shower, in the back. The interior had been customized, and no expense had been spared.

Outside, the rain became intense, streaking along the windows as the powerful engines hurtled the jet down the runway. Steven loved the way the plane seemed to shoot away from the ground, climbing far faster than anything else, like an airborne Lamborghini sports car, maybe even a McLaren. At altitude, they settled in for the two and a half hour flight over the Atlantic to the tiny island. The conversation was lighthearted and fun. It was nice, Steven thought, to have his son along for this adventure. Henry wasn't at all uneasy at being filmed by Jessie's cameraman.

As Angie was serving a small lunch, chicken chunks in a green salad with a smooth, light white wine, the G-5 began to bounce in some turbulence. After a couple of pretty heavy bumps, Tom, the copilot, came into the cabin to talk with Steven.

"Mr. Hudson, I've been on the radio with Bermuda," he said quietly. "The minor cold front that was expected to pass through is stalled and the depression is actually deepening. In fact, the barometer is dropping like a rock. We have to decide if we want to turn back to Teterboro or keep going. The landing in Bermuda will be rough but not dangerous. It's up to you."

"Well, Tom, how long do you think the storm will last after we arrive, if we keep going?"

"I don't really have a good forecast. They'll be revising now that this front is misbehaving, but it's not in yet."

Jessie had been listening intently. "Steven, if it's safe to land, let's keep going. Willard and my whole crew are there. I would like to get some footage or all the expenses are completely wasted. It will probably clear."

He accepted her request. "Okay, Tom, I agree with Ms. James. She personally knows Al Roker. Let's keep going."

When they were thirty minutes from Bermuda's airport, the turbulence increased noticeably. Tom returned and had them all buckle up. He said a strong cross wind would make the landing "different." And it sure was. As they made the final approach, Steven could see the runway lights through the open cockpit door and the windshield. They were angled sideways, "crabbing" a lot to hold course against a strong side wind. The plane seemed to be buffeted like a feather in a storm, and they all hung onto the arms of their seats. When they touched down, the plane skidded noticeably before Joe, at the controls, powered down the momentum. One of the girls screamed, and Tom came on the intercom to announce, "Sorry, for the excitement folks—all's well. The tower says we're the last flight they're going to permit to land until this front blows through. That cross wind was gusting at over forty knots."

The G-5 came to a stop near the terminal. The whine of the engines diminished to silence and their hostess, Angie, broke out umbrellas for them to use against the rain. The sound of the storm outside was loud now that they had landed.

The best part about a private jet, Steven often thought, was the speed of clearing in and out of air terminals. Usually he was just waved through, and without other planes in evidence on the ground, he expected this to be extra fast. But he hadn't been to Bermuda recently.

They encountered a woman in a bulging, blue uniform who did everything by the book. She was so slow and deliberate that Steven thought she might still be waiting for the book to be written. Passports were checked and they found out Heather and Kim didn't have passports. But driver's licenses would be accepted thanks to an "intergovernmental agreement between the government of Bermuda and the government of the United States of America." This was said in a tone clearly implying that the United States was the secondary power of the two.

Heather cleared Customs on the strength of her Rhode Island

driver's license, but Kim didn't have either a passport or a driver's license. They had reached an impasse. Clearly, the bureaucracy established by more than two hundred years of English rule was now safe in the hands of this massive official of Bermuda, a nation independent of the mother country in almost every way, save for nostalgia and resentment.

Jessie came to Kim's aid. Introducing herself, she explained about the TV crew already on the island, who Steven was— that it was his jet—and the idea of the show. This was a mistake. The woman intoned, "The filming of pornography is an illegal activity on the island, punishable by a prison term." Only after Tom sought out the lady's supervisor was an agreement reached. With the pilot's personal guarantee, Kim would be permitted to remain on the island for forty-eight hours and then only after a complete search of her baggage. Kim, Tom, and her bags were brought to a room for a thorough search, which took a number of minutes. When they returned, Kim was blushing deeply and the pilot had a very odd look on his face.

"Anything wrong, Tom?" Steven asked.

"No, not wrong—nothing illegal, I guess. Just very . . . strange," was his inscrutable answer, upon which he refused to expound.

With some difficulty, Jessie had rounded up two taxis, one for the TV group and the other for the G-5 crew and all the combined luggage. They were parked with their headlights illuminating the gathering dusk. The rain was blowing nearly horizontally in the ever increasing wind.

Their hotel was on the edge of Hamilton, the island's largest town. The whole island was only twenty miles long and a little over a mile wide, so Steven didn't think it would take long to drive from St. George, at the north end where they had landed, the nine or so miles required. Wrong again. Because of the storm blowing down branches and causing sporadic flooding, the normal short drive took well over an hour. At last they arrived at the Royal Victoria Pink Sand Hotel. They could hear the waves pounding, and it seemed like all of the beach's pink sand was blowing across the lawn and into their faces, as they hurried into the lobby and out of the rain.

The place was like a big, old English seaside summer hotel, lots of white paint on the woodwork, green walls, chintz-covered arm-chairs, and couches everywhere. The TV crew was ready for them. Willard was in pink Bermuda shorts and the most violently colored sports shirt Steven had ever seen. The lights blazed as Jessie maneu-vered Steven between Heather and Kim. He escorted them through the lobby and to the front desk. This was the first time that day that Steven had assumed his Don Juan role, and he felt a little awkward with the two girls. The manager gave them keys to the Royal suite on the top floor. The cameramen followed them up the large open cen-tral staircase (the elevator was too small for them all) to the third floor and into the huge suite. Large photographs of a young-looking Queen Elizabeth and her young Prince Philip were on the walls and in frames on the tables—mementos of a Royal visit to the island long ago, before the governor had been assassinated and the island had become a virtually independent entity, home for thousands upon thousands of "letter box" off-shore tax haven companies for the tax-allergic citizens of the world.

The suite consisted of a huge central room, with lots of over-stuffed chintz furniture, a marble fireplace, and four bedrooms with baths opening off this principal center. Steven, Henry, and Jessie each had a room to themselves and the two girls shared the remain-ing bedroom.

As the French doors to the balcony outside rattled and shook on their hinges with the blasts of wind from the Atlantic, all went to their rooms to freshen up for dinner. Jessie had given them only thirty minutes, as she needed to get on with the shoot. Everyone dressed informally, but Heather and Kim looked elegantly casual in their Donna Karan outfits that Jessie had selected for them. Henry wore his long blond hair carefully combed back and a rather tight-fitting sports shirt to show off his torso. Steven realized that his son wanted to make a good impression on the girls. Steven looked equally sharp in white slacks and a navy blue, cotton turtleneck sweater.

The cavernous dining room was devoid of other hotel guests. Jessie's crew had taken up most of the hotel's rooms, and so the camera people were able to tape at will. The five of them sat down to a classic, high English dinner of 1930's vintage. The roast beef had been cooked to a crumbling dryness and the four accompanying veggies had been put to boil, perhaps eight hours previously. Steven remarked, "The English think that you can taste germs, and if food has any flavor, cook it some more."

The idea was to capture the developing relationships between Steven and the two girls. But it wasn't coming off as Jessie had planned. Because of the shrieking wind buffeting the hotel from off the ocean, which was giving the sound technicians fits, the girls seemed withdrawn and talked mostly to each other. Growing discouraged, Jessie remarked, "Probably Henry and I should not have joined you three at the table." Yet Steven kept drawing her into conversation. He wanted to know everything about her. And even though she protested more than once, "Hey, this isn't about me," she had an interesting story to tell.

She'd grown up in Scarsdale, the only daughter of a neurosurgeon father, and a mother who taught European history at nearby Sarah Lawrence College. Both her parents were still going strong, and Jessie saw them every weekend. She said that her home had been a very happy one; she had two brothers who were married and had kids.

Steven interrupted to ask, "Hank, when are you going to oblige me in that department?" His son's blithe shrug reminded him of his inability to settle down with any woman.

Jessie had imagined a career in acting, she told them. She'd starred in productions in high school and then also at her college, Wellesley. But she gradually became more interested in the nonperforming side, particularly playwriting. She wrote a one-act play about the death of a beloved grandfather, which the Wellesley Drama Department had produced to some acclaim in her senior year, but "it was far too serious and intense to be interesting to a wide audience," she insisted. After graduation she found a job on Madison Avenue, writing copy at an ad agency. Eventually she became involved in helping to stage scripts, some of which she wrote for TV commercials. Then the big break had come at Acme Studios, starting with writing and producing drama series and sitcoms with others and rising six years ago to the Executive Producer position overseeing everything at Acme. She'd done extremely well. Her comedy drama series *California King Size* had swept the Emmy awards.

But she surprised Steven when she said that the *Trophy Bride* project was going to be her last. "I've made enough money in TV. I am going to get out and try my hand again at playwriting. If I don't do it now, I never will."

Jessie skirted the issue of her failed marriage and, most important, Mark. He was never far from her mind. She wondered how he and Steven would hit it off. Would they find more of a rapport than the void existing with Gregory?

"Anyway," she said at the dinner's end to Steven and Hank, "I would like you to assemble with the girls back up in the suite. Tomorrow we will work outside all day around the pool and the beach. Willard has dozens of ideas for scenes."

Steven was left wishing she had said something about her ex, the mysterious Mr. James. He also wanted to know more about her fiancé, since her engagement ring was so annoyingly 'there.' He supposed, however, he'd learned a lot at one sitting.

They rose from the table, following her instructions. As they approached the stairway, the hotel seemed to tremble at its foundations with an extra strong blast. At once all the electricity in the building went out, and Steven, looking out of the window, could see that power was out over the whole island. Some of the hand-held cameras still had their lights, but they wouldn't last; without power, it was obvious that the shoot would be over for the night. The hotel staff scurried about setting up candles and lamps. The techs with the hand-helds shot a little more footage, annoyed at nature's inconsideration of their plans. Jessie decided to call off further taping. Upstairs, the five of them settled in the suite's living room, now looking even more vast as the weak flickering candles failed to illuminate the corners.

It seemed, somehow, that when the cameras stopped rolling and they were left to themselves, their purpose in being evaporated. Conversation became difficult, strained. Jessie was fretting and basically waiting for better weather in the morning, when the lens caps would come off, and they again could all exist. Kim and Heather

seemed the most out of place in the group. They appeared to be interested only in each other. Far from competing for Steven, as Jessie
had hoped, they acted as if he were a problem that they had to en-
dure politely. They didn't show any greater interest in Henry.

When Henry noted that the rain had stopped, even though the
wind was still strong, he suggested, "Dad, do you want to go outside?
We can take a look at the waves crashing on the shore."

"Sure, that would be great," Steven replied. Jessie chose to turn
in, and the girls announced that they were retiring as well.

No stars were visible, but Steven and Henry agreed that the
worst of the storm was over, even though it was not easy to walk
against the wind across the lawn to the ocean. The grass was covered
with solid waves of sand blown from the beach. In some places these
mini-sand dunes were about a foot high. The waves were huge and
salt spray stung their faces as they halted before the rocks along the
shore. "Rocks?" Steven wondered aloud, "What happened to the famous pink sand? Indeed, all of the sand had been washed away, exposing the jagged-looking black volcanic rock of the island's shell. As
they walked back, Henry joked, "Management will have to change
the name to "Royal Victoria Black Lava Rock Beach Hotel."

Inside, without power, no one was around. No emergency gen-
erators, Steven guessed. They climbed the stairs to the Royal Suite.
The three women were in their rooms behind closed doors. The two
men poured themselves a couple of scotches—neat, since the ice
had melted—and toasted each other. "Here's to a long, unsatisfac-
tory day."

As their conversation lagged, Henry poured himself another,
but Steven said good night and withdrew to his chintz-empowered
bedroom, where the stub of a candle was still giving some light. He

lay down fully clothed, intending to rest for a moment, and fell asleep almost instantly.

Later on, Steven awoke with a start. The candle was out and he didn't know how long he'd been asleep. The wind was still strong and noisy, but possibly a little diminished. A faint light was coming in from the living room, and he got up to investigate. He saw Henry standing, motionless, looking into the girls' room through a crack in their door, which was slightly ajar. What was he up to this time? Steven wondered as he crossed the room. Henry didn't hear him coming, and when he touched his son on the shoulder, Henry jumped, startled. But he quickly recovered. "Shhh," he hissed with his finger across his lips. He motioned slightly for Steven to take a look through the door. No, thought Steven, to do so would be improper. But Henry stepped aside and with a small push he positioned his father so that it was almost impossible not to see.

The girls' room was illuminated by several wavering candles that cast an unsteady light over a scene entirely new to Steven's experience. Heather was nude upon the bed and Kim, above her, was also nude, but wearing some sort of complicated black leather harness. Through numerous buckles and D-rings, the straps crossed her shoulders, spanned her full breasts, encircled her waist, and passed between her legs to rise again over her firm buttocks to rejoin the other straps at the waist. She held a long, black whip in her right hand. It had a leather handle and numerous strands whirling in the air as she manipulated it over the prone girl on the bed. Heather's body was glistening in perspiration as she moaned in anticipation of the whiplash, which seemed always to be withheld. The wind, the rattle of the windows in the old building, made it hard to hear what the two were saying exactly, but Steven made out, "Hurt me, please, mistress."

Father and son watched in silence. The eroticism between the girls was transfixing. . . .

Suddenly, the electric power returned and the suite was flooded with light. The two participants and the two voyeurs gasped audibly as the electricity flashed on. The girls instantly became aware of the men at the door.

"You creeps!" Kim screamed at them. Well-chosen words, Steven thought in a flash.

Raging, the girls threw themselves at the door. They slammed it shut and shot the bolt home. Their flood of invective could be heard clearly through the suite.

Henry tried to explain to Steven, "Dad, I heard what I thought was crying. I was investigating what it was when—"

His story was cut short by Jessie, who entered in a hotel bathrobe. "I heard a door slam. What on earth is going on?" She tried to open the door. "What are Heather and Kim doing? Why are they locked in?"

The cursing had been replaced by crying, and Steven realized that their door would soon open to Jessie's soothing entreaties. It was also clear that Henry shared his father's disinclination to explain. At last Steven understood what his pilot had seen in that bag at Customs.

"Jessie, the girls can tell you. If you don't get a good answer, ask to see the special costume Kim brought."

The girls eventually opened the door to Jessie. As she entered, the two Hudsons fled to their respective bedrooms. Steven could hear, as his door closed, Henry breaking out in gales of laughter.

*I*n the morning, the green sky seemed to mirror the green walls of the suite. The weather looked decidedly unwell to

Steven, although the wind had dropped to nothing. Huge swells continued to roll in and crash upon the now rocky shore.

Not wanting to talk with the others, he had room service deliver a light breakfast to his bedroom. The friendly waiter, a dead ringer for the young Bob Marley, said that a lot of damage had been inflicted on the island by the storm, but that, according to the manager, the pink sand would reappear. It always did, sometimes with the help of a dredge and some bulldozers.

After he took a call from Tom, one of the pilots, advising that the winds were expected to rise again by mid-afternoon and that it would be best to clear Bermuda sooner rather than later, Steven realized he had to talk with Jessie. He wasn't going to continue with this S & M pair, no matter what.

He found her together with Willard downstairs in the lobby. She was directing her technical crews, who were busy packing up equipment into the battered traveling cases.

"Oh, Steven," she said dejectedly. "No shoot, no beach, no girls. Let's get out of Dodge."

"I may already understand, but fill me in, please."

"Steven, Heather and Kim don't want to continue. I don't really know what happened last night, but I guess they were more interested in finding each other than in landing you." She looked pained at making this revelation. She began rubbing her temples furiously. "I didn't see this coming. I am truly sorry. I don't know if it will make sense in the series. I am not sure that we can use any of the footage we shot last night. This isn't going at all the way Willard and I planned."

He hated to add to her woes, but he was sick of this mess. "Jessie, I think I'll pull out too. I'm sorry. I've wasted your time. This isn't going any place." He held up a hand to stop her from replying. "These girls and I are from different planets. No, that's the wrong analogy. We're from different epochs in time, to be more accurate. How can it ever work?"

To his surprise, she didn't try to change his mind. "Maybe it can't," she sighed. "The idea felt so good in the beginning. But, Steven, it's 100 percent my fault. I sent you the wrong girls! Crystal, well, she was meant to be fun, to get things rolling. You and I both know that she was never a possibility. But these two could have worked, I thought." Her eyes filled with a dark storm, and Steven realized she knew exactly what had happened last night.

"I've been on the phone this morning," she said wearily. "Remember Lynne, the tall brunette? Well, Lynne is going to meet us when we land. Please give us one more chance. Just spend a little time with her. No cameras. No pressure. Don't make a decision about quitting. Just wait until tomorrow. Please?"

Steven was still susceptible to Jessie's charm. Besides, she was asking for almost nothing.

"For you, Jessie. I'll meet Lynne for you."

Her wonderful smile in response was more than compensation.

The flight back wasn't much fun. Most of the group sat in stony silence, seemingly engrossed in various magazines or books. Henry grabbed the first glossy he saw and appeared deeply interested in *Ebony* for the entire trip. Steven sat with a copy of *The Economist* in his lap, but he couldn't keep from sneaking peeks at Jessie the entire flight. She was smartly dressed in sporty slacks and a Tom Ford blouse, working on pages of numbers. In her reading glasses she was quite attractive, Steven thought. The girls took seats as far in the rear as possible and did not talk even to each other.

The pilots had cleared them through U.S. Customs while still in Bermuda. They landed and pulled up alongside a black Cadillac limo Tony had chosen for their pickup. Standing next to him was a strikingly beautiful young woman dressed in a carefully tailored business suit. She was holding a silver tray of caviar canapés for their enjoyment.

"Hello, Mr. Hudson, I'm Lynne," she said with a winning smile. "You don't know it yet, but I'm the next Mrs. Hudson."

CHAPTER TEN

*L*ynne was indeed lovely and very smart. She had arranged a catered dinner in the penthouse entirely on her own initiative. Jeffrey, not expecting their early return from Bermuda, had taken a few days off, so Henry and Steven were happy to find everything planned in advance. They were tired from the flight and readily let this gorgeous girl entertain them.

She was classically beautiful, poised, confident, and quick-witted. When Steven said, "Lynne, you seem quite at home here," she didn't miss a beat in replying, "Well, I told you I would be the next Mrs. Hudson."

Steven laughed and sipped the martini she'd expertly prepared, but Henry was uncharacteristically subdued. Steven didn't notice how his son was preoccupied with Lynne's every move. And during dinner Henry was unusually awkward, actually letting his father carry the light bantering conversation. And he noticeably didn't laugh at

Steven's "Mrs. Hudson, that was a great meal," when they'd finished the dessert.

After the dishes were cleared, they settled around the fireplace.

Lynne smoothly led the after-dinner chatter, and at last engaged Henry in conversation. Steven watched them together. He was tired and he let his mind wander, paying only occasional attention to the young people. He was forming a decision. He'd said he'd meet with Jessie one last time, and then that would be it. He couldn't go on with this charade. And he readily agreed to Henry's offer to escort Lynne back to her apartment. After sorting through a few papers in his office, he retired for the night. He was at peace with his decision to abort his fledgling TV career. He only wished he didn't have to give up Jessie as part of the bargain.

*T*he following day Willard arrived in Steven's Wall Street office dressed in a double-breasted black suit with the widest pink pinstripes that Steven had ever seen, complete with a black shirt and pink, silk tie. His tiny feet were encased in white canvas shoes—in the dead of winter. He looked like a micro edition of Al Capone, had the Chicago gangster grown hair on his head and chosen to dye it pink and blue.

"Good morning, mate! Isn't Jessie here yet? We came separately."

Steven was in Wall Street mode this morning, all business. "No, Willard, and I need to talk to her. I've decided to bail and not waste any more of your time and money. I've made my decision."

"Hmm . . . you Yanks say you've *made* a decision; we Brits say that we've *taken* one—shows how differently our minds work. But I understand how you feel, Steven, after Crystal and that Bermuda disaster. You were so happy during the first episode . . . how those girls adored you, Steven! They're calling me all the time, wanting to know when they can be with you again."

Steven didn't look up from the papers he was signing. "Oh really?"

"Absolutely. There's something magnetic in your personality that is very compelling to women. Jessie felt it right away."

Steven stopped what he was doing and looked up. "Did she?"

"Oh, yes!"

"Well, I feel something exactly like that when I'm with her, too. I truly do."

Willard's hands began flying all over the place. "She so enjoys being with you, Steven. She thinks you're insightful and wise. She told me that she wouldn't even consider doing the show without you starring in it. She's always believed that only a man of your depth would see the true possibilities in our little endeavor."

Willard was laying it on thick, and Steven said, "Well, I don't know about that . . ."

Before Willard could get any further in exploiting Steven's weakness for Jessie—which she would have been mortified to hear—she hurried into the room.

"Steven, what a wonderful office you have." She gazed about the wood paneling in admiration. "Makes mine look like tinsel." Steven jumped from his seat behind the desk and graciously motioned Jessie toward a comfortable chair beside the coffee table. He personally took the silver coffee tray Mrs. O'Brian brought and set it down in front of her. Willard found his own place in another chair.

"Jessie, I was explaining to Steven how much you enjoy working with him on this show and how much the girls look forward to being with him still more," explained Willard.

"Yes, Steven, when you met Lynne at the airport yesterday, you agreed to continue, didn't you?"

Willard almost flinched at her direct approach—this was it! They would sink or swim with his answer.

Willard's relief was nearly tangible when Steven responded, "Jessie, it is so very good to see you. I did, I guess, sort of promise you that maybe I would, at least, have a date with Lynne. She made Hank and me a great dinner last night."

The meeting continued with Willard and Jessie slowly rebuilding Steven's confidence in the show's concept. They wound up having a richly prepared lunch together in the intimate dining room adjoining Steven's office. The electric fireplace was glowing as they entered, the rosy light reflected from the French polished mahogany panels around the room. Oil paintings of old sailing ships hung on the walls, and a particularly beautiful ship by Montague Dawson hung over the stone mantelpiece. The circular table was set for three and the cobalt blue, gold-rimmed plates complimented the cut crystal, thick linen tablecloth, and napkins.

Willard was duly impressed with this display of Wall Street elegance, but Jessie had a hard time believing that this older man, with all his sophistication and accomplishments, was still willing to play their game. He seemed like a very decent guy, and she thought she knew the answer to why he would submit to such indignity. It was evident in the way Steven looked at her. Several times when Steven wasn't watching, Willard winked at her. Once he even silently mouthed, "You." It was flattering yet disconcerting, all this attention. Could she learn to like it?

*L*ynne was no Jessie, but she was a girl Steven could take seriously. That was clear by the end of their first camera observed lunch together, the following day. As usual, Jessie and Willard hovered behind the scenes. Willard at one point had to interrupt politely to ask Steven sotto voce to stop following Jessie with his eyes all the time. It would distract the audience, he said. Steven again found it strange to be doing everything for the benefit of a future TV audience, but Lynne didn't seem to mind at all. The lunch was shot in a corner of the Rainbow Room atop Rockefeller Center—too touristy, Steven thought, but great for Jessie's script and her audience.

Steven was, a little to his surprise, very comfortable with Lynne. Her intelligence complemented her great looks, and for the rest of that day and the next, despite the camera crew's intrusion, he became increasingly at ease in her company. She in turn quickly set about virtually taking over Steven's life. On their third outing she purchased tickets to the marvelous San Francisco ballet in brief residence at Lincoln Center. Somehow, she arranged for Steven to have a glass of champagne with the director, Helgi Tomasson, during the intermission, and afterward they had dinner at Aquavit, Steven's favorite restaurant for fish. The blue ultra-modern Scandinavian decor and the spectacular indoor waterfall was as exciting as always. He was sure it was all photographing beautifully. It was very romantic—if he ignored the ever-present TV crew and the attending chaos.

Lynne looked perfectly at home in these glamorous surroundings and so confident and self-assured that Steven didn't in the slightest feel embarrassed about the difference in their ages. As the
cameras rolled, it was obvious to all that Steven and Lynne were sim-
patico, maybe clicking. They looked great together at the ballet, he
in a tux and she in an off-the-shoulder, black velvet gown. Jessie
beamed encouragement and Steven basked in her approval.

Lynne, it turned out, came from Lake Forest, a rich suburb of
Chicago. Her father owned a fleet of ready-mix cement trucks and
was very successful. She had graduated from Northwestern with a
major in business, and she'd honed her people and business skills by
working for her father during the summers, their busiest time of the
year. Coming to New York to model was a bit of a lark, she told
Steven. The longer-term plan was to return to school for a master's in
business. Her photographer had sent her portfolio to Jessie and participating in the show had been a spur of the moment decision.
Learning that Lynne had future plans of her own not involving
Steven made their dating easier. He liked her. Lynne was as cosmo-
politan as Steven in her tastes. They spoke of their enjoyment of
Manhattan's galleries, museums, restaurants, and nightclubs, and
Henry invited her to play tennis at the River Club. Steven was
pleased that she got along so well with him too.

Also, Lynne was very interested in the investment world Steven
oversaw from his downtown office. After tennis one day, Henry took
her there to see his father's domain. At her request, Steven gave her a
list of the corporations of which he was a director; it was an impressive list.

They were having fun together, but it wasn't a romance. Lynne
and Steven hadn't spent a night together. Lynne was in no hurry to

move in this direction, and she made that clear to Steven. He had a talk with Jessie about it. "Jessie, this is fun but it's not very serious," he said. "It's just been a good night kiss on her doorstep so far. What do you think?"

For once she didn't try to push the girl at him. "Just let love find its own way, Steven. We don't need to be too involved with the cameras at this point."

"What if things don't work out between us?" Steven asked, still worried about the prospect of failure. "You won't have much of a series if Lynne isn't my choice."

"Not to worry, Steven, there are other girls. It may still work with her, though." She pointed out another factor. "We don't have to be honest with the time sequence. I'll tell you what. I'll start planning some shoots with the other girls, and then we can juggle the episodes to make Lynne appear to be the final girl, if that's how it works out between you two. Meanwhile keep it going. How are your kids taking to Lynne?"

"Great. At least Hank likes her. Helen and Lynne haven't met yet."

"Don't you think they should meet soon?"

"Absolutely. Helen has invited us to her apartment tomorrow. Well, she invited me and I'm bringing Lynne—Helen agreed, more or less."

The following night, Jessie and Willard had the mobile crew follow Steven and Lynne uptown to Helen's Riverside Drive apartment overlooking the Hudson. They filmed Helen opening the door and recorded the introductions of Lynne to Helen and Ari. The professor was reluctant to sign the release form that the crew chief required, but agreed after some prodding from Willard. The glib persuasion seemed to irritate Ari, and Steven could see that Willard was not his cup of tea. The crew taped a quick sweep of Helen's large apartment. It was beautiful and filled with flowers, thanks to Jessie and the show's budget. The living room always reminded Steven of a bit of Ivy Columns, Helen had so captured Yvonne's elegant, warm, classically European style of interior design. The view was superb over the broad river, with the lights of the George Washington Bridge twinkling in the distance. Then the crew peeked into the kitchen, where Helen had returned to finish her preparations, made a final sweep of the scene, and departed quietly. Steven heard the professor mutter under his breath, "What a weird creature," as Willard left.

Ari poured a glass of white wine for Lynne and, at Steven's request, shook a martini. He might never have made one before because it was filled mainly with dry vermouth, a couple of olives, but not enough gin to taste. Concealing a frown, Steven contemplated the tall, lithe man whom Helen so admired. How, Steven wondered, could a fellow be so good-looking and yet so unattractive at the same time? He radiated a condescending arrogance.

"Ari, tell me, how's your seminar going? The one Helen is taking with you?"

"Yes, Quantum Principles in Contemporary Art." He seemed to relish the title.

"Right," Steven said, not as enamored. "Tell me. What are those principles of art?"

"The operative word is 'in' not 'of.'"

"I don't think I follow you, Ari."

"It's a concept that's hard for the students to grasp as well, although Helen is coming along nicely. Contemporary artists have absorbed the concepts of physics and incorporated them *into* their art. This consists of the duality between waves and particles, the identity of matter and energy, plus of course, relativity. Science and art have been co-embedded since Leonardo, even if the artists don't understand that they're doing it."

"Well, if they don't understand that they're doing it, how do you know that they are?"

"Oh, that's what the seminar is about," said Ari with a deprecating smirk. Before he could expand upon his vast erudition, Helen returned from her kitchen, sipping her wine, to participate in the conversation.

Steven and Lynne were sitting together on the couch. He had his hand resting lightly on hers, but as soon as he saw Helen, he instinctively crossed his legs and removed his hand.

"Tell me, Lynne," said Helen sweetly, "how old are you, and when did you have your implants?"

It took a moment for Steven to absorb this question. He was unused to venom from his daughter, but Lynne understood instantly and rose from the couch blushing and angry.

"Steven, get me out of here, now!"

"Oh, I am sorry, Lynne. I guess they are real. I just thought, if we're going to be family, we could talk about everything," Helen said with unrelenting phoniness.

Lynne started for the door. Steven caught her and began a long, soothing monologue. He was just able to persuade her to return. It wasn't his words, really, it was the withering look he gave Helen that Lynne accepted, not his apologies on her behalf.

You could have plucked high C from the tension between the two women. But Lynne's enormous self-confidence returned, and she and Steven sat down reluctantly at the table to partake of, if not to enjoy, the dinner Helen had prepared. It was a crabmeat casserole. Fortunately, Lynne had no allergies to fish—and this time it was cooked.

It was up to Steven to keep the conversation going.

"What's teaching like these days, Ari? Are students interested and eager?"

Ari gave the question some thought before he said, "Yes, I suppose that they are. They mostly want to get their grades with as little interaction with the school or each other as possible." With a frown he continued, "They're like corporate robots, I think, with their little noses to the grindstone. Grades, graduation, jobs—they never let themselves explore the poetry, the art, the abstractions of academic life." Ari was looking with disapproval directly at Steven, the personification of corporate America. He expanded on his theme, "They never look at college as the place to try out new ideas, to challenge the status quo."

Steven wouldn't let himself be drawn into anybody's activist politics. He was happy to leave the building of paradise to others, or to God in heaven, so he countered Ari's challenge with a different thrust. "Surely today's complexity requires thorough preparation, Ari. Don't these kids need to concentrate on skills needed to compete in a globalized world?"

They parried back and forth, always in disagreement, but Steven wouldn't let their conversation become openly hostile.

Lynne had fallen silent. Clearly, thought Steven, she wanted out of there, and they would leave immediately after dessert—no lingering with after dinner coffee. Helen was also silent, but once her father and her boyfriend had finished, for a moment, arguing about the students of the new millennium, she caught their attention with a small clink of her spoon against her wine glass.

Speaking directly to Lynne, she said, "I was a bitch to you, Lynne, and I want to apologize. I've had a very hard time thinking about Pop being with anyone but Mom. It seems disloyal to her." She stopped Steven's protest with a shake of her head. "I know that I'm wrong. Pop has the right to be with anyone he wants. I don't know you, but you seem nice." Tears were flowing and Helen finished in a voice choked with emotion. "I was wrong—please don't hate me. Let me make it up to you."

Ever unpredictable, Helen's unexpected but welcome gesture toward friendship caught the three of them off guard. They sat in silence as Helen's tears continued. Then Lynne rose from her place next to Steven and gave Helen a hug. "Let me help clear the table. We can talk in the kitchen while these guys decide the future of higher education."

Perhaps it was the loss of their audience, but Steven's interest in the philosophical debate dwindled away, or maybe it was Helen's apology. He changed the subject.

"Been seeing a lot of Helen, out of class that is, Ari?"

The arrogant cast left his face, replaced by a kindness Steven liked better. "Yes, we're together much of the time."

"Where are you from? Tell me a little about yourself. We need to find another topic, since we'll never agree on education." Steven tried to get a smile—and failed.

"Born and raised in Manhattan. My father is a lawyer at the tort bar, you know, personal injury litigation." He made a face before he went on, "I've got two younger sisters. I'm divorced—no kids. Mother died while visiting her parents in Israel—a stroke, unusual at her age. It was very sad. She was buried there and my father and I attended the funeral. I hadn't been to Israel before. It's a beautiful place. They've made a garden in the desert. Have you been there?"

"No, Ari. Never had the chance." He was starting to realize, a little, what Helen saw in Ari. "Where do you live now? Near Columbia?"

Ari hesitated, becoming very uncomfortable. "You and Helen haven't talked about things much lately, I guess. Mr. Hudson, I live here. I live in this apartment with Helen."

This froze any rapport that was developing between them. "No, I didn't know." They sat in strained silence. Soon the girls returned. Judging from appearances, they both had been crying.

Lynne found her coat, Steven his hat, and with mumbled good-byes, they made their way out and back to the waiting Bentley. Steven began to apologize for the way Helen had behaved, but Lynne cut him off.

"I like her, I really do. She explained everything to me. How she thought this show was a good idea at first, but when she saw all of us together in the studio for the first time, it hit her. She hadn't accepted the fact that her mother is gone. She knows now that she's possessive and jealous. When she saw us together tonight, it hit her, hard. She wanted to hurt me. She knows this, and she's very sorry and upset."

"You're very sweet, Lynne. I've never seen Helen be so rude."

"And, Steven . . . there's a little more. She's hopelessly in love with Ari." She turned toward him in the darkness of the backseat. "I hate to break the news, but you're going to have to learn how to get along with him."

*I*t was a very tough match, and Henry had really struggled before she slammed in the winning set point of the game. Gee, she played well, he thought, and God is she beautiful! This was his fifth tennis date with Lynne at the River Club, off Manhattan's FDR Drive. They wiped away their perspiration and strolled in their tennis outfits into the club's bar. Henry had found himself thinking about Lynne a lot since that first dinner in the penthouse. Unbelievably, he hadn't scored yet. She seemed immune to his charm. She hadn't even let him give her a kiss.

"So, Hank, don't put me off again. What do you really do for a living?" she asked after a couple of Coca-Colas were served in tall glasses. They were sitting at a circular table in the mid-afternoon quiet of the club.

He squirmed a little, his confident smile fading slightly. "I told you before. I do computer stuff, mostly." Sometimes he felt guilty about not working.

She had a teasing playfulness in her smile. "You mean e-mail?" She wasn't letting him off the hook.

"No, serious stuff." He became animated as he continued. "I've been playing around trying to improve network security. I program in Linux, by the way. I think everything Bill Gates and Microsoft does sucks."

Lynne sat back in her chair. Maybe he wasn't just a handsome playboy after all. She tested this improbable idea by asking, "Can you explain what you're actually doing?"

"I'll try," and he launched into a technical spiel which she found difficult to follow, though his enthusiasm was clear. "The problem with security systems is that a remote accessor is always permitted to enter the network in front of the firewall before he is challenged to present his random ID. This gives him a shot at penetrating the firewall. With my idea—which is working right now—he can't even access the system before he presents his scrambled PIN. It's a breakthrough in security."

"Wow." She'd caught some of his excitement. "Sounds great, who will you sell it to?"

"Oh, I don't sell my ideas—just publish them on the net, and if they're any good, I get kudos from my peers," he explained.

This bothered her. "But *could* you sell the idea if you wanted to? It sounds like it might be pretty valuable."

"I suppose so." The thought had never occurred to him. Ever since he could remember, money was just automatically there. The idea that someone might pay him for his own ideas was new. Maybe Lynne was right. He would have to think about it. She sure was sharp, that was certain.

They had another round of Cokes and chatted on. He felt so happy with her. She was really interesting, and it was a small wonder that she was going to be a reality TV star. But, the thought of his dad with her was chilling. He felt both inferior to and jealous of his father. His father overshadowed him in every way. Henry's charm instinctively ratcheted up a couple more notches. He didn't want this tennis date to end.

At last, he had to acknowledge that time was passing. It was after five and they had to shower and change into street clothes. He escorted her out of the bar and back to the separate men's and women's changing rooms. He decided to risk it. Without a word, he took her in his arms by the locker room doors. She responded to his surprise tactic, as he knew she would. They embraced in a prolonged kiss with rising passion. What a shame, he thought, that they couldn't shower and change together.

He didn't notice the tall, sleek-looking man a little distance away observing them the whole time.

*T*hey emerged from their showers feeling refreshed and walked together back to where Henry had parked the leased canary yellow Ferrari, which was filling in for the damaged McLaren. After they were in the leather lined interior, and before he hit the ignition to fire the throaty, rasping, twelve cylinder roar of the engine, he paused.

"Lynne," he said in a voice rich in tenderness, "come with me to my place. We really need time with each other. Let's spend the night together."

Her response was like a bucket of cold water poured all over him. "Who do you think I am?" she exclaimed in anger. "And who are you anyway? I'm going to see your father and go to the theater with him. Just because we had a kiss doesn't mean that I'm going to bed with you. Forget it! Take me home!"

Henry was grateful that the Ferrari's mechanical clatter made further conversation difficult. His mind was in turmoil. He'd been overshadowed, once again, by his father.

*I*n the world outside, spring was in the air. Even in Manhattan, where the environment was as man-made as possi-

ble, nature was showing the first green shoots of its perpetual renewal. But Steven's mood was not being lifted by the first stirrings of
a new season. Rather, he felt drained. In the days following the un-
fortunate dinner at Helen's, he tried to talk about her involvement
with Ari, but she cut him off, making it clear that she was "an adult,
leading her own life." Also troubling, his relationship with Lynne
seemed to be losing altitude. She said the dinner at Helen's didn't af-
fect her, but she didn't seem to want a romance to bloom, and perhaps he didn't either.

Still, he was pleased when Mrs. O'Brian reminded him of the
meeting Lynne had scheduled early that afternoon in his downtown
office. She wanted to talk about some business ideas she had. He was
startled when she arrived together with Henry.

"Dad, Lynne has some great ideas to show you!" Henry seemed
very pleased with himself, glowing with confidence. Steven was
happy to see them, but very surprised to see them together.

"Well, please sit down and tell me about the ideas." Steven
gave a broad smile to Lynne and seated them around the table in the
office.

"Steven," Lynne began right away, "I took the list of the companies you gave me and did some background work on them. It's the
kind of thing I may do after business school." She opened a leather
briefcase and spread a number of pages with charts and graphs on
the table. "Hank has been a tremendous help. He's great with computers and his ideas are terrific." She gave Henry a fond look with
this compliment. What was going on between them? Steven couldn't
help wondering.

"I've tried to show the matrix of data capturing where there may
be unrecognized investment opportunity." She was pointing to a

graph with lines in various colors crossing the page. "Take Space Technologies, for example," her finger traced along the paper. "Here it looks like the rate of change in earnings is exceeding the rate of change in market capitalization." She looked directly at Steven. "That could be very important."

Lynne continued to expand on her insight with an occasional supporting comment from Henry. Steven listened politely as she explained how the Internet made it easy to scan analysts' reports and even newspaper gossip pertinent to the various companies. Henry was steady in his smiling, approving of everything she said.

It was obvious to Steven that they had been spending time together. Clearly much more than tennis was involved. What was he to make of this? As to their investment proposals, well, he listened with only half a mind. It was all pretty naïve. They were just exploring the first layer of the investment onion he'd learned to peel many years ago. Steven hoped that he was disguising his lack of appreciation for their work, and more important, hiding his unease over their increasing involvement.

It was an unsettling meeting. Red warning flags were flying, but at the end he accompanied them back to the elevators, thanking them profusely, and saying how helpful their methods would be.

Continuing to be upset, Steven got next to nothing done for the rest of the afternoon, and before he left his office, he tried to ring Henry. The cheerful recording asked him to leave a number. He tried his son's cell phone and got the same message.

Jeeves served him a requested "industrial strength" martini and said, "Oh, boss, I forgot to tell you that Mr. Crowninshield called. I left his number on your desk." Steven clicked on the light in his of-

fice, wondering what was bothering Pierce now. It was always something. He returned the call.

Pierce needed Steven's opinion on a major new debt scheme
being considered for a corporate restructuring on which Hudson and
Partners was bidding. Steven was puzzled because Pierce had handled this sort of deal before. Only at the end of the conversation did
it become apparent why he'd called.

Pierce said, "How is it going with the chorus girls? Still spending your time in television?"

Steven put a positive spin on the proceedings. "A little, it's just
fun. Probably nothing will come of it."

"Too bad. In the beginning I thought it was scandalous, but
maybe not. You should find a girl like the one your son has."

"What do you mean?"

"I mean the one he had in your office today. I saw them at the
River Club last week too. She looked fantastic in her tennis outfit, by
the way." True delight entered his voice as he imparted the bomb-
shell he'd been itching to detonate. "After their game he gave her a
kiss that—well, it was a show stopper. They didn't notice me watching, so I watched—until I got . . . well, until it was time to stop
watching, if you know what I mean."

"Right, Pierce," Steven said, suddenly mortified. "Uh, it's good
that the J. P. Morgan bunch is in the group. Keep me posted on the
progress and thanks for bringing me up to speed. Good night."

Steven stood by his desk, his mind racing. Pierce was a fussy,
old hen, for sure. And he was always happy to score a point against
Steven, the founding partner, but would he concoct a story like that?
No. It confirmed all of Steven's suspicions. Henry was deceiving him.

He rang his son's number again. This time Henry answered,

and Steven got straight to the point. "Hank, you and Lynne have been doing a lot more that tennis together, haven't you?"

His dad's anger caught Henry off-guard. "No, I haven't. We haven't, I mean."

"I don't believe you, Hank. I think you're using me as another one of your ways to meet and seduce girls." All Steven's resentment of his son's prodigal life was carried in this accusation.

Henry was stunned. His father was correct in general, of course, but he hadn't progressed much beyond that tennis club kiss with Lynne. He was both innocent and guilty as charged. Still, he wasn't going to take a tongue lashing from his father. His voice began to rise, too.

"No way! I don't need your help to do that!" He softened his tone a little. "I swear to you that I haven't slept with Lynne. I really haven't, Dad. I'm telling the truth."

Steven's anger evaporated. For whatever other faults he had, Henry had never lied to him. Frustrated him, yes. Disappointed him, sure. But he'd never lied.

"I'm sorry, Hank," the mollified father responded. "Pierce Crowninshield told me that he saw you and Lynne kissing after tennis. He must be mistaken."

The heat was gone, but when they hung up after some lighter talk, each realized that a line had been crossed. Steven was determined to keep an eagle eye on his son.

Henry could only sigh, "Shit, where do I go from here?"

CHAPTER ELEVEN

*T*he following day Steven isolated himself in his Wall Street lair, torn with doubt and unhappy for being suspicious of his own son. He debated calling Hank again but decided to wait and see. He took few calls, but Jessie's was put right through by Mrs. O'Brian. She confirmed that his date with Lynne was on for that night at 21. Jessie would be meeting them at the restaurant with her full mobile camera crew. Steven groaned. He couldn't believe that Lynne would have the brass to meet him for dinner, if Pierce was right that she and Hank were an item. Should he ask her? Would she tell the truth on camera, for God's sake?

His car arrived at eight. The TV crew was already in place, with a few spectators also hanging about, curious to see who the celebrity was. Willard was chatting with some of them; he was happy that *Trophy Bride* was back on track. Jessie, as attractive as ever, was dressed in a tailored charcoal suit with a burgundy, Hermes silk scarf, offsetting her black hair perfectly.

"I know this is going to be a great taping." She was all smiles. "You have that ability to attract the camera, to fill the frame. Even in 21 you will outshine everyone else." He wished he shared her confidence.

He needn't have worried. By 8:25 Lynne still hadn't arrived or called Steven or Jessie on their cells. They sat together in the Bentley in front of 21 with its thirty-three iron jockeys lined up on the ground, staircase, and wrought-iron balcony, waiting so that the crew could tape the glamorous couple entering the famous, former speakeasy. They tried calling her but got no answer.

To Steven's surprise, Jessie excused herself. "I'll be back in a minute." She left the car to talk with two of the spectators—an attractively dressed woman of sixty and a tall, handsome boy about fifteen years old. Jessie appeared to know them, but when she returned to the car, she offered no explanation.

By 8:45, with still no sign of Lynne, Steven said, "Screw it, Jessie. Why don't you have dinner with me? We've earned a night off for ourselves."

Jessie seemed torn. "Steven, I really would love to, but I had been planning . . . let me check." She jumped out again and rejoined the woman and boy, who were still standing by the entrance. Jessie was in deep conversation with the woman—the teenager seemed totally detached. Curious, Steven decided to join them. By now he was sure he knew the reason for Lynne's absence, and he didn't care. It would be wonderful to have Jessie to himself for an evening. Jessie turned in surprise as he approached. She didn't at first offer an introduction. He plowed right ahead, though. "Hello, I'm Steven Hudson. Are you here to witness the taping?"

Jessie finally remembered her manners. "Let me introduce you. This is Virginia and Mark Waters. Yes, they are here to watch the shoot, but I guess that won't be happening."

"Well, it's chilly out here. Let's go inside," Steven suggested.

"Oh, we can't trouble you, Steven. I'll talk to the technicians and we'll cancel the shoot."

He indicated her two companions as he said, "That's your call, Jessie, but these folks have been standing here for a long time. I insist that you all join me inside."

While Jessie hesitated, the boy said, "Let's go in. I want to use the bathroom."

With a helpless shrug she said, "Why not? But let's get some tape out of this at least."

She called the cameraman over. "Please shoot Mr. Hudson escorting me into 21. We may as well get something—then that's it for the night. We'll talk tomorrow about the next scene." Jessie then fumed to Willard. "She didn't call you either? We're wasting a ton of money having the crew here for nothing. You can keep soaps on budget, but forget about it with reality TV." But then she turned her angry look into a glamorous smile. She took Steven's proffered arm and let him escort her into the restaurant while her crew filmed it all, for possible future use. Virginia and Mark followed along behind.

Steven loved 21 with its prints of horses, oil paintings, model airplanes, toy cars, and all kinds of souvenirs hanging from the beams. It had a club-like atmosphere, but with the bustle and class of one of the world's top eating places. The three adults sat in comfortable chairs around a table in the wood-paneled lounge, and Steven ordered three glasses of champagne and an orange juice for Mark, who was in the men's room. Virginia Waters, in her early sixties,

thanked Steven profusely for his hospitality, and they all chatted politely. Mark sat in silence. He appeared to listen without showing any
interest in talking. Steven hadn't the slightest idea of who they were
or why they had been among the spectators outside. Virginia's explanation that they were curious about seeing Jessica at work explained,
without answering, the question.

After a brief conversational reference to Steven's Gulfstream
jet, Mark interrupted Steven in mid-sentence. "When you're flying
north to south or south to north, do you allow for the Coriolis force?"

Steven blinked at the odd question. "I have my pilots check on
all kinds of things, Mark, but I don't worry about that. Should I?"

"Maybe," and with that Mark returned to his usual silence.

Jessie explained, "Mark is very interested in math and physics,
Steven. Most of the time his questions are over our heads."

After some further awkward small talk about the TV reality
show, Virginia announced that she and Mark would have to head
back home to Scarsdale. Steven courteously tried to persuade them
to stay for dinner, but Virginia could not be dissuaded and she and
Mark departed with her polite thank-you.

By this time it was clear that Steven had been stood up by
Lynne. "Let's not bother about her," he said. Steven indicated to their
waiter that they would be staying for dinner, and Jessie seemed to be
as happy as he was to be free of the pressure of the show for the night.
Shortly, the maitre d' arrived and conducted them into the dining
room, where tables were more guardedly allocated than positions in
heaven. Steven, as usual, had his favorite, the most intimate and select of all.

"I guess I owe you an explanation, Steven," Jessie said. "You just met my mother and my son. I try to keep my personal life very much to myself. If Lynne had shown up, we would have shot our footage outside, and some in here, and then I would have bolted. Mark and Mom have always been so curious about what I do. I thought they could have just been bystanders. I didn't plan to get you involved."

"But, Jessie, it was a pleasure for me. Your mother is charming and Mark seems . . . precocious." They were seated in a sheltered corner and the background noises were not intrusive. Steven requested a bottle of '82 Lynch-Bages from the sommelier to accompany the pepper-crusted steaks they both ordered. Jessie found it wonderful, which pleased Steven.

Then she answered the obvious question. "As you probably noticed, Mark is a boy with 'special needs,' as they say."

"Well, he just seemed very . . . quiet. And, frankly, I didn't know what he was talking about. The Coriolis force? Is that what makes the earth rotate, maybe?"

She smiled at her son's bits of arcane knowledge. "Oh, I guess I'm really pretty lucky. For years I thought Mark was autistic. As a baby, he screamed if I held him. He crawled and walked on schedule. But he wouldn't, or couldn't talk. By the time he was five years old, I had pretty much accepted that he was hopelessly autistic. Then he said his first words. I'll never forget them. 'Mother, what makes it possible for birds to fly?'"

Steven chuckled at the story. "Wow! That's quite a mouthful. You must have been relieved."

She smiled, proud of Mark. "Yes, sure. But when I hugged him, he screamed, and he was angry when I couldn't give him an immediate and satisfactory answer to his question. It turned out that he has

Asperger's syndrome. It took a long time for doctors to reach that diagnosis, and it has not been easy for him, or us, to learn to live with it. We are still learning."

The waiter served their char-broiled steaks and fried shoe string potatoes with sides of creamed spinach. It smelled great and looked delicious.

Steven picked up where Jessie had left off. "I don't think I know what that syndrome is, Jessie."

"It's a kind of autism; it almost always affects boys. A doctor told me that it's like having an extreme male brain."

"What in the world does that mean?"

Her explanation came smoothly, as though she had done it many times. "Well, if you greatly oversimplify and greatly exaggerate, you could characterize the extreme female brain as being strong on empathy, sympathetic understanding, sensitivity to other's thoughts and emotions, an awareness of feelings, and undercurrents in people's behavior." She paused, and Steven nodded in agreement.

"The extreme male brain, again oversimplifying, is the reverse of all that, showing a near total insensitivity to emotion of any kind, an intensity of logic, and extreme rationality instead. Mark has a great skill and devotion to mathematics and physics, for example, and an almost simplemindedness for literature, poetry, and a total indifference to everything subjective."

They paused in conversation while their waiter refilled their wine glasses. "Well, he seems to be okay now. Is he?" asked Steven.

She became more earnest. "Yes, in many ways he is. He's always required home tutoring. He's always had trouble mixing with other kids who have special needs, and regular school has been out of the question. I've had a lot of trouble finding tutors who can keep up with him in math and science. He's almost fifteen, and he has sailed through partial differential equations and tensor calculus, which, I'm told, are at Ph.D. level or beyond. But in English, social studies, and, really, everything that *isn't* math or science, he is years behind his age group. He thinks it's all stupid and says he doesn't care. More likely, he's simply handicapped in these areas." She scowled at this admission, and Steven could tell she had worked hard with him in these subjects.

"Decades ago," she went on, her voice low, "he would have been called an 'idiot savant.' You know, he can do cube roots in his head and all sorts of mental calculations, like Dustin Hoffman in *Rain Man*. That term puts me off, though. Mark is a genius who just can't understand and is frustrated by the day-to-day social interactions we all take for granted."

Steven was impressed by what she was telling him. "Jessie, it sounds like you've had a second career. I never would've guessed."

She waved off that idea. "Well, it's really the other way around. Mark is my career. I have devoted my life to him. That is, my parents and I have. With their help, after my beloved ex-husband bailed on us, I've been able to hold a successful job, going to work every day and spending every weekend in Scarsdale with Mark, Mom, and Dad. I gave Mark their last name, Waters, though I kept my married name, James—it was easier career-wise."

"It couldn't have been easy, without Mark's father around to help, I mean."

Jessie waited for the table to be cleared and for their waiter to take their orders for a dessert of mixed sorbets with espresso and glasses of light sauternes.

A note of contempt filled her voice. "He was part of the problem, not part of the solution. No point in trashing him, but our marriage was in trouble before Mark was born. William was so selfish and childish—I don't mean with boyish charm, I mean immature. He drank a lot. And without going into the gory details, let's just say he had scrapes with the law. He cost me plenty in both dollars and emotional capital. I tried to make it work for a long time. He sure didn't. Aside from the fact that he was a good-looking guy, I don't know what I ever saw in him.

"After Mark was born and after it was abundantly clear that he had developmental problems, William just couldn't cope. I think he was ashamed of Mark. The drinking got worse. He started snorting cocaine. Finally, I filed, he didn't object. Once the divorce came through, *I* paid *him* alimony for a while and devoted myself to raising Mark. Since then, Steven, I have been married to my career, and it's been a very happy marriage, if I do say so myself."

"But," he pointed to her ring, "you are engaged."

"Yes, to Gregory Granger. He teaches self-awareness seminars and he travels a lot doing that. We haven't been engaged very long, haven't set the date. I am trying to get Mark to adjust to him, to accept him. It could be going better between them. Gregory tries, I think, but Mark doesn't."

Steven was delighted that Jessie trusted him enough to talk about her life in such detail. Mark was, he thought, a very lucky young man to have such a mother, and frankly he envied Gregory Granger, whoever he was.

Steven was still curious, wanting to know even more about this woman with her poise, her looks, her delicious voice, and interesting background. He was captivated by her. But Jessie instead shifted their conversation back to business—ground more comfortable for her.

"Oh, Steven, I meant to tell you. The test group results are in and they are great."

"Wonderful, Jessie," he exclaimed. "Um, what are you actually talking about?"

"We have been showing the takes so far to a sample audience to get their reaction. It will help us sell the series. If the results stay this positive, the show will be a smash. And, Steven, they love you! The women want to be with you and even better, the guys want to *be* you!"

Steven arched an eyebrow. "Poor souls."

"No, really. Steven, the test audience is rooting for you. They want this to work. They want for you to be happy, to wind up with the right woman . . . and so do I."

Jessie fell abruptly silent, and Steven decided to take a chance.

"Sometimes," he said, starting slowly, "I think of happiness only in the past tense. But with you here, tonight, I see possibilities."

This was taking an unwanted direction for Jessie. She quickly deflected the conversation.

"Right, Steven," she said, flustered. "You are right. We need to plan a little, in case Lynne doesn't turn out to be the one." She glanced about the restaurant, as though Lynne would magically appear. "The fact that she didn't show up here tonight doesn't look good. Something must be wrong. I don't understand."

He couldn't bring up what Pierce had seen. Jessie didn't need to know about another setback.

"I know that Bermuda was a disaster, but I like the idea of two girls competing. Let's try it again. Could we use your yacht this time, or how about your ski chalet?"

"Either one would be fine," Steven agreed, but what he didn't tell her was that out of all the dates, he'd enjoyed this night with her the most. She was better company than the girls she picked. Gregory Granger was a very lucky man indeed.

*H*elen caught him on his cell phone while he was being driven from Wall Street back uptown the following afternoon. She wanted to talk, and Steven was happy to meet her at the Cloisters, not too far from her apartment. She would ride her bike there. It was a little warmer again today and nice to be outside.

The monastery-like museum, built by the Rockefellers, housed the world's finest collection of medieval art, and he and Helen had occasionally gone there when she was younger. She told him once that their time together in that beautiful place was what inspired her to become an artist. Today they met in the courtyard and then visited the tapestry room, where the hauntingly beautiful unicorn weavings were as inspiring as ever.

"They say, Helen, that the unicorn can only be captured by love. Maybe that's why it's extinct."

"A pretty heavy thought, Pop, even for you on this nice spring day. Well, nearly spring day." Her false gaiety swiftly came to an end. From her face Steven knew she was the bearer of bad news. "Anyway, I'm on a mission. Hank asked me to talk to you. He's too ashamed to do it himself, so I'm here to rescue my brother."

"Okay . . ." Steven said hesitantly.

Helen took a deep breath and let it out slowly. "Dad, he says he's insanely, madly, passionately in love with Lynne. I know he's talked about being madly in love before, but this seems real." Steven listened without interrupting. "I think it's true. I really do."

Steven frowned as her obviously rehearsed speech was given.

But before Helen had even finished, he realized that Lynne wasn't a fraction as important to him as having the air cleared with his son. After a pause, he replied, "I guessed this is what you were going to say. I'd heard it from another source too." Seeing her discomfort, he patted her hand. "Lynne is a wonderful girl, and I'm happy for Hank. She and I weren't in love, and I didn't really like her interest in my financial affairs, to be frank."

She peeped at him out of the corner of her eye. "So you aren't angry?"

"No, not at all. He should've told me himself, though. Why stick you with the job?"

She turned more fully toward him. "Oh, he would've done it. He isn't afraid of you, just embarrassed. We both trust you to understand us. You always have."

He took her hand. "Sweetie, that's a lovely thing to hear. And it's right, you two can always come to me about anything."

A strange quaver entered her voice. "I know, Pop." She dropped her head, unable to look him in the eye. "I also have some news of my own."

"Sure. What's up, Helen."

"Pop, I'm pregnant. Ari and I are going to have a baby."

CHAPTER TWELVE

*T*he day after Helen dropped her bomb on him in the tapestry room, Steven had to take the G-5 to Los Angeles to attend the Merry-Go-Round Ball, the biannual charity event put on by his friends Walter and Mary Smythe. Seated in the plane alone, he mulled over what his daughter had said. She truly was in love. She said that Ari was much nicer once you got to know him. Steven found that hard to believe, but he agreed to give the professor a second chance. Helen seemed determined to go through with her pregnancy, and if so, Steven would have to learn to like, or at least tolerate, the young academic, or he would be shut out of her life.

In the end, he had to stop thinking about the mess. He tried to focus on the upcoming charity ball. He intended to stay in L.A. only for the event and for the more private party afterward, a reception at the Smythe mansion in the hills overlooking the city. Walter had not been in great health recently, and Steven wanted to see him. He changed into his tux somewhere over Nevada, and after landing, a black limo whisked him off to the Beverly Hilton, where the main event was always held.

With possibly the exception of the smaller *Vanity Fair* party at Oscar time, this large ball was *the* social event for all the "in" crowd of Southern California, far more important than the annual Oscar show, which was staged strictly for Eastern prime-time television, and which Steven had found an agonizing, prolonged bore to attend. The Smythe ball, on the other hand, was really fun. Walter, a multi-billionaire former owner of MGM, and Mary screened attendance carefully for their fund-raiser to support research on diabetes, and over the years they had raised scores of millions for their favorite charity. Steven always gave generously—that and his friendship with Walter ensured him a seat at the Smythe's table, and a special invitation to their home for the party after the party.

He arrived to a traffic jam of black limousines in the driveway of the hotel. Ahead, the flashes of cameras were virtually continuous. Dozens of photographers had been roped off from the red carpet over which the "beautiful people" flowed into the building. The women's jewelry glittered extravagantly in the cameras' blinding glare.

When Steven's car finally drew up to the entry, guarded by police and dark-suited security men with wires in their ears, he walked alone down the carpet. That was so unusual that a reporter shouted, "Should we know you?"

Another with better connections in the industry called out, "Steve, where is your reality girl?"

Steven tossed off, "She's home doing the dishes," and the reporter laughed. Before anyone could follow up, Steven, his vision impaired from the exploding camera flashes, quickly ducked inside.

The hotel was filled with over a thousand indisputably Very Important People, elbowing their way among the bars, the hors d'oeuvres tables, and the exhibits of silent auction items. Hollywood stars were everywhere. Steven spotted a dozen familiar to him in his first glance: Elizabeth Taylor, Clint Eastwood, Dustin Hoffman, Sharon Stone, plus other celebrities like Larry King and Governor Schwarzenegger.

He found a small bar in a corner, a little less crowded, and ordered a martini. As he reached for the drink, he excused himself for interrupting the conversation between two very good-looking young men, obviously close friends. To his inquiry they said that they "had jobs in the movies."

Armed with his martini, Steven wandered about the crowded rooms, through the glittering throng. He noticed the southern California native fauna in abundance—old, short, fat, bald men—each with an incredibly glamorous and towering starlet on either side— producers, no doubt.

Once the martini was gone, Steven stood alone, watching the scene. New York had its big events, but this was something else. If the jewels were real, their value would have exceeded the gross national product of the Benelux block of nations. He was wondering how far off dinner was when an extremely attractive young woman intruded on his thoughts. She handed him a fresh glass of champagne.

"You look like you could use this," she said. She noticed his lack of tan and added, "You aren't from around here, are you?"

"You're right, I'm from New York. My name is Steven. What are you doing here?"

"I'm Trudi. Trudi Wilson." As she said this, a tall photographer dressed in a black tux snapped their picture. She explained, "Oh, this is Eddie Austin. He's photographing the team."

"Team?" Steven wondered aloud.

"Right. I'm on the U.S. Olympic ski team. A few of us are here tonight as guests of Mr. and Mrs. Smythe. Oh, wow! Look, that's Matt Damon and Ben Affleck." She pointed to the two guys who'd said to Steven that they had jobs in the movies.

"And over there is Nicole Kidman . . . I wonder if Tom Cruise is here."

She was so excited by all the glamour, and Steven found her youthful enthusiasm infectious. Trudi was a very beautiful girl with dark hair and blue eyes, almost violet in their intensity. With her starlet beauty, she fit nicely in this crowd, and she carried an outdoor freshness and athleticism the others couldn't match. She made the others look like exotic hothouse flowers.

They chatted amiably, collecting more champagne as they strolled through the crowds. Eddie trailed along, snapping photos of them together and in little groups of celebrities. Steven had never known many of the Hollywood set, since his financial interest in the film industry was minimal, and that night was no exception. So he was pleased to encounter a tired-looking Walter Smythe, standing with help from his bodyguard. He was surrounded by people as the throngs prepared to squeeze into the ballroom for dinner and the show.

"Steven," Walter called out, "I am so happy to see you here again. I didn't realize you were bringing a date. Introduce me, please."

Fortunately, Steven remembered Trudi's name. It was easier to make the introduction than to explain that he didn't really know her, and when Walter insisted that Mary would find an extra chair for Trudi at their table, it suddenly developed that Steven had a date for the evening and a stunningly attractive one, at that.

The dinner was miles above the typical hotel banquet food. Rack of lamb, pink and succulent, was served together with a pleasing Napa Valley merlot. On stage a star-studded series of singers and entertainers performed: Elton John, Sting, B. B. King, and Jay Leno did their parts to help the charity. The big names all performed free, for Walter and Mary were very well liked in the industry. She herself took the microphone to announce they had raised over six million dollars that night, and her short remarks on the fight against diabetes and progress at the Denver children's hospital that they supported were applauded with genuine affection.

As good a time as Steven was having, it was almost impossible to talk with Trudi between the swelling sounds from the big orchestra and the hubbub at the tables, ranging in price from ten to one hundred thousand dollars. Steven just enjoyed her company and smiled for Eddie and the other photographers, whose flashing cameras frequently had them in focus.

After another lineup for limos when they left the hotel—Don Rickles' ad lib insults to the waiting throng had them all in stitches— Steven was a little surprised that Eddie climbed in with them when their driver finally arrived. He seemed close, but not romantically close, to Trudi.

They wound their way up out of the downtown area and finally reached the Smythe mansion, where a much smaller crowd was arriving. On the way up the hills, Steven learned that Trudi was one of the country's top ski talents. She hailed from Utah and expected to return to New York after the end of the ski season and resume her courses at the Parsons School of Design.

The Smythe mansion was a floodlit-marble palace. Inside the elegant people strolled over the marble floors with their glasses of champagne, admiring the Picassos, Renoirs, and other stunning paintings—the kind museums would love to own. The tables had been set for dessert and the fifty or so guests finally sat down together, mostly old friends of Walter and Mary and some of the evening's top performing talent. By the time Steven and Trudi said their good-byes, it was after three o'clock in the morning.

Steven had planned to return to his Gulfstream, grab an hour or two of sleep, and fly back to New York, but he was having fun. Trudi, Steven, and Eddie wound up together back at the airplane. Trudi was overwhelmed when he told her it was his private jet. "You mean, it's just for you?" The guard let them aboard—the pilots were still asleep in their motel—and Steven finally figured out how to get the coffee pot going in the plane's well-equipped pantry. Eddie snapped even more shots, and they chatted together, while the soft light of dawn slowly illuminated the L.A. basin.

When Trudi, to her amazement, discovered that Steven had a ski place in Vail, she was very curious about it. "Steven, is it a condo? Do you time share?" Steven explained that he'd acquired it from a friend who had overspent building it, partly to help save the friend from bankruptcy and partly because his children, Henry and Helen, loved to ski. Steven enjoyed skiing too, but so far this season he hadn't gone.

"I love to ski so much! If I could, I would ski year-round. A place in the Rockies for our winter and a place in Chile for their winter!"

After asking her more about her skiing, Steven said, "Trudi, how did you do it? The competition must be intense for a place on the Olympic team."

She gave a broad, impish smile. "That's right. Ever since junior high school, I've lived only for the snow. I've been a waitress, a ski instructor, and done all kinds of part-time jobs, anything to keep me on the slopes during my hours off. It hasn't left me time for much else — no guy in my life anyway." She spoke in a perpetual rush, words tumbling over each other. "I hope eventually to settle down, find a place for my trophies and medals. I hope to finish Parsons and eventually become a designer. But first I want to win some gold!"

She was so bubbly, Steven was swept up in the joie de vivre. "You must have to work out all the time."

"Yes. I run, lift weights, aerobics, but being on the snow is everything." She glanced down at herself. "I shouldn't have come to L.A. I can already feel that I'm getting out of shape. I've got to get back on the snow. Soon."

Steven listened with growing interest in Trudi. Her devotion to her sport was so pure and refreshing. There was an innocent intensity about her that was appealing. This totally unexpected date had transformed an obligatory social commitment into a special evening.

The conversation drifted back to Vail and plans seemed to gel out of thin air for Trudi to join him there for skiing the coming week. By the time she and Eddie said good-bye, the sun was peeking over the mountains. When Steven's pilots arrived to fly him back to New York, Steven was wondering how he was going to explain all this to Jessie.

*I*t didn't go well. Their meeting in her office immediately became uncomfortable. Steven didn't like the steely edge to Jessie's voice—didn't like it at all. Underlying the customary velvet was a determination and unyielding resistance.

"No, Steven, I don't think we can do this. This is not in our contract. I have too much invested, in time and money, to let the show run off the road this way."

The glass walls of her office were clear. He could see out into the open area where the hip Acme people were rushing about. He was aware that, without her, he would be experiencing none of his current excitement.

"Jessie, I'm extremely grateful for what you've done for me. You have reintroduced me to life." He meant this, even though the girls hadn't panned out. Jessie had pulled him out of his slump, got him going again. She showed him that he could survive without Yvonne. Though he would always cherish her in his memory, he could try to find enjoyment in his life once again.

Jessie cut off this line of thinking. "This isn't about gratitude, Steven. It's about a business arrangement you and I have made." She twisted her reading glasses on the silver chain as she continued, "You're ignoring our deal. I have several other girls lined up for you—Stephanie and Eve, just to name two. Lynne certainly wasn't the end of the line. And now you have run off the reservation, found some girl in Hollywood, and you want to change the show to fit your own whims. Well, it's wrong."

Steven flushed with guilt. He hadn't intended to flip Jessie's script; it had just happened.

"Jessie, please," Steven said, frustrated, "you know I don't know anything about television production, but I really like this girl. She's a breath of fresh air. She isn't a model she's not an actress, not a star-let, not like any of the others."

Jessie was hearing him out, but the frown was still in place.

"Couldn't you find a way to fit her in somehow? Couldn't you fake some background shoots to make it look like she'd been in with the others from day one? I haven't talked with her about the show, but I'll bet she would love to work with you."

Jessie snorted at that. "Of course she would. Do you know how many girls I turned down?"

"Jessie, perhaps she's the one. I like her a lot. Can't you find a way? My place is big enough for us all."

"Steven . . . oh hell! I have too much at stake in this! I can't let you slip away!" Steven had never seen Jessie angry before. He was starting to understand that she hadn't become Acme's de facto boss on just sweet talk alone. Yet he wasn't exactly a wallflower himself. Trudi was special. She was genuine, not just one of Jessie's reality girls.

His voice was quiet but pure steel as he responded, "Originally, you said I could pick the girls I liked. At the time I deferred to you be-cause you knew better." He held her gaze, making sure she under-stood. "Well, those girls have all been a bust. This time I'm asking to pick my own reality girl."

Jessie didn't answer at first. She'd seen the Wall Street lion for the first time. "Okay, Steven," she said at last. "You win. Let me get busy. I'll see what I can set up."

CHAPTER THIRTEEN

*W*hile the Gulfstream soared over the blanket of light covering the Metropolitan New York area on its way west, Steven turned on his Hewlett-Packard tablet computer, which was linked to his office via the onboard satellite Internet uplink.

He was surprised to find, among a number of routine e-mails forwarded by Mrs. O'Brian, one from Mark Waters.

To: steven.hudson@hudsonandpartners.com
From: mwaters@aol.com
Subject: Coriolis Effect

Dear Mr. Steven Hudson:

Mother says that I was rude to you, seven point eight days ago, when we met at the restaurant 21 (it is named after the address it has on the street—a very good idea for naming things, I think). I did not intend to be rude. I did not intend to make you look stupid by asking you about Coriolis (Gaspard, Gustave de, born 1792, died 1843). I have since used his famous equation for combined transverse and rotational motion, using an estimated speed for your airplane of 620 knots (1.1 statute miles per knot) and proved that the predicted effect is too small to be a problem. You are correct not to worry about it and, therefore, you are not stupid.

Sincerely, Mark Waters

Steven smiled to himself; it was always nice to be reassured. He clicked to a second message from Mark Waters.

To: steven.hudson@hudsonandpartners.com
From: mwaters@aol.com
Subject: Coriolis Effect

Dear Mr. Steven Hudson:

My e-mail management system indicates that my first message has been received and opened by you or someone at your office. I like e-mail because you can communicate with people without trying to understand the information they are showing on their faces—because you don't have to see their faces. E-mail is also preferable to the telephone because you don't have to listen to them either.

I use e-mail a lot and I have a very famous e-mail friend,

Professor Steven Hawking (Lucasian Professor of Mathematics at the University of Cambridge in England, Europe).

I have an e-mail from Professor Hawking encouraging me to send my paper on quantum gravity to the letters section of *The Physical Review*.

My theory assumes that there is a minimum unit (quantum) of time and that time and space is granular, and that the velocity of light is infinite but blocked by the cyclical absence of time and space and . . .

Steven didn't comprehend what the boy was saying. The language alone was baffling, and the equations that Mark included were unrecognizable. He doubted even if Hank would understand any of it. Undoubtedly, Jessie had a genius on her hands. Steven Hawking seemed to agree. Steven laughed aloud at the concluding paragraph.

. . . so, since you were right about Coriolis and therefore are not stupid (Mother agrees with me on your stupidity and lack thereof) perhaps you could e-mail me your opinion about quantum gravity. My tutor doesn't understand it. He says that the math is over his head and he is a basketball player (I am trying to make a joke) and that I will have to wait until he gets his Ph.D. in two years. Anyway, I expect to hear from you. My e-mail is not spam. Well, back to Reimann's hypothesis.

Sincerely,
Mark Waters

Steven hit the reply button and typed the following:

To: mwaters@aol.com

From: steven.hudson@hudsonandpartners.com

Subject: Your e-mails

Dear Mark:

Thanks for your (two) e-mails. I am pleased that the three of us, you, your mother and I, all agree on the question of my stupidity. But, Mark, and I really hate to admit this, your new theory is over my head too and I am 6'2" (1.88 meters) tall. Maybe someday you can discuss it with my son Henry. He is smarter than me and a little taller. He is a computer expert. Anyway, it was very nice to meet you 7.9 days ago; this is a true fact. I met your friend Steven Hawking once at a charity benefit. He was in his wheelchair and communicating only through his computer, but he was living proof, not that one was ever needed, that there is no such thing as a handicap.

My very best regards,

Steven Hudson

Steven clicked on Send, still smiling over the disarmingly charming e-mails from a peer of Professor Hawking. What an extraordinary young man! Now all he had to do was get his mother to smile at him.

*J*essie felt guilty about being so unresponsive to Gregory's view about Steven and *Trophy Bride*. She just couldn't seem to adjust anymore to his inner-self interpretation of everything—couldn't see her lion of Wall Street as a needy child. So, she decided to treat her fiancé to a home-cooked dinner. That would be a great surprise.

She'd hoped it would lead to a stress-free evening, but the decision was a mistake. Never really at home in her own kitchen, Jessie burned the chicken breasts. They stuck to the bottom of her expensive copper pan as she struggled to save the meal. Damn, why are women expected to be born cooks? The potatoes au gratin had just been scraped into the garbage disposal and some frozen French fries popped into the microwave when Gregory entered the apartment. His "Is something burning?" didn't get things off to a good start.

But the '01 Kendall chardonnay was chilled, and Gregory helped her toss the salad. They toasted each other by candlelight, the golden wine reflecting the dancing flame. Maybe the evening was going to be okay. He didn't seem to mind that she had overcooked the chicken. In fact he cleaned his plate.

As Gregory scooped some ice cream he said, "Jessie, it's good to be with you tonight. I loved the dinner. You've been on the go so much. Remember step number four, give your inner-self a chance to be heard."

"Of course." She couldn't suppress her frown. "Unfortunately, sweetheart, I have to fly to Vail tomorrow. I'm going skiing."

"That's the first time you've mentioned snow, Jessie. I thought you hated skiing. What's up?"

"I do hate it. And I have to take time to shop for a ski outfit. Unfortunately, Steven has gone off script." In biting tones, she explained the latest development. She summed up the afternoon's meeting with growing irritation.

"Jessie, I don't see what's bothering you. I thought that Steven falling for some young bunny is exactly what you've been hoping for."

Jessie didn't answer. She just shook her head in disagreement.

"Is it that he picked one of his own and not one of the girls you've chosen?"

She stopped to think for a second. Was Gregory right? Why was she so upset about Trudi? She put her napkin to her lips in an effort to hide her expression.

"No, of course not. It's all a matter of the budget. I hadn't allowed for a lot of outdoor shooting, and ski photographers aren't a dime a dozen."

But that wasn't the reason. Gregory was probably right. As long as she was calling the shots, she was very comfortable with Steven. Now that he was pulling away from her, she found it was troubling.

Then Gregory really touched a nerve. "You know, Jessie, Steven's inner child needs a romp from time to time. Let him play. I think you're getting possessive."

"God! Are you jealous of him, Gregory? Do you want to play too? If I hear about the inner child one more time I'll scream!"

That shut him up.

The G-5 touched down in the dark of the early evening at Eagle Vail airport and parked among several lesser corporate jets already lined up there. Steven had brought Jeffrey along to cook, and they climbed together into the waiting taxi. It was only a thirty-five minute drive from the small airfield to the Vail complex. Steven's house was poised on the lower slope of Vail Mountain, past the luxurious Mill Creek development, and near the condos around the Christiania Hotel. Not quite seven years old, the house was so ultra-modern that it was difficult to keep everything in it working at the same time. Designed by a world-famous pair of Swiss architects, it was built by a dot.com billionaire from Silicon Valley. He was fabulously rich until the Internet bubble burst, making his stock nearly worthless.

Thinking of this, Steven told Jeffrey a joke he heard in the office as they rode along between snow banks on either side of the highway.

"How do you get a dot.com chief executive officer off your front door step?"

"I don't know, boss."

"Why, just pay for the pizza, of course."

Jeffrey howled at that. "Ouch! That hurts. But it's probably true, huh?" He glanced out the window at the passing winterscape. "I hope your engineering wizards have the place up and running for us. Remember last year I had to cook dinner using the fireplace?"

Jeffrey wasn't in love with the place, named Snow Cliff House. It was designed to operate mostly from solar power, but not the big black panels that most people used. Oh no, it used quartz cylinders filled with argon gas, which somehow focused light from mirrored parabolas onto tubes carrying water, which turned to steam on a good sunny day. The cellar was filled with pumps and other machinery. The house had cost a fortune to build, but it was environmentally responsible. On fuel savings alone, Steven told Jeffrey, it would pay for itself in, oh, about a hundred years.

It was really cold at the higher altitude when they arrived, but to Jeffrey's surprise the house was warm, in temperature at least. Steven knew that Jeffrey would never adjust to the coldness of the décor—steel, stone, concrete and acres of glass displaying the valley below. The only art works on the walls were photographs, huge black-and-white blow-ups, by Robert Mapplethorpe, Richard Avedon, and Helmet Newton.

Soon they had a roaring fire going in the vast fireplace, built from granite boulders, and Jeffrey served up the food he'd ordered in from the Left Bank restaurant in the town. He told Steven that he had made a date to ski tomorrow with Fran, a friend who helped out at the place. Steven sat at a big glass table alone, but he chatted with his Jeeves, who ate standing in the kitchen, screened only by an open wooden grid.

"So, boss, who's this Trudi you've been talking about?"

"She's a champion skier that I met in L A. She and her photog-rapher are arriving here early tomorrow."

Jeffrey appeared from behind the screen, his face alert with cu-riosity. "How come she has her own photographer? Isn't that pretty unusual?"

"Not really. It's part of the deal I made with Jessie. You see, we're going to work Trudi into the show, so we need photographers. Jessie has lined up one of the cameramen who shot the ski scenes in the James Bond movie *The World Is Not Enough*, and we'll also use Trudi's guy. His name is Eddie Austin, incidentally, and he'll be staying here with us. Trudi already knows him. He's the team photographer."

Jeffrey still seemed mystified, and Steven added, a touch an-noyed, "I told you, didn't I, that Jessie is flying in tomorrow night? I'm sending the plane back now to pick her up."

"Ah, the great Jessie is coming, too. What's she going to do, su-
pervise you and Trudi in the bedroom scene? 'Now Steven, you put
your arm here, and Trudi, you put your leg there . . .'" His laughter
echoed all over the cavernous space of the chalet, finally bringing a
smile to his boss's face.

*T*he morning was bright and beautiful, the snow dazzling
against the frosty blue of the mountain sky. Trudi and
Eddie drove in from Denver in a rented Jeep in time to enjoy the big
"fry-up" breakfast Jeffrey was preparing. Trudi looked terrific in her
form-fitting, one-piece dark blue ski suit that complemented her deep
blue, violet-hued eyes. She had a U.S. Olympic ski team blue and
white jacket draped loosely over her shoulders. Steven could sense her
impatience to get up on the mountain. Eddie was athletic-looking as
well, in a one-piece, black waterproof outfit, with lots of zippers.

Steven had been wondering how he would react to Trudi this
time around. He hardly knew her—they hadn't done much more
than become acquainted in L.A. He had thought a lot about her,
though. The evening in L.A. kept revolving in his mind. He knew,
realistically, that if he was going to emerge from his five years' of
mourning, he should be thinking of someone like Jessie, a woman at
least a little closer to his age. But there was something about Trudi
that was very appealing, beyond the allure of her being a champion.
He knew that he sized up people well in the business world. But
what about young women? Were his instincts right about Trudi?

While Trudi and Eddie got their ski equipment unloaded and
his camera equipment organized, Steven zipped himself up in a red
Bogner one-piece suit, which looked sharp. Steven usually gave Jef-

frey, who loved to ski, the daylight hours off, and he would join them. The cook emerged from his room downstairs looking like the Michelin Man. His normal rotund fullness was exaggerated by a white, puffy jacket that seemed to make him nearly spherical. His goggles only emphasized the effect.

They snapped on their skis outside the house and glided down the short distance to the ticket sales and lift complex. Shortly, sitting four abreast, they rode the chair lift higher up the mountain. The snow looked excellent. Even though it was late in the season, the base was still deep. As they passed the Game Club—a private restaurant two-thirds of the way up—they gained a spectacular view of the magnificent, wide-open slopes that made Vail so appealing to skiers from around the world. The area was so vast, conditions were rarely less than perfect.

As they neared the top, Trudi and Eddie discussed how the scenes should be shot. He would go on ahead to film her and Steven skiing together. Trudi assured Steven that she would not ski beyond his capabilities. Soon they were standing together before their first descent, joy in their hearts at the beauty before them.

With a whoop, Jeffrey took off. Trudi and Eddie watched in gaping amazement as the plump cook instantly transformed into a light, graceful creature upon the snow. Then Eddie pushed off. Skiing expertly, he positioned himself a few hundred yards down the first slope and aimed his telephoto lens back up to where Trudi and Steven waited. Trudi exclaimed, "Steven, let's go!" and they pushed off. She skied extremely well, but not at breakneck speed, and Steven was able to match her pace. They raced past Eddie, spraying loose snow nearly in his face, and he followed them, this time shooting from behind. Their skilled turns left criss-crossing ski trails upon the brilliantly sparkling white blanket.

Happily, they skied together all morning. Eddie and Trudi told Jeffrey that he was a wonder on the slopes, and he responded with an aw shucks grin. They had lunch together at the Game Club and sunned themselves in chairs outside. Trudi was in her element, Steven thought. She was beautiful, fun, with no pretensions or agenda. He looked forward to these next few days. Jessie would realize that he was right. Trudi was no phony; she was the real thing.

During the afternoon, Jeffrey rendezvoused with his friend Fran from the restaurant. She was a tall, beautiful girl who skied nearly as well as he did. The five of them skied hard as a group for a run, and then they split up. Eddie had more than enough video on tape, and Steven and Trudi were free to ski together—unchaperoned.

Steven was delighted to be alone with Trudi. They began to explore some of the more remote and challenging expert runs on Vail Mountain. They skied so fast that they had ample opportunity to talk on the relatively slow lift rides back up to the top. Everything she said enhanced his rapidly growing appreciation for her. She was so unlike the other young women recently in his life. She had no connection to *Trophy Bride*, only the connection that Steven had made on his own.

That was an increasing worry. He realized as she talked about the Olympics and her aspirations that the TV show meant nothing to her. The other girls had signed a contract with Jessie, accepting, in principle at least, the idea of becoming his bride, if asked. Trudi was under no such agreement.

Back on the chairlift his thoughts resumed their previous track. The other girls had known everything about Steven; Trudi knew essentially nothing. It would be great, he thought, to introduce her to all the aspects of his life. She had an indifference to his wealth, which was very appealing. In some ways, Trudi reminded him of Yvonne, who never knew, cared, or inquired about money, just trusting Steven totally in that part of their marriage.

For Jessie's sake, he had to tell Trudi about the show. Tentatively, he began to guide the conversation in that direction. He started by talking a little about Yvonne and how empty his life had been since her death. That's why he signed up for this reality TV show.

As soon as Trudi caught his drift, however, she responded, "Steven . . . I don't really know anything about you. Your invitation to come here is wonderful, but we're from different worlds. I'm a glorified ski bum and you are, I guess, a millionaire? I would never fit into your life. It's way over my head. Please don't take this in the wrong way, but I'm not going to sign any TV contract. I have too many more mountains to ski. Hey, we're at the top—let's go!"

She skied rapidly away. He followed in a troubled state of mind. At least Trudi was honest. Perhaps that's what made her so attractive to him. He decided he wasn't going to let her get away. He had several days to turn the situation around. Her no would not be the final answer.

As four o'clock rolled around and the lifts stopped running, they had to call it a day. The shadows of the tall pine trees made their last downhill run a chilly one. As they skied down, they encountered Jeffrey and Fran, continuing on to the lower slope and the front door of Steven's chalet.

While they were stepping out of their skis and organizing their poles, mittens, and so forth, a taxi pulled up. Jessie and Gus, the German ski camerman she'd hired, climbed out. She was not pleased at all to be out in "nature," as she put it. She was chilly in giving Steven a perfunctory hug and icy when introduced to Trudi.

Gus helped Steven brew a big pot of Irish coffees, and then a second batch, and the others got the fire roaring. Jeffrey and Fran organized a big buffet from the excellent food that had been sent up from the restaurant. It was shaping up to be a fine *après* ski evening, except for the frosty distance between Jessie and Trudi.

Steven chose to ignore it. Trudi looked so sexy and cute in her U.S. Olympic team jacket. Jessie was overdressed in an expensive cashmere sweater with a genuine fur collar and cuffs. She looked uncomfortable and unhappy. Her mood was not improved by Trudi's offhand dismissal of a possible TV show contract, at least for the time being. Also, in an aside to Steven, she complained that to be in Vail, she'd had to postpone and reschedule a trip to Boston with Mark for an interview with the head of the Physics department and others at MIT. They had reviewed his work and wanted to meet him.

Everyone was tired from a long day of skiing and travel, and the evening wound down before the fire went out. Goodnights were said all around and everyone retired to their respective rooms. All of the five bedrooms would be filled, with Eddie and Gus sharing a room. Although no one said anything, it did not go unnoticed that Jeffrey and Fran entered Jeffrey's room together.

*U*pon awakening, Steven checked his e-mail and was pleased to discover three more messages from his new pal Mark. They had that unique mix of rarified intellect and utter naiveté, which he found so charming. He would have to share them with Jessie. Despite the connection he felt to Trudi, last night he'd missed the easy rapport he'd developed with Jessie.

Throwing back the bedroom curtains, he was happy to see that during the night a wonderful dusting of two inches of new powder had fallen, the kind of snow that makes western skiing the delight of the world.

As they finished their breakfast coffees and looked out over the valley, the skiers realized that nature had presented them with perfect conditions. The slopes would be fresh and beautiful in sunlight with the dusting of snow on the trees like powdered sugar—and not a breath of wind to disturb the scene.

Everyone suited up and waited so Steven could say good-bye to Jessie for the day. At last she emerged looking like a real snow bunny, from her fur hat to her fur-lined aprés-ski boots. She waved them off toward the lifts. "I plan to put in an aerobic day of shopping," she said.

The first run down the black diamond slope was better skiing than Steven had experienced in years. He was having a marvelous time with Trudi, and she was thrilled with the excellent conditions as well. The base was firm, and their parabolic skis helped them carve lightning fast turns. Eddie and Gus must be shooting fantastic stuff, Steven thought, as the powder they kicked up swirled around Trudi and himself in dry clouds of prismatic ice particles, refracting the sunlight into millions of glorious rainbows.

Disaster struck on the second run.

They were skiing fast, but no faster than they had been on the first run, when Trudi caught an edge. She lost her balance and then wiped out, tumbling over and over down the steep slope before she came to a stop. Her bindings had released and both skis had sprung free. She let go of her ski poles as well. With panic in his heart, Steven skied to her side and found her unconscious. She wasn't wearing a helmet. Gus and Eddie quickly joined him. They all detached their skis and crouched by the girl. Gus had experienced many ski accidents, and this didn't look good, he told them. But slowly Trudi started to come to. As she did, her face became distorted with pain and she cried, "My leg! My leg!"

Steven called the Vail Mountain Ski Patrol on his mobile phone. It seemed to take them forever to answer. When they did, he described where they were and that they were pretty sure Trudi had a broken leg. They needed help immediately. Since the slope was too steep to land a helicopter, they would have to wait for the ski patrol to arrive with a stretcher sled.

It seemed like hours, but it was actually only twenty-five minutes before two fit-looking patrolmen arrived from the top of the lift with a sled behind them. It was difficult to get Trudi strapped in because every motion caused her excruciating pain, but the patrol guys were experienced. They even teased Trudi a little— "What's a ski bunny like you doing on the experts' run?"—to get her mind off the pain. Finally they set off on the long, bumpy slide behind their V-positioned skis, as they snowplowed her down to the bottom.

*S*teven's heart ached for Trudi. The poor kid! He'd been sitting in the reception area of the clinic, world famous for dealing with the injuries of athletes, for hours. It was six o'clock. He had telephoned Jessie and she was waiting with him. As soon as the ambulance arrived, the doctor had taken a close look and then had summoned his colleague, the best bone man in the world, to take charge. The clinic was busy. The nurse had said that the more perfect the conditions, the busier they were. "People think that they're God when the conditions are excellent. They forget that they are just flesh and bone, and they ski far too fast."

After a CT scan, the doctor returned to assure Steven. "Trudi has good clean breaks, in several places—no joints involved. Almost textbook, routine stuff. She'll be in a cast from hip to ankle for a couple of months, but she'll recover completely." When asked if she would be able to rejoin the Olympic team, he had said, "Oh, sure. The funny thing is, I don't recognize her name. Trudi Wilson? I thought I knew them all."

He and Jessie were finally admitted to her room. She was in bed, in the classic broken leg position. The cast was huge, and the broken leg was elevated above her head by means of a sandbag-weighted rope, through a pulley in the ceiling. She was dazed, loaded up with painkillers.

Something was odd about her eyes. They were brown. Trudi mumbled to Jessie that the doctors had removed her tinted contacts. Trudi's hair was damp, and her makeup was washed off by the nurses. Jessie, Steven unhappily noted, displayed little sympathy to the unglamorous, injured girl.

They sat with Trudi as she drifted in and out of sleep. Jessie checked her watch frequently. Steven was in anguish, feeling that he was to blame. If he hadn't invited her, she wouldn't have come to Vail.

Within the hour, Jeffrey arrived with a FedEx envelope, which had come to the house during the afternoon. It was addressed to:

Trudi Austin Wilson
c/o Steven Hudson
Snow Cliff House
Vail, Colorado

Steven showed the envelope to Trudi, but she was in no condition to deal with it. He thought she indicated that he should open it for her. He did, and as he slid out the letter within, a check fluttered to the floor. He picked it up. It was from *Celebrity Week* magazine and made out to Mrs. Trudi Austin, in the amount of one hundred thousand dollars.

Suspicious, he read the letter. The further he read, the more humiliated he became. Steven slumped in his chair. His breathing became labored and his cheeks burned in a mixture of anger and shame. "Steven, what is it?" Jessie asked. Silently, he handed over the letter to her.

Jessie quickly skimmed the letter. In a stern voice she read the choicest bits back to Steven out loud:

"The enclosed check represents our down payment for the feature you are developing for us, *How to Nab a Millionaire in Ten Easy Steps*, and we agree that Steven Hudson would seem to be an extremely attractive prospect."

And:

". . . it is excellent that you have opened the door to Acme Studio's reality episodes, now in production . . ."

And:

". . . if you can penetrate the Acme effort and actually become one of the '*Trophy* girls,' we will double our payment to you . . ."

And:

"... obviously, if you become the chosen bride, the payout to you will expand vastly beyond our meager purse ..."

And:

"... we acknowledge the expenses of Mr. Austin, and we will reimburse you for them ..."

And:

"... but we cannot reimburse the eBay invoice for a U.S. Ski Team Olympic jacket; we consider clothing items to be a personal expense ..."

The rejected eBay invoice was stapled to the letter. Jessie, displaying a triumphant smirk, handed the letter back to Steven. He was pale and staring blankly in near incomprehension. All of the joy and vigor of the morning was but a memory.

Then Jessie's expression turned fierce, and she snatched the check still in Steven's hand. Standing over Trudi, who watched through dull eyes, Jessie tore the check up into confetti-sized pieces and scattered them over the bed.

Steven was aroused out of his stupor. "Jessie, you can't do that. It's her property and she's got a broken leg!"

"Well, Steven, *you're* my property and she broke her leg *trespassing!*"

The following afternoon, they took the G-5 jet back to New York. Steven told the clinic to send him all the bills, over Jessie's objections that he was being too generous, by far. They never saw Eddie Austin. He had cleared out. Jessie sat with Steven in the front lounge chairs, with Jeffrey snoring contentedly in back. They were both deep in their own thoughts, but Steven knew hers. As they flew over Nebraska, he was sure her thoughts were "I could have told you so."

Over Ohio, they were "I could have told you so."

And over New Jersey, they were "I could have told you so. Oh, Steven, I could have told you so . . . I could have told you so . . . "

CHAPTER FOURTEEN

*T*he nudes painted on black velvet were gone.

Henry and Lynne lay in each other's arms, naked together on the bed in his loft. He wanted her full time in his life. In the past, the C word—commitment—was never in his vocabulary. Girls came and girls went. But with Lynne, he repeatedly offered to be hers alone, and now he was in anguish. Henry was experiencing some of his own medicine. Lynne wasn't sure that she would stay in his life; *she* was not ready to commit to *him*.

After the angry words with his father and his confession to Helen, he had courted Lynne with great energy and charm. Now, they were spending occasional nights together. But she remained troubled by the father-son relationship, plus his prodigal ways.

"Hank, two things really bother me," she said. They were having a relationship talk after a slow, passionate round of sex. "You let your dad completely support you and yet you went behind his back when you started dating me. How can you just take from him like that and not earn your own place in the world?"

She was pushing buttons that were wired painfully into Henry's psyche. "My father," he responded with a sigh. "How can I compete with him? He's one of the richest and most powerful men in New York. In the country! I can't measure up to that, and I really don't like being the son of a famous man. But I wasn't given a choice."

His self-pity didn't move her. "You resent him, don't you?" It was pretty clear to her. "Did you want to hurt him by snatching away his girl?"

"Oh, Lynne. I love you, don't you see that?" He sat on the edge of the bed, his blond hair tumbling over his forehead, with the most earnest of expressions. "I'm so embarrassed that Dad was in the picture. I never meant to get in his way, it just happened."

"What about work? Is that something you ever plan to do?" This was the question that was uppermost in her mind.

She was so beautiful. He decided that she deserved a straight answer. His worried look deepened as he said, "When I graduated from college, I wanted to find some sort of job. Dad would've opened all the doors for me, but I didn't want to trade on his name. I enrolled in a broker's training program, but I dropped out when I realized that I would be spending most of my time making calls to solicit business. The firm giving me the training expected me to use Dad's contacts, and I wouldn't do that either. Dad wanted me to join his firm, but how could I? Nobody wants the boss's son around." He paused to reach out and touch her shoulder, "You should know, Lynne, the trust funds that were set up years ago for Helen and me are very significant. Money isn't a problem."

"But doing something to earn respect is basic, Hank. Not just respect from others, but respect for yourself. You're young enough now to be a playboy, but what about when you're older?"

Henry didn't answer right away. The question had occurred to him many times on his own. "Well, I've been thinking. Remember we talked at the tennis club about my idea for better computer firewall security? I ran the idea by an engineer friend, and he thinks he could do the hardware side of it. It might be possible to put a company together in the security field. This could be the first product."

Lynne sat up. This was interesting! She loved entrepreneurial activity. She went directly to the first problem to be solved. "How much money would it take to get the business started?"

"Well, not as much as you might think." Henry was uncharacteristically thoughtful. "Nothing significant for facilities, just start-up capital to cover the programmers and engineers—we would outsource the manufacturing. Marketing would take some money, though. I think it could hit the breakeven point with less than a million dollars invested."

"But where would you get that kind of cash? Would your father have to bankroll everything?"

"I don't think so," Henry answered with a grin. "Remember I told you about my McLaren? The car that caught on fire? Well, the factory called me this morning to say they could fix it better than new, and get this, they have a buyer. If I want to sell, they can get a price higher than I paid! That cash would be enough."

She thought this could be very exciting. After showering together and cooking some pasta for dinner, they kicked ideas back and forth. The more they explored the venture, the brighter the prospects became, building upon each other's strengths. They concluded that the next steps should be taken together. Lynne would develop the management side, and Henry would oversee the technical matters.

He said, only half joking, as they rounded out their plans, "Just let me be chairman. I think Dad might respect that."

*A*t breakfast, the spring's welcome sunshine flooded the kitchen. Jessie finished scrambling some eggs and stuck a few slices of bread in the toaster. As she cooked, she went over the days schedule one last time—both for Gregory's benefit and for her own piece of mind.

"Thanks for helping out. I have my hands full at the office. I have to persuade Steven, once again, to keep going," she said wearily. "It's getting harder and harder. He has been so let down by the whole thing."

"Well, that stems from his conflicted inner self."

She fixed him with a sour look. "That, and being trashed at every turn by everyone."

He felt her hostile vibes and quickly got off his soapbox. "How are you going to do it this time?"

"With Eve," Jessie said, nodding, "she's my ace in the hole, so to speak. I have to make sure you never meet her. She is the most beautiful woman I have ever seen in my life—a professional model, tall, intelligent, and interested in Steven. He hasn't seen her since we shot the first episode. He's pretty depressed right now, but I think she'll be able to catch him, turn the tide, get him to the altar, and save the show."

"Ah, the problems of the business world!"

She slapped his plate on the table noisily. "Right." He startled at the sound, giving her a grim satisfaction. "Are you squared away for today?"

Gregory meekly took a folded paper from his jacket pocket. He was nicely dressed in a trim black blazer and white cashmere turtleneck sweater.

"Let's see," he said, recovering his usual confident tone, "Mark arrives at 10:35 A.M., lower-level, Grand Central, train from Scarsdale. We're going to meet Professor Ackerman of the A. E. Imperatore School of Science at the Stevens Institute of Technology in Hoboken. Ackerman is in charge of the Special Program for the Mathematically Gifted. Take the PATH train from Thirty-third Street and Sixth to Hoboken. Cab, bus, or walk to the school, which isn't that far. Repeat the process coming back but bring Mark by your office to say hello after his interview. Have I got it right?"

"Bravo, sweetheart," she said, regretting her outburst. "You are a life saver. I just can't do it today, so thanks in advance from both Mark and me."

Gregory thought the reception area for the math department was a little shabby, but the young African American secretary who asked them to sit and wait for Mark's interview was very attractive. Gregory gave himself a brownie point for doing his duty, shepherding the exasperatingly difficult Mark to the Stevens Institute. However, he hadn't brought anything to read and he was bored. Small talk with the boy was impossible. Mark always seemed preoccupied with inner thoughts, and every time Gregory tried to interest him in something important from Anthony Tower, Mark dismissed him with a grunt and returned to his portable Internet device.

Mark suddenly burst out in a raucous laugh, startling Gregory, who couldn't imagine that the kid had a sense of humor.

"What's so funny?" Gregory's curiosity was piqued.

Mark didn't answer. He just handed the BlackBerry to Gregory, who took it with a frown. He read:

In answer to your questions about chess, I don't play much anymore, and I am unfamiliar with Capablanca's opening—I just try to avoid Hudson's closing. That's when I get so unhappy with my opponent that I overturn the board.

Gregory couldn't believe it. "Is this from *Steven* Hudson?" Mark nodded. "You e-mail Steven Hudson about chess?"

Finally Mark answered, "Yes, we correspond about many interesting things every day." The boy showed no sign of wanting to engage in conversation, and Gregory was saved from the struggle when a tall, round-shouldered older man in a tweed jacket entered. "I am Hastings Ackerman," he said with a friendly smile. "You must be Mark Waters—I've heard so much about you. Please come into my office." He shook Gregory's hand and said that he should wait in the reception area during the interview.

Before long, Gregory was chatting with the secretary. Her name was Charonda. She was bored too, and soon he was charming her with talk about his travels around the country. She was impressed to learn that Anthony Tower's number one man was right there in her office.

Shortly, he was helping her with boyfriend troubles. "When Rayvon drinks too much and starts groping other women, it's not him that's doing it." Gregory loved to help others, especially when they were pretty girls. "No, Charonda, it's his inner child acting out boyhood compulsions."

She found Gregory's ideas reassuring, more satisfying than her own ideas—she'd been thinking that Rayvon was just an SOB—and Gregory was on a roll, enjoying every minute as he expanded on the power within the seven steps. He acknowledged Mark's reappearance in the outer office with an uninterested glance and happily carried on with his pitch. After he had written down the time and location of his next New York seminar, she pointed out that Mark had walked out the door.

Gregory assumed that the annoying egghead had gone to the men's room. After he and Jessie married, he vowed he would send him off to some boarding school for freaks. Overseas would be best. But Mark wasn't in the bathroom. He was nowhere to be seen in the corridors of the building either. Gregory hurried down the stairs to check the lobby, no luck. He sprinted back up to ask the professor if Mark had said anything about leaving. He had not. Gregory had a moment of perfect clarity: the kid had ditched him, and Jessie would be furious.

*J*essie found her desk cluttered with phone messages, including a couple from Agnes Atherton. The responsibility of somehow seeing *Trophy Bride* through to completion was heavy on her shoulders. It all depended upon keeping Steven going.

So much of her reputation and Agnes Atherton's money was riding on it. And surely, she had an obligation to Steven too. He was so . . . what was the word . . . genuine, that was it. When this was over, she was going to miss him, even though he could be stubborn and difficult. Lately, he'd been on her mind so much. He had a strength of character that she found more attractive than his good looks. Sure, there were lots of handsome men around, but how many men would be able to withstand the disappointments he had?

For the thousandth time she thought how much harder reality TV was proving to be than sitcoms and soaps.

She bit the bullet and called him. Mrs. O'Brian put the call through right away.

"Steven, good morning," she purred. "Have you recovered from the trip?" She hated to bring up Vail and mention Trudi, but Jessie had to see if Steven was in a mood to proceed.

"God, what a dope I am." He sounded even more depressed than she had feared. "Those two grifters really conned me. She should be on the U.S. Olympic *scam* team." Jessie listened while Steven vented his anger. But she realized that he was more embarrassed than wounded. When he said, "You saw through her right away, Jessie. I should've listened to you," she grabbed the opening.

"Steven, we need to get back on track. I want to reacquaint you with Eve."

"Oh, Jessie," she could hear his sigh over the phone, "I want to be with a woman . . . like you."

She felt her heart skip a beat, but she replied, "Yes, exactly. Eve is so much more mature than the others. She is a woman you will be happy with, Steven. Let me invite you to dinner at my place, to talk about the show. No cameras, just you and me."

She continued to talk with him, gradually restoring his confidence and, she supposed, building on his interest in her. It wasn't too long before she was successful in getting him to agree to dinner. By the time she hung up, Jessie was confident that the show would go on. Eve was, she reflected, fantastic. She would be certain to catch Steven. She just had to get a few more girls into the plot so there would be enough tape for the remaining episodes. That would be the only significant problem. But if Steven was happy with Eve, maybe he would play along. After all, he was pretty relaxed, even when surrounded by cameras and crew.

She hadn't been at her desk for much more than another hour when her secretary burst in. "Jessie, Gregory is on the phone. He says that it's important."

Jessie picked up the phone immediately. "What is it, Gregory?"

"Mark is gone."

"*What?*"

"We went to Stevens Institute for the interview, but at the time it ended, I went to the men's room, and when I came back—it was only a minute—he'd taken off. I looked everywhere before I called you. Where do you think he could've gone?"

A wave of panic engulfed Jessie. She didn't bother blaming Gregory. Instead, she asked him to alert the campus police immediately, plus the Hoboken police, and then to call her right back. She and her secretary worked the phones and alerted the NYPD and the PATH security office. The police normally wouldn't jump into action for a missing teenage boy, but Mark was a kid with "special needs," and they took the panicked mother's call seriously. If he didn't turn up by late afternoon, they assured her, they would issue an Amber Alert. In the meantime they would have a cop check the station for the next train to Scarsdale, which, her secretary had discovered, wouldn't start boarding until 2:30 P.M.

When Gregory called back with no news, Jessie really broke down. "How could you have lost him?" She started crying. "He doesn't have any idea of how to get around. He is a baby!"

"Jessie, your inner child is very strong. You can turn to her for strength."

"Dammit, Gregory, how can you talk bullshit like that? Mark is my life—God knows where he is or who has got him." Visions of him falling victim to some pedophile flooded her mind. "Gregory, find him! Why did he wander off? Were you quarreling?"

"Not at all. He was still in Professor Ackerman's office when I ducked into the john. I wasn't gone for more than a minute, like I said before."

"Oh, God. I am so worried."

The next three hours brought no news. Gregory retraced the path he and Mark had taken in the morning, and he called in negative reports on his cell phone to Jessie, who was frozen at her desk. She had also alerted her parents and the Scarsdale police to no avail.

Her secretary interrupted her tumultuous thoughts with "Steven Hudson is on line two. Do you want to take his call?"

Steven had only rung to tell her that the pilots had found her silk scarf, which she'd forgotten to take from the Gulfstream. He was shocked when she, in a flood of tears, told him about Mark.

By now Steven knew a little about the boy's routines, and he asked "Have you tried sending him an e-mail? He says he always carries his BlackBerry—I'll try right now."

He was sitting by his computer and he typed, "Please call your mom immediately, Mark. She is very worried about you. Thanks, Steven." He hit send.

Two minutes later, while she was still being comforted by Steven, her secretary burst in. "Mark is on line one!"

Jessie snatched up the phone. "Mark! Mark, I am frantic, where have you been?"

Mark's voice was monotone as always. "In Flushing, Queens, at 111th Street where it intersects Forty-eighth Avenue."

"What? Why?"

"That's where the New York Hall of Science is located, according to the Internet, and it is correct. They have some interesting interactive exhibits, Mother, but their explanation of Brownian motion is all wrong, as anyone familiar with Einstein's original paper on the subject would easily recognize."

Jessie flicked that information from her mind. She had a more pressing question. "Mark, did someone take you there?"

"No. I took the PATH train from Hoboken to Thirty-third Street, then the B train one stop to Forty-second Street, and switched to the number 7 line to 111th Street. It is a short walk from there. The New York City subway map was accurate."

"God, where are you now?"

"Calling you from a pay telephone near the intersection of Sixth Avenue and Forty-fifth Street in Manhattan, New York City, New York."

"But that's just around the corner from here!"

"Yes. You wanted me to come to your office to say hello. By my calculation, I am approximately six and two-thirds minutes away. Do you still want to see me?"

The Amber Alert wouldn't be necessary after all.

*L*ate that same night, back in her apartment with Gregory, Jessie was exhausted. She had insisted on accompanying Mark back to Scarsdale on the train, and they had eaten dinner with her parents. She'd only just returned.

It had not been easy to get anything from Mark—he was so preoccupied in recounting the rail signal lights. She'd learned, years ago, not to challenge him on his obsessions, but she really wanted to get to the bottom of things. What had happened at the Stevens Institute? Why had he ditched Gregory? Now and then the train slowed and Mark could be diverted from his counting, without fear of missing a signal.

It was like pulling teeth to find out anything about the interview. All she could get was that "Ackerman was okay." They would accept him, but Mark preferred physics, and he wanted to go to MIT for that reason instead.

As for ditching Gregory, he was more forthcoming. "He is an idiot. He talks about things that have no meaning. When the interview was over, I came out and found him talking to Professor Ackerman's secretary about the inner self. He saw me, but then he kept talking, on and on. So I left." He paused and turned to her. "Mom, why do you want to marry someone who is so stupid?"

Back at her place, Gregory sensed her cold rage immediately. Before she could say a word, he said, "Jessie, you look really beat. I'm so sorry that I let Mark slip away. It'll never happen again. Here, sit on the floor and I'll give you a shoulder and neck massage."

"I'm fine," she said coolly.

She took off her coat and hung it in the foyer closet. Coming into the living room, she ignored his invitation to come sit with him on the couch. She took the armchair instead.

"What did you and Mark talk about this morning?"

He tried to hide his annoyance. "Jessie, it's really hard to talk with him. You know he likes to count things. Station stops, whether more people are entering or leaving the subway car—things like that. He tells me the results, but I think he's mostly talking to himself." Gregory displayed a rare frown. "You know how I believe in the inner self, but with Mark I think it's a computer chip. We could stamp Intel Inside on his forehead and not be that far off."

This unthinking slight released a new wave of cold fury from Jessie.

"Gregory, he said you were talking with Professor Ackerman's secretary when he came out. You weren't in the men's room."

Guilt flashed in his eyes before he could look away. "Well, yes. I tried to take her through a simple version of the seven steps. She said she had boyfriend troubles, and I counseled her to discover her inner self."

Jessie grew perfectly still. "And while you were talking to her, Mark walked off."

He twisted uneasily in his seat. "That's not quite right."

"Mark said he got tired of waiting for you, so he left."

Gregory had no answer for that. After a few uncomfortable moments, he managed to recover his smile.

Jessie wasn't putting up with any more of his crap. "Gregory, what goes on inside *your* head? How do you see yourself—us?"

Smiling, he said, "I see myself in a mirror of enlightened awareness, which reflects not only me but you and the others impinging upon our resonance."

"What *are* you talking about?"

"The essence of our relationship is the absolute trust we have in our deepest thoughts and perceptions, shaped by knowledge of the inner self dynamic."

Jessie felt like strangling him. "I am not in one of your seminars, Gregory. We are engaged to be married. Do you love me?"

"Sure, that too."

How different he was from Steven, she thought. Always parroting the same old lines. "Gregory, are you a genuine person? Has life etched anything on your slate?"

"Slate? I'm not a blank slate, a 'tabula rasa.'" Gregory's smile had slowly faded away during this exchange. "Jessie, life has etched me plenty."

"How, Gregory?"

"Well, I have lived intensely and experienced nearly every emotion and interaction with the troubled and tortured souls in my seminars around the country."

"You mean you have lived secondhand."

"And what do you mean, am I a genuine person? Who are you comparing me to?"

Jessie sighed. "Never mind, Gregory. We can talk about us later." She rose to her feet. "I'm going to bed, now. Alone. Would you mind going back to your place?"

CHAPTER FIFTEEN

*W*hen Helen unwrapped it, the book nearly took up the whole tabletop at the Carnegie deli. The cover was a beautiful reproduction of Marcel Duchamp's *Nude Descending a Staircase*, and the title was *Quantum Leaps in Art*, by Aristotle Cohen. Steven leafed through the pages. The text was lavishly interspersed with wonderful photographs of contemporary paintings.

"Pop, check out the dedication and the note he wrote you." Helen was happy to be back in the Saturday routine with her dad.

The typeset words read "To Helen, the Joy of My Life—Ari," and he had written in blue ink, "To Steven Hudson, my favorite capitalist. Peace and warmest regards, Ari Cohen."

"Wow, Helen, this is quite a book!" Steven said as he refolded his reading glasses. "I had no idea this was in the works. It'll look great on my coffee table. No kidding, I look forward to reading it. I'm sure that I'll learn a lot." He was truly impressed. Ari must carry some clout in the art world to have accomplished this, he thought.

"We're excited about it. The advance sales have been very strong. Well, very strong for a $75 art book. Ari says he'll use the proceeds to set up the baby's room with everything we'll need and to hire a nurse to help."

Steven raised his opinion of the professor for the second time in the space of a few moments. "That's wonderful, Helen. . . . Ah, have you been planning a wedding?" He was at last able to ask the question that had been on his mind ever since Helen had surprised him with her news.

"Oh, don't you bug me about that too, I won't let Ari talk about it anymore. Why are weddings so important anyway?"

Well, he supposed, if Helen wasn't in panic mode, then he wouldn't be either. She was an artist. Artists were just different. Weren't they? But still, he was uncomfortable. She sensed that he was brooding about her situation and switched the topic.

"So, Pop, with Lynne and Hank shacked up, have you found another teenage stepmother for me?"

Steven shuddered at the thought of more TV girls, not to mention Trudi. "No, Helen, I haven't and I won't be finding one either. I've agreed to meet Jessie at her place tonight and she's going to try to talk me into continuing, but this time I won't let her. I'll let you in on a little secret—I wish that she wasn't engaged. That's the real truth." She looked at him with an appraising nod, but didn't press the subject.

They spent a happy afternoon in various galleries together, and they chatted about how well Henry and Lynne were doing, omitting further emotional matters of their own.

*H*adassah picked up Jessie outside the Princeton train station. She was driving an enormous black SUV, and Jessie was pleased to see that her look of panic from that day at the hospital was gone. She now looked happy and confident on this nice spring day. Jessie hadn't seen Saul since his heart attack and this visit was an overdue social obligation. But also, Jessie needed to update Saul. *Trophy Bride* was not under control by any stretch of the imagination, and she needed to level with her boss. She had dressed in an attractive suit which said success, but she felt very awkward, worried about how Saul would react.

Jessie and Hadassah discussed Saul's health as they drove out of the peaceful college town and along the roads lined with budding trees toward the Gross's place in the country. Hadassah seemed very pleased. As they rolled up the crushed gravel drive to the attractive house, covered in white weather-stained shingles, she said, "Be prepared to be unprepared."

They found Saul sunning himself in a deck chair on the patio behind the house. Hadassah had been right. The transformation was amazing, and Jessie almost didn't recognize Acme's owner as he jumped up and pulled a shirt on, smiling broadly at his Executive Producer.

"Jessie, it's great to see you—thanks for shlepping all the way out here." He had lost a huge amount of weight. His cheeks were pink; his smoker's pallor gone. There was a spring to his step and a warmth to his smile that astonished Jessie. Saul had even shaved away the long strings of hair previously combed across his bald pate. He looked at least ten years younger. Jessie was so taken aback that they were nearly finished with the sandwiches Hadassah had prepared and set on a metal table in the sun, before the shop talk began. And it was Saul who got the ball rolling.

"Jessie, I love the test tapes for your reality show. I think it's brilliant the way you leave all the bride wannabes in the running."

She tried to hide the surprise she felt at his positive interpretation—in her mind Steven hadn't gotten far enough with any of the contestants to make even a rejection meaningful. But maybe Saul was onto something she hadn't considered. He continued. "I had expected each episode to eliminate one, like every other reality show on the tube. But doing it this way, the viewers will be rooting for their favorite right up to the end!"

"Well, I am glad that you like it." But, Jessie knew it was time to enlighten the owner. Her expression turned very serious.

"Saul, I've got to confess, nothing has gone as planned. And I have a big problem. I don't think Steven Hudson will see it through. If he drops out we have—to use one of your expressions—bupkus." And Jessie filled in her boss, detail by detail, on all that had gone wrong—how Willard's prediction that reality would follow the script was completely off the mark. She rested her elbows on the table and looked Saul directly in the eyes.

"I am not laying the blame on Willard, not at all. It's my fault. I picked Steven and he is, frankly, a gentleman. He's too good for this circus." She needed to get this off her chest. "I wish I had chosen a man desperate enough to put up with our script, no matter what. I feel a lot of sympathy for him now. Saul, I hate to say it, but I may not be able to deliver on this one."

She slumped back in her seat as she got to the worst part. "We haven't even shot any of the expected stuff, like cooking contests, the shopping sprees, the bathing suit scenes." She looked dejected, defeated. She grimaced as she waited for his explosion.

But, it didn't happen. Instead, Saul leaned over the table and touched her hand very gently, with no hint of sexual overtone. He seemed almost fatherly as he said, "Jessie, I think that's exactly why I love your tapes so much. They are *not* predictable. Steven is *not* desperate. He *is* a gentleman." Saul's sincerity was total as he continued. "The show is *reality* television in the best sense." He was speaking earnestly. "I think Steven trusts you or he wouldn't have gone this far. You said he's coming to your place for dinner. Here's your chance. Build his confidence, and most important, introduce him to a wonderful girl very soon. You can pull this off, Jessie." He settled back in his chair, beaming at her. "I know it."

"I hope you're right. I am trying hard."

"I know." He began to exude a sincerity she had never seen before, as he continued. "Look, since my heart attack, I've had a chance to do some thinking. It's time, long overdue, that Hadassah and I get back on track. Without her, I'm dead. She's been so wonderful to me, Jessie, I don't deserve . . ." He choked up, and had to pause for a moment. "Anyway, we need to rebuild, to take time, and as they say, 'smell the roses.' Jessie . . . when you wind up *Trophy Bride*, I want to make you President of Acme, with a whole big chunk of stock."

Had someone kidnapped the real Saul and put this nice clone of him in his place? No, his sincerity was genuine, and Jessie felt disoriented for the rest of the visit. She commented over and over about the changes in the boss as Hadassah drove her back into Princeton. And as she rode the train to Penn Station, she was still reeling from the unexpected support and encouragement the once dreaded Saul had given her. He was transformed. But, somehow, his new nice-guy persona increased the pressure she felt. If he had exploded, she probably would have simply quit on the spot. Now, he was another decent person she couldn't disappoint, along with Agnes, Willard, and above all, Steven.

*S*ince Jessie wasn't very good at playing chef, she called in Antonio, a caterer. Antonio had trained under Lidia Bastianich at Felidia, one of the top Italian restaurants in New York. She knew Steven loved Italian food and she wanted the best for him. Tonight was important. Her job depended on it.

While the cook prepared the food in the kitchen, she nervously examined her apartment to make sure everything was perfect. The flowers looked good on the bookcase and on the dining table. Her Rosenthal, bone ivory dinner plates with their crimson and gold edges were gleaming, and the candles, in their modern silver and polished bronze candlesticks, reflected in the ebony surface of the table. Jessie lit the candles. Then she checked herself in the mirror, having taken extra time with her hair and makeup.

Jessie opened the drawer below the TV where she'd put the leather framed photograph of Gregory. He was still smiling, even if she wasn't. She stood looking down at his picture, unconsciously twisting the engagement ring on her finger. Catching herself doing this, she stopped, took the ring off, put it in the drawer on top of the photo, and closed the drawer. She was frowning, and her mind filled with conflicting thoughts. She opened the drawer and put the ring back on her finger. There was time. She had time to make the right decision.

Steven arrived promptly, and she buzzed him through the lobby and gave him the elevator access code over the intercom. She felt a surge of excitement and had the door open to greet him as he walked down the hall to her apartment.

The mouth-watering aromas of Italian cuisine greeted him as he approached. Jessie looked marvelous. She greeted him with a little hug. She always made his heart jump, but tonight she was truly arresting. Jessie must have taken extra care, he thought. She was dressed in a pearl gray, long-sleeved silk blouse and a black, raw silk skirt. Except for her ring, a long string of pearls around her neck was her only jewelry. It was an understated look that emphasized her beauty.

He liked her place. He appreciated the contemporary look, though perhaps it lacked personal touches. There were, however, several photos of Mark, both alone and with her parents. He couldn't find a trace of Gregory anywhere.

"Jessie, it's good to see you. Thanks again for all your sympathy in Vail. I'm so sorry to have wasted your time."

He made himself comfortable on the couch, and she sat in a chair opposite. Antonio served them both ice-cold martinis from the freezer. They had been prepared earlier by Jessie exactly the way Steven liked.

When the cook returned to the kitchen, she said, "Before we talk about the show, I've been wondering about Lynne and Hank. They certainly surprised us both! Can you fill me in?" She was pleased to see his face light with a smile.

"You're not going to believe this. You absolutely won't believe it. She's reformed him! He's become a businessman—an entrepreneur—and she's helping him pull together a brand-new venture in computer security. I don't understand it exactly, but the incredible thing is that he won't accept any financial help from me—says he got the money from a fire sale." He chuckled at the thought. "You know, Jessie, stealing Lynne was the best thing he ever did!"

She could see Steven positively glowing with pride, and she encouraged him to talk about his kids during dinner. Her chef had prepared a meal featuring *osso buco* to rival anything in Italy, and he served it with his own silver, bone marrow spoons. The wine was an incredible '64 vintage Barolo, velvety and rich, for which Jessie paid dearly. Steven mentioned Ari's book but not Helen's pregnancy, and she filled him in on Mark's big adventure in New York and his good luck with Professor Ackerman. But she omitted all mention of Gregory. Steven assumed that her fiancé was simply away seeking inner selves.

Antonio wound up the excellent meal with a sublime tiramisu so light that Steven told him, "I've a wonderful cook at my place, but he could learn from you: *cucina deliziosa, Complimenti*." The young chef glowed at this recognition.

Steven hoped they could sit together on the couch as they moved back into the living room, but she retuned to her original chair. Still, he felt great. It had been a wonderful meal and he was happy with her.

"Now, Steven," Jessie turned serious as she morphed back into her Executive Producer role, "I want to talk to you about Eve." She ignored his sigh and resistive body language. "I know that you are sick to death of the show and Acme and me. But you haven't dated Eve! I have been saving her for last. Steven, she is the promise I made to you in the beginning. She will sweep you away!"

It is déjà vu all over again, as Yogi Berra once said. He felt as if he was back in her office on that first visit. He could even feel the tongue-tied awkwardness returning.

"Jessie . . ." She could hear in his voice that he was wavering. "I . . . can't believe I'm saying this, but . . . what do you want me to do?"

A thousand possible answers raced through her mind but what came out was "just have lunch with me Monday to meet Eve."

"But, Jessie, even if I go nuts for her, what good will it do you?" He wanted her to succeed, but how could it work? "You won't have a series. There haven't been enough girls."

"I know, but here is the idea. Give me three more full days to shoot lots of tape. We'll shoot continuously, and I'll mix in three new girls. It doesn't have to be real—hell, it's reality TV! I can edit it all to make anything happen. It will work, Steven. It will work if you like Eve." She glanced away, unable to hold his gaze. What was she doing? What if he really did like Eve?

Steven rose and crossed over to her chair. She looked up, not knowing what he was going to do. For an instant she thought he might give her a kiss, but instead he took her hand in his and said, "All right, call me Adam. I'll meet Eve."

*S*teven arrived at the Four Seasons a little early, and the maitre d' showed him to his table. Jessie had told him at the close of their evening together that his friend Agnes Atherton was putting up most of the production money for *Trophy Bride*, and this added to the pressure he felt today. He had been rewound again, he thought grumpily; still Jessie's clockwork Romeo.

Eve and Jessie arrived together. Conversations stopped and heads turned as they passed to join Steven. Jessie dazzled in her fashionable business ensemble, and Eve was truly a sensation. She was tall, with wavy auburn hair, mysteriously compelling eyes, full lips, a wonderfully sculpted face, and a statuesque figure to match. Her walk particularly caught Steven's attention. She was a professional model, all right, with that unmistakable foot-crossing, hip-swinging catwalk slink. He had not forgotten her face.

Eve's personality was equal to her physical qualities—warm, confident, very poised, and assured. They chatted about the show, laughed about the false starts. Commenting about Bermuda, Eve assured Steven that she really liked *men*. The warm, seductive laugh that accompanied this message certainly helped to make the point. Steven found Jessie nodding with approval, every time he made eye contact with her. The afternoon slipped by rapidly. Steve thought that setting up more dates would be a good idea when Jessie suggested it.

On the way out, she told him that she would unleash Willard, who had been in a funk at not having been included in the Vail sequence, and now was frantic to get back in the action. He couldn't let the show lay an egg.

Over the next couple of days, as Jessie became convinced that Eve and Steven were really clicking, she let Willard run free. During the Vail diversion, he'd been busy filming three girls, Tracy, Katelin, and Stephanie in a number of concocted reality situations, running imaginary errands and quests for Steven, cooking meals, buying neckties, all as if Steven was actually involved. They were the episode fillers Jessie needed to slot in before the wedding scene with Eve. So, Steven found himself being dragged from one to the other, mouthing lines which would somehow, Willard assured him, knit it all together. He was getting pretty good at the game, and Willard's remark to Jessie that he'd never seen anyone better on camera wasn't just flattery. By the end of the third day, the filler was almost complete.

But, with Eve, it wasn't just filler. Steven was really enjoying her company, as Jessie had predicted.

The shoot of Steven watching Eve model the spring line of McCartney was a mega coup for Jessie. The cameras reveled in all the glitter and glamour of the fashion world, the high society audience, the stunning Eve on the runway, and a captivated Steven appreciating it all.

It was actually working. Steven was having a good time and Eve was enjoying herself too. Jessie was filming great stuff that her test groups were devouring. Her suggestion to send them next to Steven's yacht was an excellent idea, they decided, and Jeffrey was dispatched to help in the preparations.

That night Steven and Eve were alone together in the penthouse for the first time. They enjoyed champagne on the terrace with its fantastic views. Steven felt a growing desire for the delectable young woman. He showed her how to make his favorite pasta. First he put together a preparation of dried chili peppers, onions, and garlic in olive oil. The dish was a simple picante delight with the oil, minus the peppers, onions, and garlic, plus sun-dried tomatoes and shrimp stirred in over a hot flame, added to the spaghetti—cooked al dente of course. When she smiled in appreciation, he couldn't help adding, "I was a chef's helper and picked this up along with some other recipes during a summer job at Harvard. I liked working the kitchen. The place was in south Boston, and unfortunately it's long gone. It was called La Toscana, the chef, Luigi, was a great guy."

Enchanted, she moved close behind him. "I want to watch you cook," she said lightly.

After dinner, Steven turned the lights low in the sunken living room. With soft music playing from his music system, they danced together. He kept whirling her past the floor-to-ceiling windows, filled with the sparkling lights of New York below.

It was natural that they found their way into his bedroom. He turned down the bed and lit a couple of candles, while she withdrew to the bathroom. Shortly she returned, wearing nothing at all. Steven came forward to kiss her marvelous breasts, but she said, "My darling, I am so sorry, but it's the wrong time of the month for me. We will have to wait until we're on the yacht."

He was frustrated. He shyly undressed to join her in bed. He could not recall ever feeling as adolescent, as embarrassed by his erection. She blew out the candle but didn't offer relief. She just gave him a light kiss on the cheek saying, "Sleep well, Darling, I'm looking forward to the yacht."

*T*he exquisitely varnished, gleaming Riva speedboat roared away from the dock in Gustavia, through the gin clear water, in late afternoon sunlight. The warm salt spray felt good against Steven's face. He had flown down that day to St. Bart's and greatly looked forward to spending time aboard his 197-foot motor yacht, the *Green Shoe*, with Eve, who would arrive the next day. Cubby (Cubbington) Fairchild, the yacht's young British first mate was at the helm of the speeding Riva. His nickname aboard was "Bay Watch"—Cubby really was that good-looking.

In New York, winter had grudgingly given way to a bout of

cloudy, windy spring weather, which Steven had been grateful to escape. Cubby turned back to chat with Steven as they sped through the boats at anchor in the outer bay.

"We had quite a ruckus aboard last night with Jeffrey, sir. I picked him up at the airport, took him food shopping, and he had a few Heinekens after dinner with us all. He fell asleep on the foredeck and in the middle of the night, came roaring into the crew quarters. It sounded like someone was trying to kill him—so much yelling. Turned out that an enormous flying cockroach had crawled into his ear and couldn't get back out. It looked like Godzilla, and I guess it was very painful, or frightening, or both. I got some tweezers and tried to pull it out, but every time I touched it, it tried to go in farther and Jeffrey really screamed."

"Good God," Steven said. "What did you do?"

"Had to take him to the hospital. Middle of the night. No taxis ashore. Called the ambulance. Everybody was laughing and making fun of him. He was not amused."

"What did they do to get rid of it?"

"Killed it by pouring pure alcohol into his ear. Then they could extract it easily. He's fine, no damage done. The ER doctor said they get about one a year. First time anyone from a yacht, though."

By the end of this story, they had pulled alongside the beautiful white *Green Shoe* at anchor in the turquoise water. The boarding stairs were deployed and Steven climbed aboard to be welcomed back again by the suntanned crew in their summer white uniforms. He went below to his stateroom to change and soon reemerged to enjoy a Mount Gay rum and tonic in a comfortable wicker chair on the aft deck under a white sun awning. Jeffrey came aft to welcome his boss aboard. Steven couldn't resist teasing, "Jeeves, if you're so seriously into inter-species relationships, we could arrange a trip to San Francisco; the mayor could marry you to a cockroach in a jiffy."

"Very funny, boss. I'm going to ask for hazard pay if you keep sending me into these zones."

"Anyway, Jeffrey, are you okay? All set in the galley? Eve arrives tomorrow and we'll start our cruise."

"Aye, aye, boss. Don't think I'll let myself fall asleep, though, until I get back to New York. Ugh!"

Steven collected another Mount Gay and tonic from the bar on the aft deck and admired the Caribbean's red-hued sunset. Cubby was standing by to drop the naval ensign—the yacht's flag at the stern. The mate's blue eyes were on his wristwatch to get the moment of setting within a few second's accuracy.

Steven mentally recounted the happy days since Eve had entered his life. Jessie had been right. They clicked together, and Steven was grateful to have, at last, found the girl who he might very well marry. It was working out for all of them, he thought. Timing is everything in life, and now it was time for Eve. The only problem was his sexual frustration, which he hoped was temporary.

With a start, Steven's thoughts returned to the present at the sound of a cannon being fired from some yacht to mark the sunset. Cubby dropped the ensign. Steven climbed to the upper deck, where on an outside table a light dinner would be served. All his thoughts were focused on tomorrow, when Eve would arrive.

*T*here was a downpour during the night brought by the prevailing trade wind, but the golden teak decks were drying quickly in the warm sun as Steven emerged in the morning and surveyed the scene around him. *Green Shoe* was the largest yacht in the bay, but several other fine boats were also at anchor, and a number of outboard-motor powered tenders scurried about over the sparkling waves. He downed a quick breakfast and went ashore in the Riva with Cubby to meet Eve and Jessie at the tiny airport. They were due in on the first flight.

The little town of Gustavia, a duty-free port, was alive with tourists as usual, but finding a taxi was no problem and soon they were climbing the steep road to the ridge dividing the island. The propeller driven island-hopper commuter plane was on its way in and their driver stopped to let it pass—it seemed to clear the road along the ridge top only by a few feet. Jessie emerged from the small terminal with seven of her technical crew, as they arrived.

She was happy to see Steven and gave him a warm hug and kiss on his cheek.

"Where's Eve?" he asked.

Her smile curdled. "She will be on the next flight, in the afternoon. Her answer left him looking so dispirited that she hastened to explain, "I had to give all the seats on the plane to the camera crew so that they could get ready. Eve was very pleased to find out she could sleep in and take the later flight."

Steven caught the frosty edge in Jessie's voice and he wondered, was she jealous? Was she finally showing that she cared for him?

It was hard to tell because Jessie went on smoothly, "So, Steven, I have you to myself for now. You can help me get settled into the house I've rented. It's supposed to be very cute."

He couldn't tell if she was being suggestive, because she immediately went about getting her TV crew organized. She'd brought only two associate producers, and she put them and the rest in taxis with Cubby from the yacht. The mate would help to get them all to their hotel and then aboard the boat, ready for the afternoon's shoot. By that time Steven realized that he'd just been imagining things. He had sex on the brain.

He helped Jessie with her bags, and they proceeded in another taxi along the beach in the direction of the island's most posh hotel, the Eden Roc.

Her little house, nearly adjacent to the hotel, really was charming. Situated on a brilliant white sand beach within fifty feet of the gently lapping water, it was sheltered by deep green leafy shrubs of the cactus family. The interior was a studio with a bed, tiny cooking area, and a small but well-stocked bar. A large, white-bladed ceiling fan slowly circulated the air drawn in through slatted shutters, making the room comfortably cool and shaded from the blinding morning light.

"Isn't this marvelous?" Jessie said, delighted with the place.

As she gestured all about, Steven noticed that the engagement ring on her finger was gone. A phantom ring remained where it had been. It couldn't have been gone for long.

While he stared, she said, "I can't wait to see your yacht, Steven. The *Green Shoe?* Why did you name it that?"

He finally lifted his gaze. "Oh, it's sort of an inside Wall Street joke. In the early days of stock flotations—you know, public offerings—sometimes the issue would be heavily oversubscribed. When that happened, it could drive the price up out of control of the bankers. So we got SEC permission to issue extra shares, to take some of the steam out of the boiler, so to speak. The first time it was done, decades ago, was for the Green Shoe Company. It's been called a 'green shoe' ever since. When it happens, we bankers, of course, always make a ton of extra money. You could say, green shoes paid for the boat."

She peered out the shutters at the sea outside. "It's an interesting name, makes me think of the old woman who lived in a shoe with all the kids."

She whirled around, remembering something. "Oh, Steven, I have some great news about Mark. We went to MIT earlier this week, and he had interviews with the chairmen of both the math and physics departments. They'll accept him into a program for special talents whenever I decide he is ready to go."

He came toward her and clasped her by the shoulders. "Jessie, I already know! He and I e-mail each other every day. It's just wonderful! Do they understand his theory on quantum gravity?"

"Yes, I think they do. The math chairman said that Mark has ability that reminds him of the greatest of all MIT's brains, the late Professor Norbert Weiner. He said that Mark would one day be very famous. He might win a major prize."

They smiled together. "You must be extremely proud of him."

"Oh, I am. But he's still a child!" She broke away and began pacing. "Maybe in a year he might be able to cope with being away from me and his grandparents—perhaps for a few weeks at a time. His principal psychologist says that he will be, but Steven, he has been my life. How can I ever fill the void?"

Steven tried to assure her that all parents felt that loneliness, the sense of time moving inexorably on, when the day came for the kids to leave the nest. "But you'll find this more like opening a new chapter in a continuing and maturing relationship. They do come back home."

Jessie regarded him fondly. "You're a very good father. I can see why your kids like you so much."

Jessie proceeded to unpack her few things. Slipping briefly into the small bathroom, she emerged in a very becoming summer blouse and shorts, looking cool and fit. Steven mixed two rum and tonics and they sat together on the front porch in low lawn chairs under the grass-roofed sunscreen, looking out over the turquoise waters of the bay.

"Steven, I know that the past weeks haven't been the greatest for you. No fault on your part, but none of the girls have worked out, except maybe now, with Eve." Jessie was thoughtful in her tone.

"That's an understatement," he said. "What a merry-go-round I've been on."

"In the beginning I didn't think you would ever participate in our silly reality show, but now I'm sorry that it will ever stop," she said wistfully. "Sometimes I wonder if it isn't really my fault that so much has gone wrong."

He turned to her, puzzled. "I don't know what you mean, Jessie. How can it have been your fault?"

"Except for Trudi, I picked them all, Steven. Out of all the beautiful girls in the world, I picked the ones that didn't work out. Let's be honest—you would never have married any of them." Then with a warm laugh she added, "Maybe I don't want this to ever end. Just so we'll keep going, you and I. I wonder if Dr. Freud would come to that conclusion."

At the mention of the name Steven scoffed, "The only thing Freud ever said that made sense to me was 'sometimes a cigar is just a cigar.' What are you really saying, Jessie?"

"Oh, I don't know," she said vaguely. "I suppose I will miss you when this is over. I've enjoyed being with you . . ."

Steven's pulse was rising, but he didn't want to push too hard.

"Well, perhaps I'll wind up marrying Eve in front of millions, and afterward she and I and you and Gregory can be friends."

She took a long sip of her drink, then waggled her ring finger in front of his face. "Gregory and I are breaking up. I think he still loves me, but he is just not an authentic person. A near disaster with Mark showed me that. He spouts all that psycho babble, but all he cares about is *his* own inner child."

"Jessie, I am so sorry to hear this. I thought you were happy."

She waved away the sympathy. "Well, now you know everything about the executive producer." She coughed uncomfortably, then checked her watch. "Come on, lover boy, finish up your drink. It's time to go to the airport and pick up Eve. Let's get on with it."

Steven had never seen Jessie look so unhappy, so vulnerable. If, he thought, she would permit it, he would take her in his arms. But she was already moving toward the door.

"Right," he said. "The show must go on."

CHAPTER SIXTEEN

*I*f Admiral Nelson had hired TV crews to film the battle of Trafalgar, it couldn't have been more complicated than the taping of the arrival of Eve and Steven in the Riva to board the *Green Shoe*. Jessie wanted the scene shot from both the deck and the water, and with the complication of waves and the pitching of the camera crews in their small rubber tenders, the scene had to be shot over and over again until she was satisfied.

Steven was very happy to be back on his yacht with this alluring woman. Eve had stepped off the plane looking absolutely fantastic, and she hadn't seemed to mind the bouncing around in the Riva for the repeated re-shootings, though she always seized Cubby's strong shoulders for support, even for the small waves.

After a quick lunch, the taping went smoothly. Steven showed Eve and the camera crew everything. It was a magnificent motor yacht, Dutch built, and in terrific condition. For the occasion, the yacht's crew had dressed the boat in over a hundred code flags of the alphabet in a continuous line, from stem to stern.

"What do the flags signify?" asked Eve, admiring them.

"To welcome you aboard and to look sporty for the TV, I guess."

"Do they spell out any message?"

"Oh, yes," Steven joked. "Starting from the bow it says: 'Rarely does one have the privilege to witness vulgar ostentation displayed upon such a scale.' Actually, Eve, they're just for color."

Eve had a mischievous laugh that Steven loved to trigger. Appearing from behind the cameraman, Jessie joined them for the tour of the yacht's interior. With soft fabrics, deep pile carpets, mahogany wainscot, classic marine paintings, leather, and a marble fireplace, the *Green Shoe* redefined pleasure boating. It was an elegant floating palace, designed and constructed by superb craftsmen. After they had toured it stem to stern, Eve wanted to change into her boating outfit. Steven conducted her back down the wide, mahogany-banistered staircase to the master suite on the lower deck, while Jessie returned to the cockpit lounge area, outside aft, to get her people organized for departure.

As soon as they entered his elegant stateroom suite and closed the door, Eve began to strip off her travel outfit. Bridget, one of the stewardesses, had laid out her Abercrombie & Fitch yachting togs on the suite's king-size bed. With no hesitation, Eve peeled off her undergarments, and naked, she approached a mesmerized Steven.

"Darling, I'm so happy we're here together. Let's make up for lost time."

She pressed her warm, voluptuous body against him. Winding her arms around his neck, she kissed him passionately, her tongue finding its way past his lips. The taste of her was electrifying, igniting him like a fuse. He quickly stripped off his clothing, and in moments they were locked in a writhing embrace on top of the silk bedspread. She slipped him inside her and started rocking so hard that the whole thing was over in mere seconds. Steven was left panting, while below him Eve smiled broadly.

"I've been waiting all day for that," she said.

Even in his orgasmic daze, Steven was filled with unease. He couldn't remain there with Eve. Jessie was on the deck waiting for them. They had to get up there and say good-bye.

Steven washed quickly and dressed in one of the suite's two bathrooms. Meanwhile Eve continued to lie on the bed, smoking a cigarette. Then she rose, washed in the other bathroom, and dressed in her smart yachting outfit. She took his hand as they returned topside to find Jessie still fussing over the packing cases. The crew was almost ready to depart.

"Well, you two look very yachty." She glanced at Steven, but he was so confused by his feelings, he couldn't look her in the eye. "Eve, you are a sailor's delight in that outfit," said Jessie with a forced smile.

They helped her and her crew down the boarding gangway and into the waiting boats.

"You two have fun," Jessie said as the tenders pulled away from the yacht. The cameraman was standing up in the rubber boat still filming. "I'm going to take a couple of days off and do absolutely nothing—just swim and sunbathe! Bye." She looked depressed, Steven thought.

As soon as the smaller tenders were clear, Jeremy, the *Shoe's* captain, with help from Stanley, the engineer, and Cubby, the mate, plus aid from Jason and Scott, the two deckhands, lifted the Riva up onto the foredeck by means of a large hydraulic crane. Then Stanley set about firing up the ship's two huge Deutz diesel engines, and Cubby began to operate the power winch for the yacht's anchor chain.

Steven, preoccupied with thoughts about the blitz-like afternoon's sex, watched all this with Eve, standing on the bridge deck in front of the wheelhouse. He was bewildered by the haste of their animal-like coupling. He'd been so startled by her sudden nakedness. But then, he reasoned, she was a professional model. She would be naked much of the time and in front of others, no doubt, during the multiple changes of outfits she would wear during a major fashion show. She probably thought nothing about being nude in front of a man, and he had taken advantage of her. Or, he questioned himself, had she taken the lead all the way?

"Where do you find these handsome sailors, Steven?" Eve was studying the suntanned youths in their shorts and T-shirts laboring on the foredeck to get the boat under way. "They're gorgeous, like a bunch of athletes, and they're not a bit sissy, despite their English accents."

He found his voice. "Most yacht crews are Brits. It's kind of like a yachting mafia. It's hard for others to break in, though there are some Kiwis and South Africans as well."

She nodded at this information. "Well, I can't keep my eyes off them. The one you call Cubby should be a model. I could open doors for him in New York."

"Don't put ideas in his head, please. It's hard enough to keep the crew together. I don't use the boat enough and they get bored."

A vibration was felt as the anchor was secured in its pocket, and Cubby signaled to the captain, behind them in the wheelhouse, that they were clear. The bow thruster kicked in, turning the yacht toward the open water. The propellers began to turn and the powerful engines started to propel the heavy yacht forward, raising a white bow wave as they gained speed.

Since it was already late in the afternoon, Steven had decided to motor to a charming uninhabited bay at the north end of the small island, only about five miles or twenty-five minutes away. They could, he thought, sail on to St. Kitts or Nevis tomorrow.

"Look, look! dolphins," Eve cried. Sure enough, four of the friendly, wonderful creatures were traveling with them at the bow, swimming at the yatcht's speed, enjoying the fun of being alive, it seemed.

"They bring good luck, Eve. It's good that you spotted them."

The yacht soon rounded the most northern tip of St. Barts. The engines slowed and they glided into a beautiful, sheltered bay. The captain shouted down to Cubby, "Drop the hook," and with a splash, the anchor, pulling one hundred and fifty feet of chain with it, rattled down from the bow. They were soon secure in their splendid surroundings for the night.

"Come on, Eve," Steven said. "In the tropics, sunset comes on quickly."

They strolled to the upper aft deck to watch the spectacle. It was clear, with only a few clouds in the distance. Steven hoped to see the green flash at the instant the upper rim of the sun dropped below the distant horizon. He explained what to look for. They stood together, hand in hand, watching. "There!" he exclaimed. "Did you see it?" "No," she said, and he could see why the tiny green dot flash, about the size of a traffic light at a mile's distance, had not registered with her. "Well, sometimes it's really spectacular."

They armed themselves with two golden Mount Gays and tonics from Bridget and drifted down to the settees in the aft cockpit. "No green flash for me," Eve joked, "but I've got the *Green Shoe* and I've got you, big guy."

They sat down and watched Cubby and Jason carefully fold the ensign, which they had dropped precisely at the instant of sunset. Within an hour, the sky had turned blue-black and the first stars appeared. The engineer switched on the intense underwater lights that circled the hull, and the *Shoe* was instantly floating in a shimmering pool of light, radiating down and all around the yacht. Numerous small fish were attracted, and soon big, flashing silver streaks appeared to hunt the smaller fry. "Those are tarpons," Steven explained. "It looks like we'll have a good fish show tonight."

"It's so beautiful, Steven," Eve sighed. "I wish I could write a poem or sing you a song to thank you for this." By now the lights illuminating the superstructure were on as well, and the *Shoe* gleamed like a jewel in the descending darkness.

"Steven, if you could think of one word to describe all this, what would it be? Fabulous? Fantastic? Exquisite?"

"How about, *it's mine*." Steven laughed as Jeffrey and Bridget emerged together to present the fine dinner the chef had prepared. It was laid out on the outside dining table within the aft cockpit.

"Boss, no Maine lobsters—too far south, but some local fisherman sold me the Caribbean version. 'Mon, dey be good,' he said. As you can see, no claws. I mean, what was Darwin thinking? But they have these big tails. I think they'll be just fine."

They sat together at one end of the big table, which was illuminated with candles in hurricane lamps. The china carried the yacht's logo, a green, Dutch wooden shoe, as did the silverware and linen napkins also embroidered with the logo. The lobsters were wonderful, as was the wine, the dessert, and the after dinner drinks.

Leaving the table, Eve and Steven strolled hand in hand around the entire yacht, frequently looking over the side to watch the frenzy of the darting fish in the shimmering blue-green light in which the boat appeared to hover. They stopped near the boarding stairs. The door in the bulwark was open, giving access to the gentle little waves below.

"Are there any sharks? Would it be safe to swim?" asked Eve.

"Oh, quite safe," he answered, thinking it was just an idle question.

Without hesitation, Eve stripped off all her clothes. Nude as a newborn, she stepped onto the teak grating at the top of the platform and made a clean, perfect high dive into the sea.

"Oh, wonderful!" she called, laughing, upon emerging to the surface. "Come on in—it's great." Eve, like an aqua ballerina, shot below the surface again with her glorious long legs sinking straight above her.

Steven furtively glared around to make sure the coast was clear and stripped down to his boxers. He walked down the steps to the water, and with a small dive, joined Eve. He couldn't believe he was doing this. Together they splashed about in the waves and then swam beneath the surface to look up at the yacht above them. The hull was black, but the dozen intense underwater lights on each side gave the *Shoe* a fantastic appearance, like an alien spaceship descending into a new world. As they frolicked, Steven was in awe of Eve's perfect body—refracted, shattered, and recombined in the light reflected from the emerald waves—like the nude on the cover of Ari's new book.

After about fifteen minutes, they climbed the swim ladder back up to the platform and returned to the deck. Cubby was standing there with two huge bath towels. Eve took one and, with no embarrassment, dried the glistening beads of water from her firm, toned body. It was hard to tell in the ambient darkness, but Steven thought that the young mate was blushing deeply.

Back in the master suite below, they each jumped into their showers to wash off the salt from the warm sea and emerged dry and feeling very healthy, stimulated by the swim. Eve was nude as she approached, and Steven dropped the towel that he'd wrapped around his waist and joined her in a long embrace.

He was both excited by her and grateful that she was giving him a second chance—a chance to prove that his impetuous coupling of the afternoon, that of an adolescent really, could be trumped by the skill of a mature man.

He gathered her up in his arms and carried her to the bed. Sweeping the bedspread away, he rested her on the sheets and began a gentle caressing, his hands flowing over her warm, enticing skin, followed by soft kisses to her lips, her breasts, and nipples. She moaned as she responded, digging her nails into his back hard enough that he wondered if he would be able to appear shirtless in the morning. He continued using his tongue to excite, descending in between her toned thighs. She writhed in gathering waves of passion and demanded he enter her at last. He controlled the rhythm until she was gasping and crying out in pleasure. With every thrust she implored him to his own climax, until, at last, he matched her ecstacy.

He thought he'd done okay.

Steven lay by Eve's side, her head resting on his arm. She lit a cigarette and began smoking, not inhaling deeply.

"This is only the second time I've seen you smoke," he said, turning to look at her, lovely against the white pillow, her shining hair framing her beautiful face, her green eyes lit in the afterglow of passion.

"I only do it after lovemaking, my darling. I suppose I should give it up. The smoking that is, not lovemaking." She stabbed the mostly unsmoked remainder in the ashtray.

Steven gave her a light kiss and again rested his head on his pillow. Without meaning to, he drifted away into a relaxing sleep.

He awoke hearing voices, thinking others were in the room. But as his mind started to clear from the brief embrace of sleep, leaving him a little groggy, he realized that Eve was up, had put on a DVD, and was adjusting the sound and picture for the plasma screen on the bulkhead opposite. It took a moment for him to realize that the machine was not playing anything from the *Shoe's* extensive library. It was playing . . . a porno movie? Yes! Two huge-breasted women were cavorting on a bed, giving fellatio to a Latin-looking guy who was generously endowed. They were all moaning in pleasure.

"Eve, what on earth . . . ?"

"Oh, darling, you're awake."

"That video," he said, pointing. "You brought it with you?"

"Yes, it's a new one that I haven't seen yet. I thought that we could give it a review together." She returned to the bed, giving Steven a full kiss on the mouth, her tongue slipping inside.

Steven, wondering if he was dreaming, furtively pinched himself. It hurt. He was awake. He was aboard his yacht in bed with a stunning woman who seemed only to want more of his body. What could be wrong with any of that?

In spite of the banal monotony of the pornography, the various swapping of positions, the girl on girl scene—which reminded him sourly of Bermuda—he found himself partaking, increasingly, in Eve's enthusiasm. She began to play out the video, with him in place of the cinema stud. Spurred by her caresses, her little bites to his nipples, her lips and tongue sliding on his rising member, he and Eve joined the porn stars in exact imitation, Eve on top, riding Steven's erection. They climaxed, with Eve adding her own loud gasps and erotic sobs to the soundtrack.

Eve lit another cigarette, and Steven headed off to his bathroom, turning off the meretricious, shabbily seductive porno on the way. He took a shower, dried himself and surveyed his reflection in the mirror. "Well mon, never too late to be de boy toy, I suppose," he said wryly to his mirror image.

Eve knocked on the door to the bathroom. When he opened it, he found her in one of the ship's terry cloth bathrobes embroidered with a green shoe. Smiling, she held out her hand revealing two blue diamond-shaped pills. She had a glass of water in her other hand.

"Some Vitamin V for us, my darling," she said.

"Vitamin V? What are you talking about? There's no such thing."

"I know. We girls don't need much more than shopping for shoes to make us feel sexy, but you guys need a little help from time to time. It's Viagra," she cooed. I'll join you and take one as well, to make you feel more comfortable, if you want."

This reference to his potency and maybe his age, offended him. "Jesus. I haven't ever taken anything like that in my life and I seem to be doing all right. Why don't we just turn in and leave something to do for tomorrow?"

But Eve would not be denied. Playfully, she tried to grab Steven below the belt. He jumped back and she advanced into the bathroom. Soon she was tickling and teasing him everywhere, spilling the water as she played. Finally, laughing with her, he became a little less defensive.

"Really, Steven, take one of these. They take a while to work. We can relax in the sauna you showed me this morning while we wait. I've got some more DVDs too—you can pick one you like. A couple of them have a whole bunch of people doing bi, straight, and kink."

Dubious about that proposition, Steven put on his bathrobe. He led Eve back into the suite and sat her down in a soft leather chair. If there was one thing he was certain of, it was that he wasn't going to take that blue pill. He started to talk seriously about his resolve, which didn't waver.

Until she started to cry.

"Oh, darling," she whispered with trembling lips, tears starting to form, "the best way to get to know each other is in bed. We're still strangers. To know you, I have to understand you, and this is the way to get to know me too. I only want to make it easier. I only want you to *know* me."

As her sobs intensified, Steven began to feel helpless. A crying woman had always confounded him. He would do anything to make the crying stop.

He took the pill.

Eve was delighted. "Thank you, my incredibly handsome darling. I promise it works better than oysters. I'll make sure you enjoy it. But it takes a little while. Do you want a sauna?"

"It also takes a while, to warm up, that is. I'll turn it on now for later. Let's take a stroll on deck."

It was very late and the crew was nowhere to be seen. The underwater lights and the lights on the superstructure had all been turned off. The only light showing was a small bulb hanging to illuminate the hoisted black ball at the bow, indicating that the yacht was at anchor. Above, a waning moon had risen and was reflected in a sparkling silver path on the dark surface of the sea. The land of the surrounding bay was black. The peeping of the tree frogs had stopped. It was a lush Caribbean night, and the *Green Shoe* was rising and shifting softly with the motion of the sea, in that feeling of being alive that man has loved about boats since he boarded the first floating log.

They stood with elbows resting upon the teak capping rail of the bulwark and looked out into the nighttime beauty. Was an emotional rapport with Eve developing as fast as the physical? He was sure it was not. And he couldn't shake off his guilt. He had thought about Yvonne. And he couldn't stop thinking about Jessie. Their murmured conversation was punctuated by longer silences. Then Eve took Steven in her arms in a long embrace and kiss of slowly escalating intensity. And Steven responded, somewhat to his amazement. He could feel arousal beginning to stir in his loins. Hand in hand they returned to the stateroom.

"Shall I put on a new disc, darling?" Eve asked.

"Sure, I've got some great J. S. Bach somewhere."

"Oh, silly, you know what I mean." Eve slid in another porn video, this one mostly exploring the apparently endless permutations possible in group sex.

Thanks to the pill, Steven was proficient. Eve, on the other hand, climaxed multiple times and seemed totally abandoned, lost in a delirium of sensuality.

In his robe, he returned from washing up to find Eve still slowly smoking a cigarette. He hoped the yacht's soundproofing had shielded the crew from her cries.

"That was magnificent. How do you do it?" she said, as he punched the off button on the DVD player.

"I don't know, Eve," he said, and he truly didn't. "But now it's really time to get some sleep," he added with a trace of irritability in his voice.

"Of course, darling, after our sauna. It'll be very relaxing. Just for a few minutes, please, before we go to bed. Okay?"

He had turned the damned thing on, he remembered, and it would be plenty hot enough by now. So he accompanied Eve through the full-width gym behind their stateroom to the cedar-lined cubicle, which was indeed very hot. The warmth was penetrating, relaxing, and Steven began to feel his tension and exhaustion mellow into a languorous anticipation of a long sleep. Soon their bodies glowed in perspiration and they returned to their respective showers.

Steven, now nearly zombie-like in his need for rest, donned his monogrammed pajamas and robe. When he left his dressing room, he found Eve still naked, sitting on the bed.

He sat on his side of the bed and switched off the light, leaving only the reading light still burning on Eve's side. He leaned toward her to ask for it to be turned off as well and noticed that she was looking intently at him with a sly smile. She was holding a slender plastic syringe in her hand.

"Christ, what's that?"

"Darling, it's prostaglandin. I get it from a doctor friend."

She slipped off the plastic sheath on the end, exposing a very sharp looking needle.

"It works much faster than Viagra. You just inject half of the syringe in each side of your penis—about midway down."

The thought of the sharp needle penetrating him—twice!—in that most sensitive of all places hit Steven like a fist.

"God damn it, are you out of your mind?!" His fury rose like a suddenly unleashed spring. He jumped up trembling, clenching his teeth. He didn't dare speak. His words wouldn't be able to keep pace with his emotions. After a deep breath, he said, "Stick it in yourself— wherever you like! I'm out of here." He stormed out of the suite, trying to slam the door behind him but all he could achieve was a modest thunk. This only increased his anger.

He disappeared into one of the guest cabins, where he tossed and turned between luxurious sheets, sleep was now out of the question. The more he thought about Eve, the reality show, and himself, the angrier he became. Particularly galling was the idea that earlier he had been grateful to Eve. Grateful for the sex! He now realized that gratitude was the first victim in any relationship.

He had just drifted off to an uncomfortable sleep when a shaft of sunlight, reflected from the wavelets on the bay, entered through the porthole and danced about the ceiling overhead. The insistent flashing made any further thought of sleep impossible.

*S*till in his bathrobe, unshaven and grumpy, Steven sat alone at the small breakfast table on the upper deck. He finished a hard-boiled egg and toast and started on his second black coffee. He had a headache, and he was exhausted. He wasn't so much angry with Eve this morning, as he was feeling trapped. He didn't want a scene with her, he simply wanted her out of the scene. Period.

She emerged from the companionway stairs from the lower deck, looking gorgeous, fresh, rested. Her hair fell softly in waves about her perfect face, made up with a professional's minimal but skilled touch. She was wearing a very stylish new sailor's outfit, by Ferretti.

"Darling, still angry?"

"Eve, I'm just tired. I hate to admit it, but I'm too old for a night like that."

She slipped into the chair opposite him. "You were wonderful, a god. Try to get some rest this morning before we take our afternoon nap. Darling, to know you is really to love you."

Steven was sure that her idea of a nap had nothing to do with sleep. Still, he sat with her as she had her tea, fruit, and Rye Crisp—a model's breakfast. She put on a big, attractive straw hat as protection against the blazing sun.

While they watched, a yacht almost as big as the *Green Shoe* rounded the point and maneuvered into position to anchor nearby. It was an impressive vessel and carried aboard a cluster of "toys." The masts of small sailboats could be seen, plus a speed boat on the aft section, but most prominent of all was a small helicopter carried high on the top deck, just aft of the wheelhouse, which was bristling with radar dishes and antennas. Steven recognized the boat immediately. It was the *Sixth Sense*, owned by his younger French friend, Jacques Santos. The yacht dropped anchor, and her busy crew hurried about, washing down and freeing up the various toys for use. The boat was a beehive of activity, characteristic of the intense and restless personality of the boat's dynamic, charming owner.

After a few minutes, Cubby brought a hand-held VHF radio to Steven. "Mr. Santos on Channel 72 for you, Mr. Hudson." Eve cast a caressing eye over the handsome young mate's superb, buffed physique, Steven noted.

"Hello, Jacques, good to see you here. *Sixth Sense* is looking as wonderful as always. Over."

"Roger that and to you the same compliment, Steven. Will you be here for a little while? Over."

"Plans are a bit in the air at the moment. Over."

"Got time for a ride in my new chopper? I'd love to show her to you. She has pontoons, can go anywhere. Only room for one passenger, though. Over."

"Jacques, that sounds just great. I'd love to take you up on that. Over." They agreed to have Steven picked up by one of the *Sense's* runabouts immediately.

With scarcely a word to Eve, Steven hurried below and changed into a pair of red swimming trunks and hustled back to the main deck, where a small rubber tender was already approaching their landing stairs. He climbed into it and in no time was boarding his friend's splendid yacht. Jacques gave him a warm greeting as he came onto the deck.

"Steven, what a pleasure! You'll love my little Robinson. It only carries me and one other, but it's light. I got rid of the Bell—too heavy to carry at sea, I thought."

Jacques was an experienced pilot, Steven knew. He had no hesitation in climbing aboard the craft and buckling up while his friend started the engine, checked the instruments, and flipped a number of toggle switches. As soon as Jacques saw that the exhaust temperature was where he wanted it to be, they virtually jumped off the deck of the yacht and almost immediately circled the *Shoe*, looking pretty at anchor.

It really was fun—Jacques loved to flit about. Soon they were hovering over the harbor in Gustavia, then they climbed above the hill and descended toward the Eden Roc hotel with its splendid long beach. Jacques settled down, almost touching the clear water. Steven could see straight to the clean sand below and even spot fishes darting about under the surface, now ruffled from the blade's down draft.

As Steven looked shoreward, he spotted the little house Jessie had rented. He tipped his head to Jacques, indicating to go closer. Then he saw her emerging from under her sun porch to look out to see what was making all the noise. Steven shouted above the roar: "Can we set her down here?"

"*Mais oui.*" In a moment, they were floating gently, fifty yards off the beach. Puzzled, Jacques killed the engine. The quiet was like being released from a pressure cooker.

"Jacques, can we call channel 72 from your radio?"

"Of course, *mon ami.*" Quickly Steven raised Cubby back aboard the *Shoe*.

"Listen, Cubby, I have been suddenly called away. I'll contact the boat after a couple of days, or so. Over."

"Roger that, sir . . ." was the puzzled answer.

"Pay attention, please. Cruise the yacht around the island for Eve a little, and Cubby, listen carefully—I am counting on you for this—give her everything she wants. And I mean everything. Out." Steven switched off before the mate could reply.

"Jacques, you're a prince, you truly are." Steven was unbuckling as he spoke. "I'll explain later." In one little motion, he dove overboard from the chopper.

Steven was a strong swimmer and before long his feet touched the bottom. Up he waded out of the sea. Brushing the water out of his hair with his hands, he walked toward an astonished Jessie, who was standing just in front of the charming cottage.

"Honey, I'm home," he said.

CHAPTER SEVENTEEN

*S*teven's salt and pepper stubble was more prominent three days later. In those seventy-two hours, he and Jessie had reached a complete union of minds and souls. More accurately, Steven thought, he'd simply acted on feelings that had been in place from the beginning, but which had been thwarted by the machinations of the reality show.

After their first long embrace on the beach, with Steven sopping wet from his swim ashore, they separated from each other, laughed at their good luck in coming together and embraced again, this time kissing long and lovingly. When they began to talk, back in the shade of the porch, they each had to get through the other's apologies. Steven's ran something like: "I was a fool to date any of those girls. Even the nice ones seemed like daughters to me. The others—a waste of time." He grabbed both of her hands in his. "I knew that you, Jessie, were the one and the only one."

He didn't intend to make her cry when he added, "And, Jessie, I really look forward to having Mark in my life too. He's a genius, I know, but also a teenager, and I miss all the turbulence teenagers bring in the house. I can help you with him. I want to help. We'll share in his Nobel Prize glory someday, I'm sure."

She had apologies of her own. "It was all my fault. In the beginning I was ashamed of you for agreeing to participate. Now I am ashamed of myself for asking you to keep going. I wanted a great TV show, I wanted a feather in my cap for my career, and I let that get in the way of my growing feelings for you."

Steven was still exhausted from his night of exertions, and he fell asleep holding her hand while lounging in one of the deck chairs. When he awoke hours later, her hand was still holding his. Her beautiful eyes were still watching him, bathing him in a wonderful warmth.

What followed were three days AWOL from the *Shoe* and its cargo of trouble for Steven, and three days of hooky for Jessie from *Trophy Bride*. They used those days carelessly, without an agenda, and that was exactly the right thing to do. They adjusted to each other got to *know* each other. Steven found, not that he ever had doubted it, that the power of love trumped that of any blue diamond-shaped pill.

They wandered the beach, swam in the crystal clear water, strolled together to the local open-air market to buy a couple of shirts, flip flops, a pair of white cotton trousers, and a toothbrush for him. One night he cooked a dinner of freshly caught snapper in the tiny kitchen, and it was delicious, she said. Steven knew that Yvonne was no longer laughing, or worse, pitying him. He knew he had her blessing.

Their idyll was ended when a taxi pulled up outside the cottage. Jacques had told the *Shoe's* captain, Jeremy, where the boss was, and Cubby had been dispatched to bring Steven a leather bag full of shore-going clothes, his shaving stuff, and a letter from Eve, sealed in one of the ship's envelopes.

Cubby looked awful, with dark circles under his eyes and a weariness, rarely seen in youth, overlaying his handsome features.

"Jeremy says he's going to fire me, Mr. Hudson, unless you tell him otherwise."

Steven steered him toward the door and onto the beach. "Come on outside, Cubby. Let's have a chat." He had a sense of what might be coming. "No need to trouble you with the mundane minutiae of the day-to-day boat stuff," he said to Jessie as they left.

"I told Jeremy what you told me, and, for the last few days, we have just been anchoring, from bay to bay, around the island. Showing Eve a good time, like you said to."

"Exactly, Cubby, just as I asked," Steven said encouragingly. "You won't be fired over that."

"Well, that's not what Jeremy is angry about. It's . . . well, I have spent some time in your master suite, a lot really. He says a crew member isn't supposed to do that, and certainly not with the boss's girlfriend." He hung his head. "I know he's right, but Eve—she asked me to bring her a 7-Up and she got between me and the door—and she took all her clothes off, and . . . If I get fired, well, Eve says I can stay with her. She can get me a job modeling in New York." He looked up in anguish. "But, Jesus, I can't stand those *needles* anymore!"

Steven stopped in his tracks. He had a very clear image in his mind—the mound of cigarette butts piling ever higher in the bedside ashtray.

He put a friendly hand on the troubled mate's shoulder and said, "Cubby, I understand completely. I asked you to take care of things and you did. There won't be a problem with Jeremy, I promise. I'm putting you up for a pay raise, wounded in action—no, wounded to cause action would be more accurate."

"Thanks, Mr. Hudson. Thanks a lot."

"And Cubby, take the day off. Got your radio with you? Good. I'll call Jeremy, get it squared away for you. I'll get Eve on a plane out of here before you go back on board."

That's exactly what Steven did. In less than five minutes, Jeremy called back confirming that Eve had reservations on the next flight out. A relieved first mate took the waiting taxi back to Gustavia.

Steven returned to the cottage wondering what to do about the letter from Eve. It was lying on the table under Jessie's nose.

"Everything okay with Cubby? He looked tired."

"Oh sure, probably standing too many anchor watches," Steven said with false concern. "Um, could you open that note from Eve?" He decided to walk directly into the line of fire. If he was going to take a hit, let it be from Jessie's hands. She tore open the flap and read.

"Steven, she must be nuts. This doesn't make sense to me. She starts by telling you that she loves you passionately, that you are her god, whatever that means. Then she complains that you are not 'a man for the distance.' Again, I can't imagine what she is talking about," Jessie adjusted her reading glasses and returned to the letter. "She continues to say that your crew 'can't go for the gold either'—is she raving? Then she winds up with a crazy paragraph that she is going to sue you and *me* for not completing her contract with the show." She gave the paper a loud tap before setting it aside. "Forget it, Steven. I wrote that contract and she signed it. There is not a millimeter of space for her to move in. Even the lowest ambulance chaser would laugh her out of his office."

"That's good, Jessie. She and her chain smoking will be off this island within the hour. Do you want to stay here? Or would you like to go aboard the *Shoe?*"

*I*t had been great aboard the yacht. Jessie had loved everything about the boat, and she had sorted out the turmoil Eve had created. Jessie's soothing voice never lost its magic. Cubby was even whistling again. But after only a few days she had to return to her responsibilities at Acme Studios. They laid plans to return to the *Shoe* when it reached Italy.

Back in Manhattan, Jessie faced the problems of the derailed project.

The test groups really loved what they had seen and wanted more. There was great curiosity over who would be the chosen bride. Jessie had everything going except the bride—hardly a detail to be brushed over. She explained to Steven that they had so much action on tape that they could cut and edit to develop the "plot" to keep everyone guessing until the last episode. The problem was, she explained, "I'll be damned if I am going to put any other gold-digging babes in your path. Now that I've got you off the market, I am going to keep you there."

Also, she had a potential morale problem on her hands with her staff. How could she keep everyone eager to make *Trophy Bride* a hit, if the word got out that she was sleeping with Steven? How long could she sustain the illusion of indecision on his part when he was obviously smitten? As happy as a lamb in clover, he said. They kept their love a secret as best they could. Jessie didn't move in with him. At least it had gone very well with Mark. He was delighted that the man who wrote such excellent e-mails liked his mom.

Jeffrey, of course, figured it out right away.

"Boss, I love Jessie—she's a keeper, that's for sure. When are you going to marry her?"

"As soon as I can. But she's trying to rescue her show and I have to tell my kids first. Children frequently resent new stepmothers, as Helen has shown once before. Please clean and press my kid gloves—I may need them before this is over, Jeeves."

*H*e had coffee with Helen in her apartment, just the two of them.

"Ari is pushing me to marry him, Pop. What should I do?" He noticed as they took their seats in the living room that her slim figure was beginning to show her pregnancy. It seemed obvious to him what she should do.

"You two are very much in love with each other. What's holding you back?" He put his arm around her shoulder as they sat together on the couch. To his amazement, she began to sob.

"I'm scared that I can't do marriage right. I wish I could talk it over with Mom." She cuddled against his shoulder, as she'd done as a little girl.

He gave her a loving hug. "I'll talk it over with Mom for you. She gave me her permission to marry Jessie. What do you think of that?"

Helen sat up straight and looked intently at him, blinking back her tears. "Pop, that's great. I've always liked Jessie, from the first time

I met her. You're not kidding, are you?" He shook his head no. "Terrific news. It was those homecoming queens chasing you that I couldn't stand."

"Helen, you've been known to change your mind. Do you mean what you're saying?"

"Pop, be fair. I've always said that I thought you were too lonely since Mom died. Remember the Arthur Murray dancing lessons I wanted to get for you? It was only when I saw you with girls my age that I flipped. You told me once that Mom was a beautiful woman who made beauty in every way. So is Jessie. If she'll have you, go for it!"

She sat in silence for a moment looking at her father. Her eyes began to glisten again as she said, "Pop, let's do it together." She smiled through her tears. "I'll get married, too. You're right about Mom. I think that's what she wants."

He left the apartment feeling very good about his daughter.

*J*essie was with him when he brought up the subject with Henry. They were invited for dinner by Lynne at Henry's loft. The place had changed since Steven had last been there. Henry's bachelor art was gone and even more computer equipment had been installed—racks of disk drives and telecommunications gear were linked by cables snaking across the wide-planked wooden floors. A giant inflatable plastic penguin was prominent—something to do with Linux, they were told. They sat on bean bags with glasses of champagne and watched Lynne bustle about with deft efficiency at the cooking island under its copper hood.

Henry made the first move. "Dad, Lynne and I are going to tie the knot. We're so happy together; want to have lots of kids, don't we, babe?" Lynne giggled in agreement as she tossed the salad.

Steven said, "Hank, Lynne—what great news!"

"That's wonderful, Lynne," Jessie chimed in. "I remember you saying that you would be the next Mrs. Hudson. I just didn't know which one you meant. Have you guys set a date?"

Lynne started to explain that she hadn't coordinated a time and place yet with her parents. "We've been so busy with Hank's business plans."

At the phrase business plans Jessie jumped to her feet. "That's it! That's it! The show is alive! I can see it clearly. Picture this: Hank and Steven standing side by side in front of the altar. You *are* ready to marry me, aren't you?"

Steven nodded eager assent.

"So there you two are and all of the *Trophy* girls walk down the aisle together. I'm there, walking with them as their chaperone, as usual. A nationwide audience watches in excitement! Only, what is Hank doing there? Is he the best man? The viewers on the edge of their seats, not knowing who is the one, the winner, Steven's choice of a bride!"

"Then I stand by Steven's side and Lynne by Hank's. The other girls move to either side, like bridesmaids. We bring the cameras in close and shoot a double wedding! There are *two* Mrs. Hudsons. The viewers get a doubleheader—oh, they will love it. Love it!"

*T*here were a million details for Jessie to arrange. Mrs. O'Brian ably handled about a hundred thousand. Willard flew in, of course, to assist, and his energy accomplished the work of dozens. There was a big surprise, too. All of the Hudsons would take their vows. Helen insisted on herself and Ari being included.

The nuptials would take place at the Bellagio Hotel in Las Vegas. Mrs. O'Brian, who had flown out some days in advance to coordinate with Jessie, had secured the most prized suite. Jessie settled there for three days along with Helen, Lynne, and all of the *Trophy* girls—even Eve, who had wisely decided to drop her threatened lawsuit.

The gowns—identical so as not to give away the choice of bride—were designed by John Galliano of Christian Dior. Jessie had considered Vera Wang at first, but decided Wang was too conservative for TV. Dior sent their top fitter from Paris to work with Jessie and all the girls. The shoes were by Manolo Blahnik, with little glittery rhinestones worked into the straps.

Steven surprised Jessie with an incredible Graff diamond necklace that had all the girls gasping. Lawrence Graff had discussed it with him from London on the phone, saying that it had taken him six years to locate so many large type D, flawless diamonds to create the masterpiece. Jessie cried in delight when Steven, on bended knee, presented it to her.

The girls were great at keeping Jessie's secret. True, each had hoped to snare Steven and become the Trophy Bride, but Jessie was popular with them. If they had to lose, losing to her was somehow okay.

With everyone's help, it was coming together. Jeffrey was on hand to coordinate food with the caterers. Mark astonished the multitudes with an on-the-spot mental calculation of what horsepower was required for the pumps driving the hotel's spectacular water jets so high in the air.

That evening, toasts were made all around. Jessie, standing and raising her glass to Steven, made a little speech.

"Here is to the best sport in the world—my own Trophy prize, my dearest Steven."

There was a murmur of "here, here" from the guests.

"He has put up with me and my stream of sweet young things for months. They are all here in the hotel with us tonight, so we are posting guards—to make sure he doesn't change his mind."

A wave of laughter followed as she turned to her beloved.

"Now, Steven, admit it. You would have preferred our nuptials to have been in the dark woodwork of one of your clubs. A few flowers, a few friends, a string quartet playing something soft and unrecognizable in the background. Am I right?"

He admitted it was so.

"Instead, we are in the glitz capital of the world, Las Vegas. We are pandering to the bad taste we in television have cultivated over the years. We are here because, dearest Steven, you are marrying a TV producer. And a girl gets to pick her own wedding!"

The son of a world-famous televangelist was on hand to officiate in a ceremony almost denuded of religious overtones. Jessie didn't want the traditions of any particular church to ruffle the feathers of the diverse viewing audience. Steven had forgotten how hot it would be under the banks of lights. Henry and Ari stood with him in front of the quickly whacked together plywood altar in the hotel's Grand Ballroom. They were perspiring in their black Armani suits, but they each looked very handsome and their nervousness didn't show much on camera.

The place was packed with family, friends, and a pick-up audience in shorts, flip-flops, and sports shirts, delighted to be part of a "happening" and to take a break from the slots. The murmur from the audience was silenced by an organ swell beginning Mendelssohn's wedding march. Jessie, Helen, and all eight girls slowly glided down the long red carpet to the three men waiting at the altar.

They moved slowly enough for the cameras to focus in on each radiant face. They were all gorgeous; Jessie's attention to the gowns was well worth the effort. And her surprise for the TV viewers played out perfectly. There was an audible gasp, then whispers of approval among the live audience when Jessie took her place next to Steven, Helen next to Ari, and Lynne next to Henry. Then rings were exchanged, vows taken, and rice thrown as the three newlywed couples exited the hotel in a whirl of excitement. . . .

Jessie got out of bed, wearing her white satin dressing gown and switched off the TV. "Well, sweetheart, there you have it," she said to Steven who was in his pajamas propped up in bed. They were back in the penthouse. "That's the first cut of the wedding scene." She was nodding her head in satisfaction. "A couple more weeks and we'll have all the episodes wrapped up. What do you think?"

He grinned and patted the bed inviting her to return. "I think it's terrific, wonderful, and the best part is that we get to consummate the marriage all over again."

She laughed and joined him. Before he doused the lights, he added, "Who would've believed all of this could come from that crazy letter of yours?"

ACKNOWLEDGMENTS

First, I need to thank the people at the studio who sent me the letter, even though they don't wish to be named publicly. Their letter set the wheels in motion. Then, most importantly, huge thanks to Danielle Steel who prodded me, urged me, encouraged me—nagged is too strong a word—to write the book. She did the preliminary editing and guided me through the whole process. The book would not exist without her.

Thanks also to Kathy Jewett, my assistant, who suffered through all the mechanics of writing and rewriting. Plus too, an important thank you to Fred Hill, the esteemed San Francisco literary agent, who took me on for this debut novel, helped with some plot ideas, and finding a publisher.

Fortunately, Judith Regan liked the book right out of the box and she put me in the capable hands of senior editor Doug Grad; John Paine was also involved in the project. These two skilled guys worked patiently with me and did the heavy lifting in showing me how to get the manuscript ready for print. We even had fun in the process.

And thanks to Sir John Blaker and Robert Rodriguez for ideas on the Willard and Crystal characters, respectively. Also, thanks to Richard Mondzak, my Jeeves, right down to the cooking, the skiing, and the cockroach. First Mate, Christian Trutor inspired Cubby, and could double for him in the role. My son, Tor, and daughter, Elizabeth, have kindly not taken offense to Henry and Helen, probably because my kids have absolutely no flaws, unlike their fictional counterparts. Their late mom, Gerd, is the inspiration for Yvonne. I am still looking for Jessie.

Finally, I wish to thank Al Halliday at Harvard, my copyright lawyer, Shelly Alpert, and Chris Goff, Chief Legal Council at HarperCollins, for figuring out how to give all my royalties to the University. Steven Hudson might agree that, sometimes, giving money away is more complicated than making it.

T. P.

ABOUT THE AUTHOR

Newsweek calls Tom Perkins a "Titan of American business." He is one of Silicon Valley's pioneers and the venture capital firm he founded has financed many famous companies including Genentech, Compaq, Amazon, AOL and Google.

Danielle Steel has dedicated a book to him and she is an editor of this novel. Author Patrick O'Brian was a friend and sailing companion. Their adventures can be found online under "Cruising with Patrick O'Brian—the Man and the Myth."

Perkins divides his time between the San Francisco Bay Area, East Sussex and one of the world's great sailing yachts. He is a Knight of the Kingdom of Norway. This is his first novel.